Bookweirdest

Bookweirdest

PAUL GLENNON

DOUBLEDAY CANADA

Doubleday Canada and colophon are registered trademarks

Library and Archives of Canada Cataloguing in Publication

Glennon, Paul, 1968-
    Bookweirdest / Paul Glennon.

Issued also in electronic format.
ISBN 978-0-385-66549-0

    I. Title.

PS8563.L46B673 2012   jC813'.6   C2012-902363-9

Cover and text design: Jennifer Lum
Cover art: Gillian Newland
Printed and bound in the USA

Published in Canada by Doubleday Canada,
a division of Random House of Canada Limited

Visit Random House of Canada Limited's website: www.randomhouse.ca

10 9 8 7 6 5 4 3 2 1

Contents

Bookweirdest

Uncle Kit's Dreamworld

The sound of sparrows arguing outside the window was very familiar. These birds had woken him before.

"The Shrubberies," he muttered to himself. He was back in his own room. The idea was comforting. When you've woken up in as many strange places and times as Norman had, waking up in the real world was a relief.

Norman sat up in bed and raised his hand to tap at the window to shoo the birds away, but before his hand fell on the windowpane, he saw the grey sweater he was wearing.

He lowered his hand as it all came back to him. The grey sweater was the one that George Kelmsworth had lent him, the one that he had been wearing when he fell asleep on the steam train. But Norman hadn't been alone on that train. He began to bat the crumpled sheets around him to see if anything else had come through from the other side. Under the covers he found the canvas knapsack. He fished around inside it with one hand and found his blue Rams sweatshirt and . . . nothing else. Beginning to worry now, he pulled the sweatshirt out and shook it as if something might be hiding in there. Nothing was.

He wasn't going to panic. Instead, he opened the window and stuck out his head and called out in a loud whisper, "Malcolm? Malcolm, are you there?"

The only reply was a more urgent fluttering and chirping of sparrows evacuating the tree. But that's right—if Malcolm was out there, the sparrows would have fled long ago.

Norman continued his search of the bedroom that had been his for the summer, standing back to see if there was anything on top of the wardrobe, wafting his arm under the bed, rifling through his pile of discarded laundry—all the while whispering the name of the missing stoat.

"Malcolm, where have you got to?" he muttered, frustrated with his furry friend's wanderings. Norman's mother knew a little bit about his own bookweirding travels, but she didn't need to find out who he sometimes brought along on the journey.

They weren't even supposed to be here at the Shrubberies. Comforting as it was for Norman to be back in the real world under the same roof as his family, this was not where he'd meant to wake up at all. He and Malcolm were supposed to have woken up far away from here, in a dark library, in the tower of a Crusader outpost, in the middle of a desert . . . in a book.

For most normal twelve-year-old boys, waking up in a book was just a fantasy, but Norman's experience of sleep and waking was anything but normal. Since the day he first ate a page from a book, falling asleep had been . . . well, let's say troublesome. That first book was *The Brothers of Lochwarren*, set in a world called Undergrowth, the place where Malcolm was born to be king. Eating that page had unleashed something called the bookweird, a force Norman only partially understood and could almost never control. The bookweird got you *into* a book. It had taken him to many strange places, and into the lives of his favourite characters. Without it, he would never have met Malcolm, or George Kelmsworth of the Intrepids adventure series, or the boy monk Jerome, who was the hero of *The Secret in the Library*. He wouldn't trade those friendships for the world, but the bookweird had its difficulties. It got you into a book, but getting out wasn't always easy. Getting out without making a terrible mess was almost impossible.

The thought of the boy monk Jerome, reminded Norman of

the urgency of finding Malcolm and getting out of here. He had made a serious mess of Jerome's book. They needed to get back there to make things right. Compared to the disaster unfolding in *The Secret in the Library*, Malcolm running loose through the house was a minor setback. Nobody's life was at stake here. But still, the last thing Norman needed was for his family to find out that he was friends with a talking medieval stoat.

He didn't bother to dress—or rather, to undress and redress. He didn't bother to take off George's grey sweater. There was no point hiding it from anybody anymore. His mother would know by now that he'd disobeyed her and bookweirded off to Kelmsworth Hall.

He tiptoed down the corridor. The house was quiet except for the usual creaks and squeaks of its worn floorboards. If he was lucky, he was the first one awake. (There was a first time for everything.) The library was the obvious place to start. Back home in Undergrowth, Malcolm was stoat royalty. He had a castle and a library of his own, but it was a medieval library with just a few dozen books. For Malcolm, the library at the Shrubberies was a marvel. Norman just had to hope that his father wasn't already in there working. He tried the door handle gingerly. The knob barely turned. He leaned into it and pushed harder, but still it stuck. Locked. That was strange. His father never locked the library.

A noise somewhere downstairs startled Norman, interrupting his thoughts. It was the clang of cups or dishes. The kitchen, of course! If there was one thing that Malcolm loved more than books, it was food. Norman descended the stairs warily. He had a picture in his mind of the tiny woodland creature sitting on the kitchen table with his face in a cereal bowl or his whiskers full of jam. Even as he worried about it, Norman couldn't help smiling. Malcolm was an annoying little creature at the best of times, but he was also his best friend in this or any world.

At the bottom of his stairs, Norman paused to listen. There was the ring of a spoon against a porcelain bowl and a low singsong kind of chattering. These didn't sound like stoat noises. They sounded decidedly human and annoyingly familiar. He dared a peek and then took a tentative step into the kitchen. There, sitting at the kitchen table, was his little sister, Dora. She was dressed in her riding clothes, ready for her morning ride, and was singing a song to herself while she scarfed her breakfast—the biggest bowl of ice cream ever consumed by man or child. Norman smirked a little at the thought of what his mother would say when she found out his little sister had been eating ice cream out of a mixing bowl for breakfast.

Dora didn't look up immediately. Norman let her continue to eat and sing blithely away while he began a surreptitious exploration of the kitchen cupboards. He quietly opened doors and examined the cupboard contents as if he were looking for something to eat. What he was hoping to see was Malcolm, sitting there with his head in a granola box or something, but there wasn't even any granola. Something strange must have happened on his parents' last shopping trip. The giant glass jars that his mother usually filled with granola and muesli were now packed to the brim with several varieties of colourful sugary cereal. They filled nearly every cupboard. Norman checked the pantry next. It too brimmed with jars of the stuff. Maybe they had won a contest for a year's supply or something. It was the sort of thing Dora would enter. There was just one small pile of granola bars left on a high shelf. Norman grabbed two—one for himself and one for his friend.

"Hey!" Dora yelled, so loudly that it made Norman jump. "It's about time you got up."

Norman had a comment about the ice cream on her lips, but he kept it to himself. It would be more fun to wait to hear what his mother had to say.

"Are Mom and Dad awake?" he asked.

Dora just squinted at him as if he had said something incomprehensible. After a moment, she reached up to her ears and pulled out a pair of tiny white earbuds. The wire led to a little pink MP3 player that matched the colour of her ice cream. That was new.

Norman took a good look at her. People said that Dora looked like him, but he didn't see it. She was skinny and pale and had too many freckles, and her hair was blonde whereas his was plain old normal brown. This morning she had on a full riding outfit, from boots to jacket. Even Norman could tell it was expensive. It looked like she had had the best birthday ever, what with the MP3 player and the riding clothes. But the tiara on her head just looked silly.

"Aren't you a little old to be playing princess?" He couldn't resist.

Dora flicked her head to turn her nose up at him. "I'll have you know that this crown belongs to Princess Cara of the Talingi," she huffed. "It was given to me to look after." She adjusted it on her head proudly.

"Whatever," Norman replied. He had no time for Dora's imaginary princess games. He had a medieval stoat to find and a Crusader outpost to stop from burning down.

"Listen," he began, wondering how much was too much to tell Dora, "have you seen any strange animals around the house? Something like a weasel or a ferret?" He left out that he would be wearing a green hunting cloak and would have a sword belted around his waist.

"I've seen lots of strange animals," Dora replied matter-of-factly.

"Like what?" Norman asked eagerly.

"Like you!" She snorted at her own lame joke, put the earbuds back in her ear and resumed her very unhealthy breakfast.

Norman decided that he was asking for that. It was best to leave Dora out of it anyway. He pocketed the granola bars and headed out the back door. He had an idea where Malcolm might be waiting for him.

A movement at the far end of the back garden caught his attention—a shadow of black behind the bright blue stands of delphiniums, an animal movement, large enough to startle him into a defensive crouch. Norman still imagined wolves stalking him sometimes. Being chased by wolves was something that stayed with you for a long time. But this was no wolf. Far too large to be a wolf, it stood above the tallest flowers in the flower bed, its head nibbling an apple from the tree. Chomping away methodically and loudly was the biggest horse Norman had ever seen. It was almost pure black—so black it glistened, its hide as glossy as the big grand piano Norman had used for exactly four very frustrating lessons last year.

He could only shake his head. A horse? His parents had let Dora get a horse? It was probably only on loan from her English friend, Penny, who lived up the valley, but a horse? Not even a pony, but a giant midnight-black stallion. It was the sort of thing a knight should ride, not his snotty little sister. If Dora got a horse, he decided to himself, he was going to ask for a PlayStation.

He hurried through the back garden towards the path. If he was right, Malcolm would be waiting for him at the footbridge. That was where they'd met before. It made sense that he would expect them to rendezvous there again.

6

Norman sat on the footbridge for a long time, dangling his feet over the edge, watching the water run slowly over the rocks. It gave him time to think about the work they had to do and the dangers they had to face. It was nice to be back in the real world— back in a world without vengeful wolves or desperate poachers, where you weren't kidnapped by power-crazy French knights— but he couldn't stay here. He had to go back, back into the most dangerous book of all, *The Secret in the Library*. It was the story of the boy Jerome, who had been brought to the Crusader outpost of San Savino as a young child; of his enemy, Black John of Nantes; and his father, Johan of Vilnius, whom everyone presumed dead. It was obvious that Johan and Jerome were supposed to find each other, but now that might not happen. Because of Norman, the book might be wrecked for good. He might never be able to put the plot right. Getting the plot right didn't seem to matter as much anymore. His mother might disagree, but what mattered to Norman was saving Jerome from the fire and the siege.

He could go there himself, he supposed, back to the burning fortress of San Savino, but Malcolm had promised to come with him. Malcolm had his own reason to go to San Savino—a valuable map to save from the flames, the treaty map that proved his claim to the Lochwarren throne—but Norman wanted him there for selfish reasons. Everything seemed more possible when Malcolm was there at his side. The stoat was as brave as he was short, and he was a useful ally in a fight. Norman sat thinking on the bridge long enough to eat both granola bars. He felt a little guilty about the second one, but it wasn't his fault. Malcolm should know better than to wander off and keep him waiting.

The sun drew higher in the sky, and Norman rested his head against the railing of the bridge. The sound of the water was making him sleepy. He closed his eyes and listened to it while the sun warmed him. It was almost musical. It reminded him of something he'd heard before. He could almost hear the song in his head:

> *Something, something the towers of Logarno,*
> *Something, something tall ships of Cayturke,*
> *Something, something books of Oviedo.*

Okay, he was daydreaming now. It was time to face the fact that Malcolm was not going to turn up—not on this bridge, not in the kitchen, not in his clothes hamper. He might never even have made it to the Shrubberies. The bookweird might have stranded him back at Kelmsworth with George. It might have carried him back home to Lochwarren. If the bookweird was really acting up, it might even have taken Malcolm to San Savino alone. It was time to find out. Norman shook his head and jumped up on the bridge. At the sound of his feet on the bridge deck, the music stopped. So much for that daydream.

Norman made his way slowly back to the house. His parents were probably looking for him anyway. He was probably in all sorts of trouble. And at the edge of the garden, he found another reason for them to ground him: the gate was wide open.

"Great," he told himself. "Now the horse has probably escaped too."

"The *horse* doesn't need a child to open a gate for him."

Norman turned towards the unfamiliar deep voice. There was no one there but the horse himself. He stood motionless in the shade of the apple tree, eyeing Norman with his giant but calm brown eyes.

"Who said that?" Norman asked. He turned around in a circle. Maybe some trick of echo had made it sound like the voice was coming from the horse's direction. Nobody showed himself.

He gave the horse a long look.

"I hate to ask, just in case this makes me more crazy," he said in a low voice, in the event anybody heard him talking to a horse, "but you didn't just say something, did you?"

The horse took a step out from underneath the apple tree. Up close the animal looked even taller, more majestic. The big black stallion let out a deep sigh from its nostrils. It almost seemed to roll its eyes. It was then that Norman saw it. It was as plain as the nose on his own face. It looked absolutely natural, as if it had always been there. It was the colour of old bone, spiralled and veined with silver. It looked indescribably precious, as only a unicorn's horn could.

"You've got to be kidding me."

The huge black horse—or to call it what it was, the unicorn—placed a stern hoof on the ground and spoke once again in that deep, commanding voice. "I never kid."

"Does my mom know there's a unicorn in the backyard?"

The unicorn never had a chance to answer. Dora had appeared at the kitchen door.

"Are you bothering Raritan?" she asked proprietarily. "He doesn't appreciate stupid questions, you know."

She skipped down the back steps towards the mythical beast beside the flower beds.

Norman opened his mouth to speak, but a retort did not come. This was all too much to think about. Malcolm had disappeared; he could be anywhere. Now a unicorn was sitting in their back garden, and his sister seemed to think this was the most normal thing in the world.

"Do Mom and Dad know about this?" It was all he could think to ask at the moment.

8

Dora barely looked at Norman. She drew a couple of bright red apples from the inside of her riding jacket and offered them to the creature. "Here are some nice fresh apples. Much better than those nasty crabapples."

Norman couldn't say for sure, but the unicorn seemed to roll its big brown eyes again. He took the apples anyway.

"I can't wait to tell them," Dora continued. She stroked the unicorn's muscled neck as it ate the apples from her hand. "They might call, if their cellphones work there."

"Where's there?" Norman asked. He had a queasy feeling in his stomach. He was certain that there was no cell coverage inside a book.

"Paris, of course. That honeymoon sort of thing." She said it as if he should know all about it. "I don't see why. They've been married for ages." She shrugged, as if it was a mystery but not a very interesting one.

"And they left you here alone?" Norman wondered what he had missed while he was away at Kelmsworth and San Savino. Was *he* supposed to be babysitting? Mom and Dad sometimes left him in charge when they went to the store for half an hour, but was he really supposed to babysit while they went to Paris? Wouldn't they at least have told him?

While he muddled through this, Dora kept talking—mostly to the unicorn, partly to herself. Norman was slipping back into his usual habit of ignoring her. She disappeared around the other side of the unicorn. The big creature bowed and huffed, lowering his horn to let her touch it.

"He said that Raritan would have to go back but he could come for visits maybe."

"Who said?" Norman asked, suddenly and strongly suspicious. "Who said Raritan could come back?"

Dora reappeared from the other side of the unicorn. "Uncle Kit, of course. Who else?"

Norman could actually feel his jaw drop. It seemed to him that the unicorn snickered as he watched.

9

"Uncle Kit?" he began slowly, in a low voice. "Uncle Kit is here at the Shrubberies?"

"Of course he's here. He's looking after us while Mom and Dad are in Paris. You'd know that if you didn't sleep all day. Uncle Kit is awesome. You should see if he can bring a unicorn for you. Raritan might let you ride with us."

As if on cue, the unicorn dipped his head again, bowing very low and kneeling on the ground, in a way that was not very natural. Norman watched in dumbstruck awe as his sister leapt onto the back of the kneeling beast and flung her arms around its neck as it rose again to four feet.

"Where to, Acting Princess Dora?" he asked in the deepest of unicorn voices.

"To the flower meadow!" Dora commanded gleefully.

Raritan exhaled once, then leapt into action. Norman had seen thoroughbreds and show jumpers during his time in Dora's horse book, *Fortune's Foal*, but nothing quite as magnificent as this. The big creature cleared the hedge without as much as two steps of run-up. He was off and onto the wood path before Norman could say anything more. Within moments, the only trace of them was the heavy thumps of hooves along the sandy path to the bridge.

Norman hurried back to the house and tried to tell himself that the rumbling in his belly wasn't panic but hunger. There were scones in the cupboard and eight types of jam in the fridge. The lingonberry jam made him think of Malcolm. The scones reminded him of his dad. If he were here, his dad would be having a coffee right now, the first or second of about six cups he'd have in a day. The smell of coffee would be reassuring right now. There were a few too many people missing from the Shrubberies, and one person he wished was not here at all.

Uncle Kit—or Fuchs, as Norman had known him for so long—was like a signpost for trouble. If Uncle Kit appeared, you knew something had gone wrong or was about to.

Norman piled a dozen scones onto a plate and ascended the stairs to confront his uncle. Either Kit was behind all this or he was letting it happen.

"Fuchs?" he shouted as he came to the top of the stairs. "Or is it Uncle Kit now? What would you like to be called today?"

He stopped at the landing and listened to the silence. "Fuchs? Uncle Kit?" he yelled again. He still wasn't used to the idea of Fuchs being his uncle. He'd known him so long and in so many different disguises. It was actually Kit who had introduced him to the bookweird, long before Norman had understood that Kit was his mother's brother, and that both his mother and his uncle shared his ability to get into books. Kit kept turning up whenever Norman bookweirded. He'd appeared as Malcolm's abbot in *The Brothers of Lochwarren*. He'd been George Kelmsworth's duplicitous lawyer in *Intrepid Amongst the Gypsies*. He'd even helped Norman out of a few scrapes with the bookweird. Unfortunately, his crazy uncle tended to create more problems with the bookweird than he solved.

Norman stomped down the hall, braver now that he had convinced himself Fuchs wasn't actually here. "Fuchs!" he called, ever louder. "Kit!" And he pounded on each door. The study door was gapped. Norman pushed it open, expecting to see his mother's laptop there on the desk, surrounded by neat stacks of paper. But the desk was empty, as were most of the shelves. Norman put the plate of scones down on the bare desk. He couldn't put his finger on what was missing, but there seemed to be less stuff in the room, as if someone had moved out.

His brain tried to figure out what was missing, but there was just too much going on to think properly. He closed the study door and tried his parents' room. It would be just like Kit to take over the master bedroom. He was about the worst house guest you could imagine. He had taken over George Kelmsworth's entire manor house once. That was the thing about Kit—he didn't care if he messed up a book or even someone's life in a book. He just wanted to be part of things. He thought books were his own private theme park.

Norman half expected the master bedroom to be locked, like the library, but the handle gave way to his pressure and the door opened without a shove.

11

"Mom? Dad?" he whispered. He still couldn't completely believe that they had left for Paris without telling him, left him in the care of crazy Uncle Kit. Norman had never even met his uncle in real life. His mother ground her teeth if she even heard her brother's name mentioned. Still, Kit wasn't exactly bad. Norman wasn't afraid of him the way he was afraid of wolves or Black John of Nantes. Kit didn't deliberately try to hurt people, but people tended to get hurt anyway when he meddled with the bookweird.

There was no response from the master bedroom, so Norman stepped inside. The bed was made, the furniture arranged and the bedside tables tidy. Norman squinted and tried to figure out if it was "Mom tidy." There was a difference that Norman had never been able to see between his version of tidy and his mom's.

There was no telltale sign of Kit's occupation. He hadn't changed the pictures or redecorated. But then, why would he? This was his house, after all. He lived here most of the time— Norman's family was just staying here for the summer. Norman circled the room, on the lookout now for the *removal* of his parents' stuff. Dad's glasses weren't on his side table, but then, he would have taken them to Paris. There were no empty coffee mugs, but he was pretty sure Mom would have cleaned them before leaving. He felt a little guilty sneaking around his parents' room. This was way worse than looking for Christmas presents. You were *supposed* to try to find your Christmas presents. Were you supposed to try to find your parents if they went missing?

Norman's fingers hesitated on the drawer of his mother's bedside table. The last time he'd spoken to her, she had warned him about the bookweird, hinted that she knew much more about it than he did. She had taken *The Secret in the Library* away from him and put it into this drawer for safekeeping. The book was special to her, something from her own childhood that she didn't want destroyed. She had made herself clear: he was not to touch *The Secret in the Library*.

He didn't like disobeying his mother, but she didn't understand. She thought hiding Malcolm's map in Jerome's library would keep Norman from using the bookweird, but she didn't know how important the treaty map was. Malcolm needed it to prove his right to the throne, and Norman would do anything for his friend.

They'd needed the book then—just as he needed it now—to get to San Savino and Jerome, so Malcolm had snuck in through the window during the night to "borrow" it for them. The stoat was supposed to put it back later, but you couldn't always count on Malcolm to do exactly what you told him.

Norman held his breath as he pulled the drawer open.

It was more cluttered than he'd expected. There were tubes of ointment and makeup, an ornate silver jar full of pins, three book-marks, tons of pens and pencils, some scarves, an old personal CD player and a stack of books on CD, but no actual book. *The Secret in the Library* wasn't there. Had Malcolm not returned it? Had his mother taken it to Paris for safekeeping? Or had Uncle Kit taken it?

"Snooping around again?"

The voice at the door startled him. Norman shut the drawer guiltily and turned to look.

"I always liked that about you. I enjoy a good snoop myself. Do you want any help?"

The figure in the doorway was strange but familiar. He was taller than Norman remembered, about as tall as his dad, he guessed, but skinnier. He looked younger than when Norman had last seen him. Partly it was the black jeans and T-shirt. Mostly it was because he'd shaved off the ridiculous moustache and muttonchops that he'd worn as George Kelmsworth's lawyer. His red hair was dyed jet black. It hung over his eyes like it had when Norman first met him in the public library back home. The earrings were back too—not the huge ring that was big enough to pass a pencil through, but a row of tiny silver hoops.

"Fuchs!" Norman half shouted it, surprise and annoyance mixed in his voice.

"Aw, Norms, don't call me that," he said in a voice that was meant to be chummy. "Call me Uncle Kit."

Norman wrinkled his nose. This was typical Kit—pretending they were in this together. Kit was like that weird kid at school who got you in trouble by talking to you in class and wondered why you ignored him the next day.

"No? Just Kit, then. Just not Christopher. I never liked that. Call me Kip even, or K-dawg. We'd have to fist bump on that. What do you say, Norms . . . Spiny?" He held out his pale knuckles for a fist bump, big silver rings flashing on his fingers.

Norman stiffened and clenched a fist. He couldn't have explained why the nickname bothered him. "Only my dad calls me Spiny."

Kit took a second to process the response. He lowered his hand, realizing that the fist bump was never coming, but the smile never left his face. "Fair enough, Norms," he concluded.

Norman took the time to assess Kit. There was usually some clue in his costume. The rings on his fingers had skulls and cross-bones. The T-shirt he wore was white with a black print of some old guy's head and two birds holding a scroll that said "Nevermore."

"What are you supposed to be? Some sort of emo rocker? Is that supposed to impress Dora, like the unicorn?" Norman had no idea what Kit actually looked like. The bookweird changed him. Norman was always himself in every book he visited, but Kit changed physically so that he blended in. In Undergrowth, he was a fox. At Kelmsworth, he was the lawyer with the ridiculous mutton-chop sideburns.

"Aw, Norms, don't be like that. Can't a guy just be himself?" He spoke in a mild British accent. It didn't sound fake, like Dora's did when she copied her friend Penny. It sounded natural, like George Kelmsworth's.

"I dunno, can he?" Norman asked rhetorically. He followed it up with a real question: "Where are my mom and dad?"

"Hasn't your sister told you? They are off to Paris for a lovely romantic getaway. Eiffel Tower, Champs-Élysées, Jim Morrison's grave and all that."

"And they left you in charge?" Norman asked skeptically.

"Of course. Who else? This is my house, after all."

Officially, Norman thought, his mom had inherited half of this house too, but you had to pick your arguments with Kit.

"Aren't you and my mom still mad at each other?"

Kit shook his head soothingly. "Water under the bridge. All sorted out now. We're one big happy family. All down to you, Norms. You really bring people together."

Norman grimaced. Kit always said everything in a voice that dared you not to believe him. The crooked smile did not leave his face. It only relaxed when he winked and asked, "Did you leave those scones in the study for me?"

The rest of the day might have been just another one of the long, boring days of his summer vacation. Norman was alone in the big English house once more. Dora was off riding, and the responsible adults were in town running errands. Except that Dora wasn't at Penny's riding a tame old pony, and the responsible adults were not his parents but a haughty black unicorn and his crazy uncle. After his confrontation with Kit, Norman hadn't run out of questions— he'd just run out of the energy to ask them. Kit could do that to you. None of his doubts and suspicions had gone away, but he just needed to find Malcolm and *The Secret in the Library* and bookweird out of here.

He searched the house again, but it gave him no clues as to what had happened and how he'd apparently slept through it. Another tour of the garden also revealed nothing. There were no more mythological animals in the yard, no centaurs in the flower beds, no dragons in the tool shed. Inside, only the locked door of the library indicated that anything was different. It had never been locked while his parents were there. Locking it must have been Uncle Kit's doing. There was something in there that he didn't want Norman to see.

As he jostled the knob and leaned all his weight on the panelled wood door for what seemed like the millionth time, his imagination started to run away with him. What if Malcolm was in there? What if Kit was keeping Malcolm captive? What if his parents were in there, bound and gagged and straining to make themselves heard? At the thought of it, Norman dropped his hand from the handle and pressed his ear fervently to the door. Nothing. Just the creaking silence of an old house. No, he reassured himself. Uncle Kit was crazy—dangerous too—but he wasn't actually evil. He wouldn't hurt anyone on purpose. When Uncle Kit messed things up, it was because of some crazy plan. He had taught Malcolm about the bookweird because he'd thought the stoat king would enjoy an adventure. It never occurred to him that you shouldn't tell people their world was a book. He'd taken over Kelmsworth Hall just because he liked the idea of owning a big English manor home. He didn't think about the consequences for George and the Intrepids. Norman had to figure out what Kit's game was this time.

The library doorknob seemed to stare at him defiantly. Below it, the keyhole was black. Norman put his eye to it, expecting to see something inside, but the room was dark, the windows and blinds drawn. A locked room and an empty keyhole suggested a key.

Back down in the kitchen, Norman rummaged through the many kitchen drawers. There were fascinating things in these drawers; besides regular cutlery, there were dozens of implements Norman had never seen and could not fathom how to use. He recognized about three: a pizza cutter, a melon baller and a kebab skewer. The rest were clearly intended for prying open or cutting foods that old English people used to eat, but were now extinct. There was no key either.

There was no more luck in the dining room. The sideboard was mostly for china and glassware. One drawer contained a cribbage board and an ancient wooden board game, but again no keys.

The best bet, and the place he should have looked first, was the master bedroom. Kit had interrupted him as he was searching the bedside table. Maybe he was closer to finding something than he thought.

Within minutes, Norman was rifling the bedside tables again: jars of makeup, ointment, hair scrunchies on his mom's side; a digital voice recorder, some reading glasses and a pack of gum on his dad's. But no key. When he was convinced of it, he sat down on the side of the bed and considered his next step. Something was very strange here, and it wasn't just that his parents were missing and there was a unicorn in the backyard. There was something else. All day as he searched through the house, the feeling had grown. Something else was different about the place. Something had changed—something he couldn't put his finger on.

The sound of car tires on the gravel outside interrupted his thinking. He rushed out to the landing to peer through the window, hoping to see his parents' little yellow rental car. It would have made him feel a lot better if they were home, but it was not the yellow hatchback that pulled up in front of the house. Norman didn't know much about cars, but it looked fast. It was low and silver and with scoops on its long pointed hood. He didn't have to guess who was driving it.

He was downstairs and at the front door just as the silver machine skidded to a stop on the gravel. Its engine growled as it shut off, and its two doors opened upwards with a hissing sound, like the hatches of a space vehicle, to allow Uncle Kit to step out. Kit grinned at Norman as he pressed a button on the key fob to close the doors again. They retracted slowly, tucking in like wings. Another press of a button caused the silver vehicle to bleep and a small hatch to open at the back.

"Dinner is in there. There's something special for you too, Norms." Kit motioned to the hatch with his head.

Norman didn't budge. "Where did you get the car? Let me guess: some spy dude just finished his mission and is wondering where he parked it. Did you leave him some bus tickets?"

Uncle Kit smiled conspiratorially, enjoying the joke, or perhaps thinking this was very close to the truth. "You pick things up on your travels, as you well know."

Norman glared at him. Of course, the silver car had come out of a book, just like Raritan had come out of a book, just like his sister's new tiara.

"Did you pick up anything of mine? *The Secret in the Library*? Malcolm's treaty map?"

17

Kit wagged a finger at him. "Don't get grabby, young man. That's *my* book. An old family friend gave me *The Secret in the Library* for my birthday one year. Didn't you see my name on the flyleaf? I thought you were more observant than that."

"You wrote your name in it yourself," Norman countered. "My mom told me so. It's her—"

Kit cut him off. His face, usually smooth and condescending, became pinched and angry like a spoiled child.

"Meg is a sneaky, lying—" He caught himself and stopped. "A childish disagreement. We laugh about it now."

"How about you let me borrow it, then?" Norman bit his lip as he asked. He should have waited. He should have found a time when Kit wasn't looking for an argument.

Kit let his wagging finger drop and smiled a knowing smile. "Oh, don't worry, Norms. You'll find I can share my toys. Why don't you take the SL3 for a spin?"

Norman reacted just quickly enough to catch the keys that were tossed to him.

"I've dismantled the rocket launcher, but the other evasive features are still active. Give the oil slick a try."

"What?" Norman asked.

"Or the smokescreen or the tire-slashers. The buttons on the centre console. You do drive shift, right?"

"I'm only twelve!" Norman replied. It was dawning on him that Kit actually intended him to get behind the wheel of the silver car.

Kit appeared puzzled for a moment, then seemed to understand. "Your mum won't let you drive, huh? I should have guessed. So overprotective. I'll teach you tomorrow. In the meantime, grab the bags from the back?"

Norman was about to reply that he wasn't a servant, but his uncle had disappeared into the house.

Norman grabbed the bags from the hatch. The first contained a stack of about a dozen personal-sized pizza boxes, the next a giant tin of biscuits. The third was a box the size of a basketball, wrapped in brown paper and inscribed to him: "To my favourite nephew, Norman, with love, Uncle Kit." He didn't want to but he couldn't help guessing.

Even before Norman had ever met him, his uncle had always sent the weirdest gifts—an Indian headdress, strange glowing gems, toy guns that seemed way too realistic. He'd always thought that his uncle was some great world traveller, sending these things back from places Norman had only read about in books. Until he'd experienced the bookweird himself, Norman could never have believed that his uncle was actually collecting souvenirs from the books themselves.

He resisted opening the box. He put all three of the bags on the dining room table and went in search of his evasive uncle.

He found his sister first. She came in from the garden, flushed and excited, starting to talk before she was even in the house.

"You should have seen the waterfall! It must be, like, ten storeys high, and it shines like silver. It really shines, Norman. It does. It glows like moonlight. Raritan says it might be a passage. We've been looking all week for a passage. We're going to try to go behind it tomorrow. Do you want to come?"

"Stop, stop." Norman held up a hand. "Why are you looking for a passage?"

Dora sucked her lower lip into her mouth and looked around to see if anyone was listening. It was just her brother and the unicorn, who was still close by outside the open door. He cast a wary eye to the kitchen as he grazed on the herbs in the window box.

"We're looking for a passage back to Diadora. Raritan says he's spent too long here and it's time to get back to the Talingi. Only you can't tell Uncle Kit yet. We want it to be a surprise."

Just a slight exhale from the unicorn caught Norman's attention. He looked out to see the animal staring at him with those giant serious eyes. Norman felt like he was being tested. He just nodded at the unicorn slowly.

"Listen, Dora, you said you've been looking for a passage all week. How long has Raritan been here? How long have Mom and

Dad been gone?" It was hard to keep track of time when you went off bookweirding. Time in the real world passed differently.

A puzzled look overtook Dora's face, as if she had not really thought about it much and was surprised now that she had.

She had just opened her mouth to talk when Kit poked his head in from the dining room. "Come on, the pizzas are getting cold."

Norman had never had pizza that good. When he asked where he'd ordered from, Kit just winked at him and grinned. The guy even went to a book for takeout. Norman couldn't blame him. Pizza in England was pretty bad.

He figured he needed a different approach with Kit. He was getting nowhere with obvious questions. He needed to be a little sneakier, like his sister and her unicorn.

"Are Mom and Dad going to call from Paris?" Norman asked. He purposely did it with a bite of pizza in his mouth, so it would look casual and off the top of his head.

Dora lifted her eyes anxiously from her own pizza. Despite the distractions Kit had brought her, she obviously missed their parents more than she was letting on.

His uncle nodded, and chewed his own slice. "They weren't sure that their cellphone would work there. They are probably having a hard time finding a phone card. Plus, you know . . . Paris."

Norman didn't "you know . . . Paris." He'd been there only once, at night, in a pretty creepy old book.

"Doesn't their hotel have a phone?" Norman asked.

"Who knows? French hotels. They're probably staying at some ancient old place. You know Meg. She loves *atmosphere*." Kit bit into his pizza to avoid saying more. The more his uncle explained about his parents' vacation, the more suspicious it sounded.

"They sent a postcard," Dora contributed brightly. "I think they are taking lots of carriage rides. That's the romantic thing you do in Paris. That's what was on the card anyway."

Norman grabbed his cup of juice and hid his face behind a big swig. "Can I see?"

Dora's face clouded again. "I don't know what happened to the card. It was on the fridge. Have you seen it, Uncle K.?"

Their uncle spread his own look of confusion across his face. "You know, I can't say I have. It probably fell down the side or something. I'll put that on my shopping list for tomorrow: better fridge magnets. In the meantime, I think it's high time Norman opened up his present."

He placed the box on the table in front of them.

Norman wasn't buying it. His parents hadn't gone to Paris. Kit was up to something again.

The last thing he wanted right now was a gift from his conniving uncle, but he played along. His uncle was trying to keep them happy. That's why Dora had a crown and a unicorn. And it would be easier to figure out what was going on if he just played along. Besides, he really was curious. With Uncle Kit, there could be anything in the box.

Norman went at the package the way he knew he was supposed to: like an excited kid on his birthday. The brown wrapping paper tore off in strips and floated to the floor. Uncle Kit didn't seem to mind the mess. He grinned picking up the scraps as they fell. Norman dutifully worked his way through the layers of packaging, the cardboard, the plastic bags, the Styrofoam padding, until he came to what was inside. There were four pieces. The goggles were obvious enough, and so were the gloves. The black box with the plug was probably the main unit and power supply. Norman's own gaming system was languishing back home. For weeks, he had been begging his parents for something to kill the boredom here in England. This thing looked like it had come from the future, or at least from Japan. It had to be some next-generation thing that only three kids in the world had yet. The regular Norman would have been all over it.

"Try it out," Kit urged, plugging in the main unit and placing the goggles over his nephew's eyes. Norman was plunged into a star field. Blue and red streaks of light flashed by in his peripheral vision. A staticky radio voice summoned him. "Pick up that bogey on the right, newbie. If you let him get a bead on you, you're space dust."

Kit helped him on with the gloves, and Norman felt the controls of his space-fighter at his fingers. He flicked a finger and the star field lurched, the fighter moving at his commands. It took his breath away. It was the most realistic VR he'd ever seen. He managed to keep his ship flying for about five minutes until one of the bogies sliced his right wing in half and he spiralled down towards an asteroid crater. He didn't even wait for the crash to remove the goggles.

The disappointment on Uncle Kit's face when Norman put the goggles down and sighed was so convincing that Norman felt a twinge of guilt.

"This is cool." He made it sound like he was saying it just to be nice. "Thank you. This may be your best present yet. Better than the blowgun, even."

Kit didn't seem to notice Norman's tone. He took it at face value and brightened up. "Want to play a two-player game?" he asked.

"No, thanks," Norman replied glumly. He rubbed his stomach and winced as he got up. "I'm going to go outside for a second. I think I might have eaten too much pizza." He felt his uncle's eyes on him as trudged out the back door. Good, Norman thought. Feel sorry for me.

Outside in the garden, he caught the looming shape of the unicorn in the evening light. He hesitated at the back door before he approached it. The animal had done nothing to suggest that it wanted to help or even wanted anything to do with him. Before, in the garden, it had given him a look of pure disdain, but even so, Norman was drawn to it. Raritan seemed to care about Dora. The unicorn was, in fact, the closest thing to a responsible adult in the house.

"Don't stand behind me like that. It's annoying." The deep voice startled Norman. He'd somehow imagined that the unicorn hadn't heard him. He should have known better.

He approached tentatively. The creature seemed even bigger when you were close to it. Norman raised a hand to pat its neck as he might with a regular horse, but he stopped himself. This wasn't a regular horse. Stroking its neck was probably about as appropriate as patting the head of your neighbour or your teacher. The unicorn's sombre brown eyes watched Norman's confused approach but betrayed no reaction. They stared openly for what seemed like minutes and then blinked. His long black lashes seemed to wave Norman away.

They just stood there silently for a long time, each of them staring out at the woods. Norman was watching the forest for some sign of Malcolm. He had no idea what the unicorn was watching for. Perhaps it was something less fruitless than looking for a stealthy forest creature in the failing light.

As they stood there, Norman could almost feel Raritan's annoyance. His huge breaths sounded like gigantic judgmental sighs. Raritan obviously knew something was wrong. He had been brought here somehow. He knew he didn't belong. He probably knew that Kit was behind it, but he suspected Norman too. Why? Had Kit said something, or could the magical creature sense the other magic? Did he know about the bookweird?

"Sir," Norman began, not sure how to address the magnificent creature. "Mr. . . . uh, Raritan, can I ask you a question?"

Raritan turned his head just barely to acknowledge him and blinked the slightest blink. Norman wondered how to begin. Raritan might distrust him, but it was because he knew something about the bookweird, had been a victim of it. It made the unicorn a potential ally and the only one he could really confide in, but it was difficult to know how much to tell him. Telling people that they belonged in a book usually didn't help much. Unicorns probably didn't like it any more than anyone else.

"I know Kit brought you here," he began. "He did the same to me. I'm supposed to be somewhere else, helping a friend who needs me."

Raritan had turned away again, but from the way his ears flicked, Norman could tell that he was listening.

"Thank you for looking after Dora. She needs someone to look after her. I think Kit sent my parents away. He claims they're on vacation, but I don't believe anything he says."

A loud exhale from the unicorn seemed to indicate that he agreed vehemently with this last statement.

Speaking his suspicions aloud somehow made it worse. He had no idea what Kit had done or how he could have done it. Kit had messed up a book before, but to mess up real life . . . well, that was something new and dangerous. Just how much had changed at the Shrubberies?

"How far have you been from here with Dora?" he asked the unicorn. "Have you been to the village? Have you seen other people?"

Raritan turned and regarded him for a long time. Norman watched for any little movement, but when he spoke, the unicorn hardly moved his lips. Only his nostrils moved, as if he used them to speak.

"Dora keeps us away from the village," he snorted. "The little one who holds the tiara has some sense."

Norman bristled at the implication but suppressed an argument.

"Have you seen any other talking animals?"

"Other than your sister and your uncle?"

Norman twisted his mouth. It wasn't easy being scolded by a unicorn.

"I mean forest animals. I'm looking for my friend Malcolm . . . King Malcolm." He hoped that his knowing animal royalty might make up for his last gaffe. "King of the stoats."

The unicorn stared back for a long time. His huge, unblinking eyes seemed to take Norman in. It made him wonder if unicorns could read minds. He tried to fill his mind with all that he needed the unicorn to know—about Malcolm and his rivals for the throne back in Undergrowth, about the map that would resolve his claim for good, but mostly about Jerome trapped in the burning tower at San Savino by Black John and his knights.

Finally the unicorn looked away. If Raritan could read minds, he didn't seem to care what was in Norman's.

He could think of nothing to convince the unicorn. Dora could probably talk to him, but that would mean explaining the bookweird to her. That was not something he was ready to do.

"Goodnight," Norman said finally, giving up on his watch and his attempts to befriend the unicorn. Raritan exhaled dismissively but kept his words to himself. Norman returned, defeated, to the house.

Uncle Kit's idea of chocolate eclairs for an evening snack was tempting, but Norman had committed himself to playing sad. If Kit wanted him to be happy, Norman wasn't going to oblige. It put the ball back into his uncle's court. He said goodnight to his sister and to Kit and climbed the stairs dolefully.

About an hour later, he heard his sister go to bed. Kit seemed to putter around the house for a while longer, but eventually he too climbed the creaky stairs to bed. By that time, Norman knew what he had to do. He couldn't wait around for Uncle Kit to feel sorry for him and put things right. Kit was useful sometimes, but he never put things right. His specialty was putting things wrong.

No, Norman was going to have to bookweird himself out of this. He needed to find *The Secret in the Library* and get back to Jerome in San Savino. Norman had seen the flaming arrows of Black John's archer setting the wooden towers of the library alight. The boy monk had lived hidden in that library all his life. He wouldn't think to leave before it was too late. It was up to Norman to save him.

It would be easier with Malcolm at his side. The stoat king knew his way around a medieval siege. He could sneak into strongholds no human could penetrate, and he was deadly with a longbow. Norman's gut told him to find Malcolm first. He had promised to help Malcolm retrieve the treaty map from Jerome's library, although maybe his gut was just afraid to face the siege of San Savino and the machinations of Black John of Nantes alone. But where to start? Kit had brought Norman home to the Shrubberies. Did that mean he'd sent Malcolm home to Lochwarren?

The best place to start was with some paper. It was crucial to Norman's ingress. An ingress was how you got into a book. It was Uncle Kit who had taught Norman the word, and who had told him that his ingress was unique. Norman could get into any book. All he had to do was eat a page.

It wasn't an exact science. The bookweird had a mind of its own sometimes. It didn't like being messed with. When you altered a book, you altered the universe, and that sometimes affected other books. All too often, Norman woke up in the wrong book. He was getting better at it, or so he told himself. He had even been able to write his way back to reality. He'd written himself out of the siege of San Savino in *The Secret in the Library* after Black John had caught him, mistaking Norman for Jerome. The vengeful knight had left him tied him up in a tent while he commanded the siege. Norman had managed to scrawl a description of the Shrubberies on some borrowed paper and then had eaten that. The bookweird might not be predictable, but he felt safer with a stash of paper and a pen in his pocket.

When he judged it safe, he flicked the light back on and opened the drawer of his bedside table. There should have been a notebook in there. His mom had bought it for him to use as a travel journal. So far he had used it only to play dots and boxes and to draw pictures of castles, but he could put it to better use now . . . if he could find it. The drawer was as cluttered as ever, but there was no notebook. Where had he left it?

He climbed out of bed as quietly as he could and began rummaging. The notebook was nowhere to be found. The backup plan would have to be to go into another book—back to George at Kelmsworth in the Intrepids series, maybe, or to Undergrowth to look for Malcolm—except that he couldn't find any books either. This was weird. He'd brought a couple of Undergrowth books with him on the trip, and his mom was always bringing new books from the town bookstore. Where were they now?

It finally dawned on him that the reason he couldn't find *The Secret in the Library*—the reason he couldn't find *any* book, and the reason the library was locked—was that Kit knew it was his escape route. Kit was trying to keep him trapped here. His crazy uncle had locked up the library and hidden every scrap of paper in the house. It had taken Norman all day to realize it, but that's what was going on. The gaming system was supposed to distract him. Kit knew that a book would have done a better job, but he also knew that every book was an escape hatch for Norman.

It was hard to hate Uncle Kit more. He'd messed up a lot of books before, but to take all the books away . . . well, that was low even for him. And to think that he'd believed Norman could be distracted with a gaming system. That was insulting.

The thought of the gaming system downstairs triggered a memory for Norman, and a triumphant grin began to spread across his face. This contest wasn't over yet. Uncle Kit hadn't thought of everything. He had made one mistake.

Norman didn't bother about the creaking step as he descended the stairs. Uncle Kit could say what he wanted if he caught him. If Kit wanted to admit that he was keeping them captive here, that was fine. Norman's mood became more defiant the closer he came to the dining room. He knew exactly what he was looking for, and he knew exactly where to find it. Uncle Kit's mistake had been to wrap his present.

The gaming system was sitting exactly where he'd left it, the main unit on the floor, the glove and goggles discarded on the table. The Styrofoam and plastic packing was still there in a pile beside the main unit. But the cardboard box that had held it all was nowhere to be seen. Nor was the brown wrapping paper that he'd shredded so enthusiastically for Kit's benefit. Did Kit actually clean up? Norman rushed to the kitchen to check the only garbage can he knew of. It was filled with pizza crusts and chocolate eclair leftovers. There wasn't a single pizza box or scrap of wrapping paper to be seen. He circled the kitchen anxiously and racked his brain. Was there another garbage can, or even a recycling box? He circled the bottom floor, checking the pantry, the bathroom, the front foyer.

Maybe the sitting room. Why did he think he'd seen a pile of paper there? He padded to the sitting room, moving more quietly now that he wasn't so sure of his escape. When he saw the magazine rack there, beside the sofa, he realized what pile of paper he must have been thinking of. By the faint, blue-tinged light of the moon, he could tell that it was empty now. He scanned the room, looking for anywhere that Kit might have disposed of the wrapping paper. Nothing. Not a recycle bin or wastepaper basket, not the crumpled ball of brown paper that Norman now desperately needed.

His eyes tracked back to the fireplace. No one had used it since they arrived here, but now the fire shield had been moved aside and the grate was open. When he knelt in front he could feel no heat, but he could tell from the smell that there had been a fire there very recently. A small pile of black ashes was left on the hearth. Only fingernail-sized scraps of paper remained. They would be useless for writing on, but all the same he plucked one out using the tips of his fingers. It crumbled to ashes the moment he touched it. Uncle Kit had closed the escape route. He was trapped.

Walking in Circles

It wasn't the easiest of sleeps. Visions of San Savino ablaze tortured him all night. It was as if he were still there, held captive in Black John's tent, watching helplessly while the siege engines lurched and hurled their fiery missiles into the undefended town. His dreams were filled with the sounds of whistling arrows and barked orders. He dreamt that Jerome was calling out to him from the library as the flames engulfed his hideout. It was one of those dreams where you try to speak but can't. He wanted to shout, to tell Jerome to get out, to tell him that he was coming back to save him, but somehow his voice wouldn't rise above a whisper.

In the morning his sheets were wrapped tightly around him as if he'd been rolled up in them. He didn't wake up rested, but he did wake up determined. Kit was not going to get away with this! His crazy uncle might be able to hide all the paper in the house, but he couldn't keep Norman from leaving.

There wasn't much in the kitchen worth taking, but Norman filled the canvas knapsack he'd borrowed from George Kelmsworth with granola bars and bottled water. It was warm out, but he kept George's sweater in there too. It made him feel better having something from inside a book. It reassured him that it was all still possible.

He had no idea how far he would have to go or how long he would be away. The nearest village was Summerside. His mother had taken him to the bookstore there. His pockets were weighed down with all the British money he was able to scrounge from around the house, mostly one- and twenty-pence pieces, and a few one- and two-pound coins. Uncle Kit had even hidden all the paper money. Norman hoped the coins in his pocket were enough to buy a book at the bookshop in Summerside. Something from the Undergrowth series would be perfect, but even a pad of paper would do.

Dora caught him just as he was sneaking out the kitchen door.

"Where are you going?" she asked absently as she opened the freezer and reached for the ice cream.

"For a walk," he replied cagily. He couldn't risk her ratting him out to Kit.

"Can I come?"

"Nope," he replied curtly. He'd learned long ago not to give excuses or reasons. It only gave her something to argue against.

Dora wasn't even bothering to get a bowl. She scooped ice cream directly from the tub. "You know, Raritan and I could catch up to you if we wanted to," she taunted.

He tried not to look worried, but a moment of doubt kept him there at the door. If Dora brought her pet unicorn to Summerside, things could get out of control. It was on his tongue to warn her, but he remembered his rule: Don't tell Dora not to do something. He managed a casual shrug. "Whatever," he said, and then ducked out the back door before she got even more curious.

He almost ran into Raritan as he fled. The unicorn stood on the garden path, much closer to the house than he'd been last night. Norman gasped and tripped as he stopped himself short. "Jeez, listen at doors much?" he asked, trying to cover up his embarrassment. As usual there was no reply from Raritan. If possible, the unicorn seemed even taller this morning, more imposing. Norman tried to stare him down, but he couldn't hold the gaze of those unblinking eyes.

"Still no sign of my friend Malcolm, huh? About this high." He held his hand down around his knee. "Wicked bow shot, kind of a smart aleck?"

Raritan blinked a long blink as if considering the question, but Norman didn't really expect a reply. He was just being a smart aleck himself.

"No?" he said, shaking his head. "Well, thanks for all your help. It's been nice chatting." He turned and stomped away.

When he looked back Raritan was still watching him. The unicorn would see him go around the front of the house. If Raritan told Kit that he'd gone by the road instead of the back path, his uncle would guess where he was heading. But there was no point asking the unicorn to keep quiet about it. Keeping quiet was, thankfully, the only thing the animal did naturally.

Norman trod as lightly as he could on the gravel driveway. Malcolm could have done the whole getaway noiselessly, but Norman was a little more heavy-footed. When he reached the road without anyone calling him back, he took one brief look back towards the house, then broke into a run, pelting down the road in the direction, he hoped, of Summerside.

At the start, he was pretty confident of his sense of direction. The fields on either side of the road looked familiar. The low rock walls looked familiar. Even the hay bales looked familiar. But as he slowed to a walk to catch his breath, he realized that all fields, all rock walls and all hay bales look pretty much the same. The road wound away from the house, never in a straight line and never flat. Hills, walls and high hedgerows seemed always to obscure his view, so it was difficult to get a bearing and he became less and less sure he was going in the right direction.

He'd figured that if he followed the road, he would arrive in Summerside eventually, but after an hour he was less certain. When the road just stopped in the middle of a hayfield, he realized he'd missed a turn. It took him twenty minutes to track back to the fork he'd missed, and he followed that again for another forty-five. It was nearly noon and he'd eaten all his granola bars and had started looking for houses. At worst he could ask for directions; at best he could ask for a few pieces of paper. That wasn't too weird, was it? People asked for a cup of sugar from their neighbours all the time.

What was weird, now that he considered it, was that he hadn't seen a single house or cottage, or even any sheep or cows. Norman didn't think he'd ever driven for more than five minutes in England without seeing a sheep or a cow, and there were houses everywhere . . . usually. He was getting that queasy feeling that something was more deeply wrong than he'd first guessed when he arrived at the second dead end. But this wasn't just an empty field at the end of the road. A few feet beyond, the asphalt fell away completely. There was nothing but sky. It was as if the world just ended there.

Norman inched slowly forward until he could see over the edge. What he saw made him dizzy with vertigo. He was on the edge of a huge cliff. The drop was almost vertical. Many, many feet below, the sea crashed against the rocks, but from this height, Norman could barely distinguish the sound of the waves from the sound of the wind across the fields. Something felt wrong about this. Norman knew England was an island, but this cliff didn't seem right. It just felt as if it didn't belong there. He was certain that the Shrubberies was more than a few hours' walk from the sea.

It was dawning on him that Kit might have changed more than the occupancy of the Shrubberies. Doubling back again, he gave the stone walls and empty fields a closer look. They looked normal, unremarkably normal, but maybe that was the point. Maybe they were supposed to look real. Norman was beginning to wonder if this wasn't the real England or the real Shrubberies. His sense of direction wasn't that bad. He ought to have at least seen Summerside from one of the rises on the road, but the hedges and walls were always in the way. He ought to have passed at least one house or one person in half a day of walking, but the country seemed remarkably empty today.

The further he walked, the more convinced he was that this wasn't the real England and the real Shrubberies but a book set in

England and the Shrubberies. How else could he explain why the countryside was so empty and all the roads went nowhere? Uncle Kit wasn't a magician. He couldn't actually distort the earth, or at least Norman hoped he couldn't.

It was almost better, he decided. If this was all just another book, Kit's meddling might not be so bad. It might mean that back in the real world, Norman's mom and dad were going about their business as usual, and there was no unicorn in their backyard. But in another way, it was worse. If this place was a book, then Kit had more control over it. He couldn't get rid of all the paper in the world, but he might be able to banish all the paper from a book.

The nature of Kit's bookweird powers was still a bit of a mystery. His uncle seemed jealous of Norman's ability to get into a book just by eating his way in. Kit's own ingress required props and memorization, but his uncle had been at this much longer and seemed to understand it better. Norman had thought he'd reached some sort of agreement with him back at Kelmsworth—that Kit had learned his lesson about messing with other people's books and other people's lives—but it seemed now that he didn't know any other way to live.

When the third road ended in yet another empty field, Norman stood and watched the grass for a long time before retracing his steps down the road. It was hot again by English standards and the coins in his pockets felt heavier all the time. He stopped by the wayside and relocated the money from his pockets to his knapsack, but that only reminded him that he'd eaten all his food. It would be time soon to think about giving up for the day. He hadn't planned to be away anywhere near this long. If he didn't find a house soon, he would have to return to the Shrubberies and try again another day.

It was a relief when he came upon the train tracks. It was not that he expected a train to come along. Not a single car or truck had passed him all day, so why would trains be any different? No, by now Norman was certain that this was not the real world but some sort of strange, empty book without people in cars or on trains.

It was probably a poem or something. That might be Kit's worst trick yet, to trap him in a poem. Nothing ever happens in poems.

The tracks at least told him that he was on a different road, since he hadn't crossed any tracks that morning. They also gave him an idea. He hadn't been able to see much earlier because of the walls and hedgerows that lined the winding roads, but there were no walls alongside the tracks. The rails ran along a high embankment that would provide a perfect lookout. With renewed enthusiasm, Norman hoisted his knapsack and set off down the tracks.

To begin with, it wasn't much different than being on the road—more empty fields and bits of forest—but as the tracks gradually climbed, he began to get a better view of the surrounding countryside. He came to the stop on top of a stone railway bridge and scanned the view. The hills did indeed stretch out as far as he could see. There was nothing like a village in sight. If there was a Summerside in this book, he was nowhere near it. Just one square of red stood out among the green of the hills and the yellow of the hayfields. Just one tile roof, glinting a little in the summer sunlight. The house below it was covered in ivy. From any other angle, it would have blended in with the woods. It was just one house, but it was all Norman needed—just one house with one piece of paper and he could get out of this.

There was no point taking the road. That was his mistake all along. Kit had figured that Norman would make a break for it and had twisted the roads around like a maze. But Norman wasn't going to let Kit determine his route any longer. From his vantage point on the embankment, he could see a narrow path along the edge of the hills. He leapt down from the embankment and set off along the path towards the house.

He couldn't say that he was happy—he was too tired to be happy—but he was relieved. This book made him nervous. It was too much like the real world. It made him wonder if he would be able to tell the real world if he saw it again. When he thought of this, it made him feel a little sick to the stomach. His mother had warned him that the bookweird was dangerous. Maybe this is what she meant. Maybe it made you so crazy that you could never tell what was real and what was made up. Maybe that was Kit's problem. There was certainly *something* wrong with him.

Norman had sworn to give up the bookweird, and it was Kit who'd drawn him back in. Norman had had no choice, really. His uncle had bookweirded Malcolm into *Intrepid Amongst the Gypsies* and left him to be captured by the Kelmsworth Poacher. He'd known that Norman would follow him into the book. It was a game for Kit, and he didn't seem to get that Norman didn't want to play anymore. Norman needed to settle things with his uncle if he was ever going to be done with the bookweird for good.

Maybe it was the worry that distracted him, or maybe it was because everything had looked so familiar today, but he didn't recognize the fields and paths he followed towards the red-roofed house in the distance. When he saw the unmistakable black shape of the unicorn standing at the edge of the field, however, he realized where he was. It wasn't just any ivy-covered, red-roofed house—it was *his* house, the Shrubberies.

Raritan wasn't in his usual spot in the back garden. Instead, he stood on a small rise at the end of the neighbouring field, staring out as if on lookout. He looked for all the world as if he was waiting for Norman to return, as if he'd expected him to come back empty-handed and defeated.

Norman didn't even meet the unicorn's eye as he trudged past him towards the back gate. Raritan let out a little whinny as the boy passed him, almost like a human's exasperated sigh, but Norman refused to acknowledge him. Nobody likes to hear "I told you so," not even from a unicorn. Raritan turned and followed Norman up the path to the garden gate, as if he had been waiting for him.

Norman took his frustrations out on the garden gate, slamming it open aggressively. Then he stood aside and held it open for Raritan to go through. He glared at the unicorn now, almost daring the creature to say something. Raritan, who had no need for gates, was already rearing to leap the fence when Norman turned to him. He seemed to stop mid-leap and acknowledge the gesture with a twist of his horned forehead, before striding through the gate.

Mollified a little by the unicorn's polite gesture, Norman closed the gate a little more gently behind him. He really just wanted to go into the house. He was famished now and exhausted. He needed to lie down on the couch with whatever junk food Kit had stocked the pantry with.

The unicorn stopped him with a little nicker, almost like a polite cough to catch his attention. Norman turned to stare at him. The frustration was clear on the boy's face, but he said nothing.

"Aren't you going to ask me about your friend the talking stoat?"

Norman lifted his hand from the doorknob and shook his head. He had been ready to call a truce with the unicorn, but he didn't need to be teased like this. Raritan just stared back, however, his big brown eyes as inscrutable as ever.

"Okay," he said, exasperated, "let's get this over with. Have you seen my friend Malcolm, king of the stoats? He's about this high, and he doesn't like to be made fun of either."

Raritan continued to stare. His eyes always seemed to be assessing the boy. Up close, his horn seemed to wave in judgment over Norman's head.

Norman closed his eyes briefly and shook his head. What was the point of this? He turned back to the door.

"Rabbits," Raritan murmured. His voice was low and secretive. It was almost like he didn't really want to say it.

"What?" Norman asked, not sure he'd heard right.

"Rabbits," Raritan repeated in his grumbling horse-whisper. "Not stoats but rabbits. Singing in the woods."

Norman couldn't contain his surprise. "You heard rabbits singing? Where?"

Raritan backed up, drawing him away from the kitchen door, and continued in his reluctant tone. "You won't harm them?" It was half a question, half an order.

"Harm them?" Norman replied, offended. "Why would I hurt them?"

Raritan turned his head and pointed his horn towards the window of Kit's bedroom.

Norman scowled. "I'm not like him."

Raritan exhaled a dismissive whinny. "Yes, you are." He stomped a foot emphatically. Norman felt the vibrations through the ground. "Very like him. Meddlesome and dangerous."

Norman wasn't going to stand there and take this. "I'm not anything like him! Kit messes up things for fun. He doesn't care. I'm trying to help." His voice squeaked in protest, but he didn't like to be lumped in with his uncle. Calming himself, he asked, "What were they singing?" He'd heard singing himself yesterday by the footbridge. He'd told himself he was imagining it, but he had recognized the tune.

He hummed the tune to himself again now, trying to remember where he'd heard it before. "Mmm . . . mm, mmm . . . the streets of Cuaderno." It was there, on the tip of his mind. "Sound the trumpets from the towers of Logarno . . . mmm . . . mmm, mm . . . the tall ships in port." He got louder as the words came back to him, realization coming as fast as the tune. "The Great Cities!" he almost shouted.

Raritan actually shushed him.

"It's a song from The Great Cities of Undergrowth," Norman insisted in a whisper. "I heard it the other day by the bridge. You have to take me to those rabbits."

Raritan gave him another of those long, evaluating unicorn looks, then nodded and tossed his head towards the back gate. Norman followed him back down the path. He suddenly wasn't quite as tired anymore. Even his hunger could wait. The Great Cities were from the Undergrowth books—Malcolm's world. Norman had assumed that he and Malcolm had been separated— that the stoat king had been sent back to Undergrowth and Norman to the Shrubberies—but if there were talking rabbits here, rabbits who sang songs about the Great Cities, didn't that mean *this* was Undergrowth? Was it possible that Uncle Kit had managed to bring the Shrubberies to Undergrowth? It would explain the complete absence of people. It would mean that his friend was closer than he realized. But it would also mean that Kit was far more powerful than he thought, and that he was messing with Norman's favourite book again.

Outside the gate, Raritan stopped, halting Norman in his tracks. Had the fickle unicorn changed his mind again? But Raritan hadn't changed his mind. In a one strange, majestic movement he lowered his head and bent his front legs so he was kneeling. Norman watched dumbfounded, unsure what to do.

Raritan made up his mind for him. "Get on before I change my mind," he commanded.

Norman shook himself out of his reverie and climbed onto the kneeling unicorn's back. He had never actually ridden a horse before. That was Dora's thing, and he had a whole new appreciation for it as he wobbled on Raritan's giant neck, feeling around for something to hold on to. But he had little time to think about where to put his hands—Raritan was already rising and springing away. It was so sudden and so fast, it was almost like flying. Norman lurched backwards and grasped at Raritan's mane, his fingers clutching strands of hair. It was the only thing stopping him from hurtling to the ground. They turned and moved in a blur of motion away from the house, and as they did, Norman just caught sight of his sister at the back door. He might have imagined it, but he was sure that her mouth was open and her jaw dropped, as if seeing her brother riding *her* unicorn was a great and terrible outrage.

They were at the footbridge in a matter of seconds. Norman counted two footfalls on the wooden planks—*the-thunk, the-thunk*—and they were on the other side. Nothing could have prepared him for the speed. He wished he could see himself to get some idea of just how fast they were going. Wind whistled in his ears and stung his eyes as they hurtled across the meadow. At the first fence, he closed his eyes and nearly lost his stomach as Raritan leapt over it. It was like being on a four-legged roller coaster. Somehow, Norman had imagined that the rabbits would be close—he'd heard them by the bridge, after all—but Raritan kept

38

riding, across field after field. He covered more distance in a few
minutes than Norman had covered in an hour.

Between the slits of his half-closed eyes, Norman caught a
glimpse of the brick arches of the railway bridge. They ran alongside the railway embankment for a while, then plunged into the
river gully. Norman inhaled deeply as the water loomed ahead.
He heard himself gasp, "Oh no," as Raritan dispensed with the
bridge and galloped right at the river. The water hardly slowed him.
The unicorn must have known exactly where to ford it. They were
across it in a few splashes. Norman again closed his eyes as the
water sprayed up around them. This was no longer a roller coaster
but a flume ride.

Norman could not have said how long the ride lasted. He was
breathless when Raritan finally slowed to a canter. After the river
there had been more fields and some woods. Now they emerged
onto the lawn of a great house. Who knew rabbits travelled so far?

The great house was boarded up now, but it had once been
magnificent. Norman knew he recognized it from somewhere. It
reminded him of Kelmsworth Hall, but this house—made entirely
of pale grey stone and surrounded by a formal garden with a hedge
maze and a tiny ruined church—was even grander. It was the church
that brought it back to him. He had been here with his parents on
one of their boring old house tours. He had stood with his mother
on the balcony and stared out at this lawn, but now the balcony was
boarded up and the house seemed long abandoned.

Just weeks ago Norman had lain down inside this little church,
which was not even a real church but a rich person's garden orna-
ment. Now the grass around it had grown long and the hedge
maze was tangled with vines. Norman loosened his grip on
Raritan's mane and patted the unicorn's neck gratefully. There was
something else about this church—something Norman had dis-
missed as a dream, but it was coming back to him now. He slipped
off the unicorn's back and approached the ruin. It reminded him
of a church he'd seen in Undergrowth. That day on the tour, he'd
slipped away from his parents for a closer look, crawled inside and

fallen asleep on the moss-covered slate floor. As he dozed there in the shade, he'd heard voices, tiny little English voices arguing about something, and when he'd opened his eyes, there had been a rabbit in a monk's cloak and cowl. He'd only seen it for a moment. He'd blinked and it was gone.

"That was real," he whispered, mostly to himself.

Raritan couldn't have known what he was talking about, but he seemed to nicker in agreement.

Norman turned to the unicorn. "When did you see them? How many? Did you talk to them?" He blurted out his questions without stopping to listen for an answer.

Raritan, by contrast, was not to be rushed. He glanced at the church as if he was reconsidering the wisdom of what he had done. Before he answered, he exhaled deeply and solemnly.

"You will not harm them." Again it was an order, not a question.

Norman shook his head. It was unthinkable.

"They are timid creatures. I followed them from the bridge, but I did not speak to them."

"So far?"

"They have a shorter route through the woods, too narrow for you or me, but yes, it is a long way to go for herbs."

"They are here now? In the church?" Norman took a step towards it, but Raritan shook his head.

"In the grass. They are afraid. They are waiting for you to leave. If you approach them, they will scatter."

Norman surveyed the long grass but stayed where he was. These rabbits had to be from Undergrowth. He'd heard them by the footbridge, singing about the Great Cities. Either the rabbits had escaped from their book or he was in Undergrowth now. Either way, they could lead him to Malcolm.

He knew that people could escape from their books. He had seen it happen with the wolves that hunted him into *Fortune's Foal* and the thief from his mother's crime novel who'd turned up at Kelmsworth. Raritan too had come from another book, though Norman didn't dare ask him about it.

He took a deep breath and considered his words before he spoke. He knew quite a bit about the Great Cities. In fact, he probably knew more about their homeland than the rabbits themselves. Two Undergrowth books were set there, and Norman had read *Exiles of the Ultima Warren* twice. He knew the secrets of the displaced kings from Far Warren, who had founded the Great Cities. He knew about their long wars with the Sea Otter raiders and the longer truce that ended *The Rescue of Isla Wake*. He'd actually met someone who'd grown up in the Great Cities, Malcolm's Uncle Cuilean.

He cleared his voice again and turned to address the long grass.

"Rabbits of the Great Cities," he began—too loudly, he thought. He held his breath and waited to hear the sound of fleeing rabbits, but there was nothing but the whisper of the wind in the grass. "Rabbits of the Great Cities; citizens of Logarno, Cuaderno and Santander; people of the Book and the Tower—I hail you in the name of Cuilean of the Mustelids, fellow of the University of Santander, thrice champion of the Palio of Archers, proud bearer of the blue cloak and the banner of silver towers, lord protector of my liege, King Malcolm of Lochwarren."

It was an impressive speech. At least Norman thought so as he stood back to assess its effectiveness. But though he stared long and hard, there was no movement in the grass, save for the blades themselves swaying back and forth in the breeze. The whispering sound built though the wind itself was dying down, until Norman finally realized that it was the lowered voices of the rabbits arguing in the grass.

"Have you seen the size of the liocorno with him? He'd trample us to death."

"Or gore us with his horn."

"But he says he's with Cuilean from the old stories."

"Anybody can say he knows Cuilean. If I told you I was best mates with Mad King Boris, would you believe me?"

"I'd believe you if you said you *were* Mad King Boris," another voice snickered.

"Shush, you. I believe the boy. No human would know about Cuilean and the Great Cities unless he'd spent time with a civilized rabbit."

"Maybe he's come to take us back. Mightn't it be a sign of the end of our exile?"

"More likely a sign of us at the end of a liocorno's horn."

Norman knew this was the sort of argument that could go on forever if he let it.

"Please," he interrupted. "I need your help."

The rabbits in the grass went silent. He fully expected them to scatter now, but it didn't matter—he would stay here, sleeping in the ruined church if he had to, until they trusted him.

He didn't even hear the rabbit's footsteps as she emerged from the grass. He saw her before he heard her. She was smaller than Norman had expected. He wondered if she was even fully grown. Having hopped out from the grass, she came no farther, just stood there at the edge of the lawn. If not for the tiny crown of buttercups woven between her tall, attentive ears, no one would have thought her anything other than a wild animal.

On some impulse, Norman dropped to one knee so that he was closer to her height. At this level, he could see by her eyes that she was different. A wild rabbit never looked at you directly like this. A wild rabbit's eyes were always elsewhere, focused on the point of escape. This rabbit didn't look ready to run just yet.

"I'm Norman." He introduced himself in the kindest, softest voice he could muster.

She stared back for a long time, assessing him before answering. "I'm called Esme," she replied. "You'd better come with us to Willowbraid."

Norman rose slowly and took a step forward. The rabbit's ear flicked. Suddenly a dozen other rabbits appeared behind Esme at the edge of the tall grasses. She was the smallest of the bunch, but only she dared hop all the way out.

"You'd better leave your liocorno," she told him. "The boys are terrified."

Raritan snorted defiantly. Nobody was going to tell him what to do. Only Dora seemed to have any influence on him.

The thought of his little sister, alone back at the Shrubberies, gave Norman a little pang of guilt. "I need you to stay here," he told the unicorn. "Look after Dora, please," he asked. "Don't trust Kit. He's up to something."

The unicorn stared back defiantly before dipping his horn in assent. "I could do no less," he declared. Raritan's eyes flicked to the rabbits once more, as if he was still wondering if he'd done the right thing. He gave them a solemn nod before turning and trotting away. Norman and the rabbits felt the thud of his hooves as he moved to a gallop at the far end of the field and was gone.

"Willowbraid is this way," Esme said, her tall ears bending to indicate the woods at the edge of the great lawn. "We've sent someone ahead to tell the magistrates. They'll be arguing about you already, I expect."

Norman had some experience following woodland animals. They paid scant attention to the requirements of human travel. While the rabbits darted, barely seen, through gaps in the tall grass, Norman waded after them through the weeds. Burrs clung to his jeans and sharp leaves cut at his hands as he tried to make a path for himself. An abandoned rake lying hidden in the grass tripped him, nearly sending him headlong. He managed to stay on his feet, but a peal of rabbit laughter told him that his trip hadn't gone unnoticed.

It wasn't any easier when they got to the woods. The rabbits must have had paths down there in the brush, but they were no good for humans. The paths went through brambles and thorn bushes for a reason: rabbits don't like to be followed. The more Norman struggled, the braver his travelling companions became.

"Try to keep up," one insolent fellow told him.

"Watch out for the br—" another called the moment before a branch cracked him on the forehead.

Esme remained patient. "You'll need to crawl from here," she told Norman, and he followed her instruction, falling to his knees and moving forward on all fours. It didn't make him any faster, but it was the only way to proceed. The brambles had closed in over his head. It was almost as if they had been grown that way on purpose, arched over the path like a vaulted tunnel. Just enough light came through the cracks to illuminate the way. It made little diamond patterns on the firmly packed soil beneath. For the rabbits it was a broad, protected avenue. For Norman it was like trying to crawl through the Tunnels-O-Fun at Dora's last birthday party.

Seeing Norman tattered and gasping on his knees did wonders for his companions' confidence. They hopped back every now and then to encourage him, darting between his legs as they came up behind him and passed him. It would have been more discouraging if Norman hadn't felt so at home. He'd been through this before. It was like his first time in Undergrowth, trying to keep up with Malcolm and his father, Duncan, as the fearsome River Raider led his band of rebels back to Lochwarren. The thought of reuniting with his lost friend made the difficulties of the path easier to take. Despite the scratches on his arms and the twigs in his hair and the friendly insults of the rabbits, Norman was happy. He was back among the people of Undergrowth, and he was sure that he would soon see his friend again.

Even so, it was a relief to finally emerge from the tunnel and rise from his knees to stand again. But he could only just stand. A canopy of woven branches arched upwards, forming a huge dome that just grazed his head. It was like standing inside a huge over-turned wicker basket. Vines of flowers and ivy twisted through the weaving, providing a decorated canopy for the wide clearing below. Norman, still capable of being surprised by the ingenuity of the Undergrowthers, gasped as he surveyed it all.

There was a whole village in there. Beneath the canopy the clearing was laid out with streets, each of which was lined with little wicker dwellings, modest huts towards the edge, growing in size and grandeur towards the middle. In the centre was a single building that looked like it had been made of scavenged brick. A broad avenue led from this building to the stone cathedral. It was a perfect

Undergrowthian town. It wouldn't have been out of place in the Borders or the Windward Dales, but here it was instead, hidden in the woods, just a short distance from Norman's house in the country-side of England. It made him want to cry out with joy.

"Welcome to Willowbraid," Esme called up from beside his foot. "You'd better wait at St. Peter's. It'll be about the only place you'll fit."

Norman skirted the edge of the village until he reached the square in front of the cathedral. The two tall doors at the front might open wide enough for him to fit his head inside, there was no way he was going to fit his shoulders through. Instead, he just sat down cross-legged in the square.

A delegation of rabbits approached, following the avenue from the brick hall, where they had evidently just finished meeting. Many of the rabbits wore brown monks' robes, which were almost indistinguishable from their fur. At the head of the delegation was a dark brown rabbit in red robes. He wore a black hat and had a gold chain around his neck. As he got closer, Norman could see that his hair was grey beneath his ears and about his whiskers. Norman could also see that he wasn't happy. He carried a tall staff that he jabbed angrily into the ground as he walked.

Behind the official party, all of Willowbraid seemed to have come out. Rabbits young and old poured out of their houses and onto the street, rushing to the square to see the spectacle. The crowd halted when they reached the edge of the square. No rabbit seemed to want to get any closer than two human arm's lengths, and yet none of them could take their eyes off the human who sat cross-legged in the middle of their church square.

The members of the official delegation also kept a wide berth, skirting the edge of the square around to the steps of the cathedral, where they all gathered in rows as if they were assembling for a group picture. The old rabbit in the red robes climbed the steps last and took his place at the front of their ranks.

"Who is responsible for bringing the two-legger here?" he demanded, rapping his staff on the stone steps as he did so.

The rabbits in the crowd took their eyes off Norman for just a moment to look around. Their eyes flitted madly as they tried to guess who would be mad enough to bring a human here.

Esme stepped forward. "I am, Father. I brought him here."

The crowd gasped.

The old rabbit frowned, but his voice softened. "Esme, you should know better. There are rules against talking to the two-leggers, and they are made for good reason. You want to end up a martyr like St. Peter up there?"

Norman hadn't noticed the mosaic on the front of the cathedral. It showed a little rabbit in a blue coat being stuffed into a burlap sack by a giant human hand. The human boy turned around to look at the crowd that had gathered. There were a lot of wary faces and a lot of baby bunnies cowering behind their mothers' aprons.

"He's going to bake us all into a pie!" one tiny voice cried out in a panic. It was greeted by muttering and grumbling. Somewhere a baby rabbit started crying. It was about the most pitiful thing Norman had ever heard. Humans, he realized, were the stuff of rabbit horror stories. He was their bogeyman.

"I'm a vegetarian," Norman whispered to no one in particular. He was starting to realize that he was not in Undergrowth—that this was the human world and the rabbits were as lost as he was.

Esme, still standing beside him, repeated his assertion earnestly. "He's a vegetarian."

If the crowd heard her, they didn't show it. Their voices continued to rise in panic and anger.

"Blind him!" someone cried.

"Throw *him* in a burlap sack, Alderman," shouted another.

More children started to cry.

Esme tried to mollify the crowd, but they pressed in closer, and her protests were drowned out by the din. Norman watched nervously as the rabbits closed in. The bigger ones pushed to the front of the crowd; some of them held pitchforks.

A flick of Esme's ears alerted Norman to a movement at the top of the cathedral. Behind the steeple crouched two rabbits in silver-grey hoods. They had unslung their longbows from their backs and were reaching for their arrows. Norman went from nervous to panicked very quickly. The rabbits and hares of the Great Cities were renowned archers.

"This two-legger is special," Esme shouted. "He has heard the old stories. He knows the legend of Cuilean of Lochwarren." Her tiny rabbit voice went unnoticed.

Only Norman saw her struggling to be heard. Being too quiet had never been his problem, and now it was time he spoke up. He'd talk some sense into them, he thought, pressing his hands to the ground to raise himself to his feet. He'd hardly raised himself an inch off the ground, but the crowd gasped and took a step back.

"Esme!" the old man called nervously from the stairs. "Step away from the two-legger. Come to safety."

But Esme didn't move. Norman could tell from her twitching ears that the archers were getting into position. He didn't dare turn around. They would aim for his eyes and might be the last thing he saw. He let himself down to a seated position again.

"Rabbits of Undergrowth," Norman began, as calmly as he could. There was a murmur of disbelief as he spoke, but he did not yet hear the whistling of arrows. "People of Willowbraid, citizens of the Great Cities," he continued. He tried to look a few rabbits in their eyes, like they teach you in public speaking, but they averted their stares. "My name is Norman Strong Arm," he said, using the name the stoats gave him and trying his best to duplicate the formal language of the books he loved. "I come here to ask your help. Long ago, the people of the Great Cities took in Cuilean of the Stoats. You fought at his side in the war with the wolves. I come here as a friend of the stoats, as the protector of my lord, Malcolm, heir of Lochwarren. The stoat throne is in danger again." A hundred little rabbit jaws dropped as he spoke. "I need your help to return to Lochwarren, to the side of my friend and king."

There was a long silence after he finished his speech. Esme looked up at him, her whiskers twitching and rippling in puzzlement. When still no one said anything, Norman screwed up his courage and turned his head slowly towards the cathedral. He couldn't help squinting instinctively to protect his eyes.

The delegation of rabbit dignitaries stood in stunned silence. Esme's father opened his mouth to speak, but no words came out and he closed it again.

At Norman's side, Esme raised her voice again. "He's been to Lochwarren, Father. It means we can go back. It means the exile is over."

For a long time, Esme's father just stood there. A hundred decisions seemed to be made and unmade in that silence.

"We'd better have the whole story," he concluded finally.

The Rabbits of England

It took some time to get the rabbits of Willowbraid to return to their homes. The younger ones lingered, approaching Norman cautiously and sniffing him tentatively, daring each other to touch him, until Esme shooed them away.

The meeting was held in the cathedral. The rabbits opened the two main doors, but it was still only wide enough for Norman to fit in his head and his forearms. He rested his chin on his hands, but the rest of his body lay on the square outside. It was a vulnerable position. The archers had been moved indoors and stationed on the catwalks and stairs. He was an easy target lying there, and he would not be able to get out quickly. The sight of Esme at his side reassured him. They were on the same level for once and he was able to look her in the eye again.

"Your father is in charge?" Norman whispered.

"He's the alderman. They usually listen to him." She gave him a quick rabbit smile, but Norman wasn't sure that this was necessarily a good thing.

The magistrates filed in through one side door. A line of robed monks filed in the other. When they had assembled, Norman assumed it was time to speak and cleared his voice to tell the whole story. Esme's father stopped him with a raised hand.

"We'll hear more from you later. First let us rabbitfolk talk."

He called Esme, and she told the assembly how Norman had summoned them from the edge of the grass field. The rabbit elders grumbled and harrumphed as she told them how he had called out the names of the Great Cities. When she mentioned Raritan, they gasped and nearly shouted in outrage.

One of the magistrates rose in protest. "Get him out of here now, Alderman Morgan. We must leave the village. It's the rule that's kept us alive: when the two-leggers find us, we move on. And this one has a liocorno. It does not bode well for us."

Esme's father held up a hand to silence the other magistrate and turned to Norman. "Why did you come to the great house?" he asked. "Who told you we would be there?"

"The unicorn, Raritan, told me, and I remembered that I'd seen rabbits there before . . ." Norman tried to recall exactly what he'd heard and seen when he woke up from his nap inside the folly. "Two monks talking about celebrating St. Peter's Eve."

The delegation turned to stare at one of the brothers, who coughed nervously and tried to look away.

"Brother Timothy? That would have been you, I presume?" Alderman Morgan asked.

"Yes, yes," the monk began, stuttering apologetically. "I believe I recall stumbling on a young two-legger sleeping in the old ruin."

"That's right," Norman affirmed excitedly. "The ruined cathedral. It looks just like the one at Edgeweir—the one the foxes started but never finished."

There was a loud grumble of protest.

"Where did you hear about the Great Cities, and about Lochwarren and Edgeweir?" Alderman Morgan's voice rumbled with suspicion.

Norman paused before answering. He'd learned to be very careful about this. You couldn't just tell someone they were a character in a book you'd read. Nobody wanted to believe they were from a book. Everyone thought theirs was the real world.

"I've been to Edgeweir and Lochwarren. Cuilean himself told

me the stories of the Great Cities as we warmed ourselves by the campfire. I was there when the stoats were freed from Scalded Rock and when they won the Second Battle of Tista Kirk. I saw the wolves routed and the stoat flag raised again at Lochwarren."

"This is an outrage!" someone called. It was the magistrate who had spoken earlier. There was a murmur of agreement behind him. "How blatant must his lies be? He speaks of ancient history. Are we to believe that this pup is a thousand years old?"

Alderman Morgan turned to stare. He seemed to have no answer to this question. Esme furrowed her brow and twitched her nose, as if trying to puzzle it out.

"Father, the chronicles tell us of the exile," she began quietly, gaining confidence as she formed her understanding, "when our ancestors came here generations ago. They passed from a world where the citizens were wise and spoke in many tongues to this place, where all animals are dull and only the two-leggers have the power of speech. Isn't it possible for a two-legger to go the other way?"

Norman saw what she was getting at. "Yes, it is possible," he asserted. "That's what happened. I travelled to Undergrowth the same way you travelled here."

"But that was centuries ago! Our people have been exiled among your kind for centuries."

"I can't explain it," Norman said. "I don't understand it, but this travelling between worlds is like travelling in time too. It's weird."

The word seemed to resonate with the rabbits. They mumbled and argued about what it meant.

"It *is* weird," Brother Timothy interjected. "No one has ever been able to explain how we came here or why. There are those who think that our exile is a punishment or test. There are those, even after all these years, who think that the old stories are legends—that there never was an Undergrowth and we have always been the only thinking, speaking animals in the forest."

His comments were greeted with more shouts of outrage and protest.

The rabbit monk continued, "Of course no one here questions the chronicles, but you understand our skepticism. For a human boy to say that he has been through the same weirdness—for him to say that he has seen our homeland—it seems a little . . ."

Alderman Morgan finished his thought: "A little too good to be true."

"I can show you," Norman protested. "I can go there and bring something back as proof."

"Can you take us?" Esme asked eagerly. "Can you show us the way back?"

The magistrates and monks waited for Norman's answer.

"I don't know," he answered finally. He wanted to tell them yes. He wanted to tell them he could get them all back to Undergrowth. But the bookweird wasn't that predictable. He had a hard enough time bringing *himself* to the right place, never mind a whole village of rabbits.

Brother Timothy nodded solemnly, as if he thought as much. An easy answer would have been too suspicious. "What do you need, boy?"

They took Norman to the scriptorium. He lay down on the grass behind it, happy to be out of the cathedral. Although the archers on the catwalk had eventually relaxed, he'd still felt vulnerable—and it wasn't exactly comfortable lying there with his head through the door.

"Can we bring you some food, boy?" Brother Timothy asked now.

The offer made Norman nostalgic for Undergrowth. "Do you have any lingonberry pie?"

"Ha," the monk laughed. "You aren't in the Borders now, lad. You'll have to make do with good old English raspberry tarts. Ambrose, you fetch him a dozen or so. Esme, why don't you bring your vegetarian friend a dandelion salad?"

Esme and a young monk hopped off to bring him some food, leaving Norman alone with the older monk. There would be sentries somewhere, of course, but they kept themselves well hidden. The sun was descending now and just a dim purple light fell through the cracks of the Willowbraid dome.

"Tell me," Timothy asked quietly, "the ruin at the great house? Is it really just like the Abbey Church at Edgeweir?"

Norman nodded.

"It was supposed to be ours, you know," he said confidentially. "That's how the story goes. The brothers accompanied the Rabbit Legion to the Highlands. Once the war was won, we were to finish building the church at Edgeweir and found a community there."

"But what happened? How did you end up here in England?"

"It is the weirdness of which you spoke. Five hundred legionnaires marched from Logarno along with armourers, blacksmiths, healers, cooks and our brothers. We heard that Cuilean and his young nephew, Malcolm, were gathering their armies to meet the wolves at Tista Kirk. We followed the old highland road, but we never reached the battlefield. We emerged from the forest on the edge of a cliff next to a sea. We could not understand it. We saw warriors massing, but they were neither our stoat allies nor our wolf enemies. They were creatures we had heard of only in books: giants; hairless bears; two-footers; monsters from fairy tales and legends."

Brother Timothy's story made Norman queasy. There were hundreds of years of history in the Undergrowth books, dozens of kingdoms and dynasties, and yet the rabbits had come from the very same time when Norman was there, from the very same forest he himself was lost in.

"And the church—the copy of Edgeweir—did you build it?"

"No, we discovered it here, many generations later." Brother Timothy spoke quickly, as if he'd found a favourite topic. "We always felt the church was special, but we never guessed that it was a copy of the one at Edgeweir. Did you really see Edgeweir? Did you meet the last of the fox abbots?"

"I met *a* fox abbot," Norman answered cautiously. "And I slept one night on the moss inside the church."

Brother Timothy just shook his head in appreciation.

Norman didn't tell Timothy that the fox abbot of Edgeweir was no ordinary fox. He was his uncle, Kit. It made Norman think. Was it possible that Kit had brought the rabbits to England?

"How long have you been here?" he asked cautiously.

Esme's soft voice interrupted. "The rabbits of England are an ancient line." In the growing darkness, Norman had not seen her return. She placed two trays on the grass between them and continued as if reciting a history lesson. "Our forefathers arrived on these shores during the times of the Anglo-Saxon kings. We have seen Vikings and Normans, Tudors and Yorks. We have endured the clearing of the forests and the coming of the railroad—"

It sounded like this recitation went on for a while, but Norman couldn't help interrupting. "During Viking times?" His voice squeaked just a little as he asked.

Esme and Timothy both nodded.

"Near Maldon?" Norman barely dared to ask.

"How did you know?" the monk said, surprised.

Norman stuffed a raspberry tart into his mouth to avoid answering. He was struggling to get his head around what he had just realized. It wasn't Kit who'd brought the rabbits here. It was Norman. After all, characters had followed him out of Undergrowth before. Three wolves had pursued him into *Fortune's Foal*. The rabbits must have been pulled along into that old Anglo-Saxon poem of his father's, *The Battle of Maldon*. Only *The Battle of Maldon* was about a real event. He had brought the rabbits into historical reality—into the *real* England—and they been here ever since. His mind twisted and contorted to hold on to the idea.

Esme and Timothy watched in silent amusement as Norman devoured the food in front of him. It was fully dark now, and he had not eaten all day. Malcolm would have been proud of the way he scarfed the tarts, and even the dandelion salad was surprisingly good. Brother Ambrose brought a second round of tarts and stayed to marvel at the giant eating machine. When Norman was done eating, they continued to watch for some time, exchanging glances, as if waiting for one of the others to say something.

It was Esme who finally broke the silence. "Father says we'll have to move from Willowbraid now. He says it doesn't matter if you are friendly. Humans can't help telling, and that means disaster for us."

She looked to the monks as if hoping they'd take up the topic, but Timothy and Ambrose let her continue.

"You said you wanted our help." She paused to frame her thoughts. "You said you wanted to help the stoats. That means you know the way back. You know the way to the old countries. Father doesn't believe you, but I do. I want you to take us with you."

When Norman looked into her glossy brown eyes, he didn't know what to say. She seemed so hopeful, so expectant. He didn't want to disappoint her, but he couldn't count on his ability to control the bookweird. He'd brought Malcolm with him once, just that once. It didn't work every time he tried, and he couldn't imagine how he would transport a whole village with him. It was the sort of thing he seemed to be able to do only by accident.

He wiped the crumbs from his lips and surveyed the three expectant rabbits. "I'm not sure, but I can try."

The rabbits could not control their joy, and there is something impossibly cute about smiling rabbits. Norman half expected them to break into song.

"I'll need some paper and some sort of pen or pencil." He paused to think if there was anything else that would help. It was more than a year since he'd been to Lochwarren, long enough for him to wonder whether he could describe it accurately, or whether his dreams had started to dilute his memory. "And any books you have that describe the Highlands, especially the lands around Lochwarren."

"Is that where you think the passage is?" Brother Timothy asked.

Norman nodded, not knowing any way to explain it better.

"Are you going to draw us a map?" asked Esme.

That was a harder question to answer. "Sort of," he replied. "It's something the fox abbot taught me—a way of moving between this world and the world of your ancestors."

The rabbits hopped away to fetch the writing materials. They emerged from the scriptorium with several blank scrolls, an inkpot and a tiny quill. To Norman, who had been looking for pencils and paper for two days, it was almost as welcome as the food. He took the quill between his thumb and his forefinger. Only a tiny fraction of the feather stuck out. It was worse than the shortest mini-putt pencil.

Esme laughed when she saw it. "We could make you another one, but you'd have to wait until tomorrow, when we can find a bigger bird."

Norman made a face. He didn't like the idea of waiting.

"Is it hard to draw?" Esme asked. "If you drew the map in the dirt, I could copy it for you."

"It's not actually that kind of map. It's more like directions."

"Well, we can take dictation," she suggested. "Ambrose is the expert. He works in the scriptorium."

At that moment, Timothy and Ambrose returned carrying a stack of books. At a nod from Timothy, Ambrose rolled out a reed mat. The older monk separated a few volumes from the pile for Norman. "These are the ones you'll want," Brother Timothy said. "They're the oldest chronicles of our arrival here."

They were tiny books. Norman opened one gingerly, afraid of ripping a page. The dim light made it difficult to read. Even squinting, Norman had trouble picking out the words. Timothy brought an oil lamp and held it over the boy's shoulder, but Norman still struggled. He shook his head.

"It's too small. I can't read it."

"I'd heard this. You humans don't see well in the dark," Timothy said. "Ambrose, you read it."

The younger monk had hardly said a word all night. Now he stood back, some steps away from them, and shook his head slowly.

"Ambrose has heard too many campfire stories about two-leggers eating up little bunnies," Esme teased. "Never mind, I'll do it."

It didn't take them long to find the right passage. The Under-growth rabbits were obsessed with the details of their arrival in

England. It was a huge mystery to them, and they'd been trying to puzzle it out for centuries. They went over the story again and again, trying to retrace their path and figure out where they went wrong.

Esme had a very sweet reading voice. She read like his mother with a bedtime story, with just the right pace and emphasis, as she related the first accounts of the Rabbit Legion's march down the high road out of Logarno and through the plains to the Highland foothills. It almost put him to sleep right there, but he kept himself awake for just a little while longer. The legion followed the king's road from the lowland stoat villages into the high country, where the wolves still held ground, then headed down a hunting track towards Tista Kirk. At one turn, the path emerged into a high meadow, from which the rabbits looked out across Lochwarren to the castle itself on the other side. Norman could imagine it well. It was Malcolm's castle. In the rabbits' chronicle, the wolf flag still flew over the towers. The Second Battle of Tista Kirk had not yet been fought and won, and Norman Strong Arm had not yet led the conquest of the castle.

"Can you copy this out for me?" he asked, looking from Esme to Ambrose, not sure if the little monk had overcome his fear of humans. "But take out everything about the wolves."

He did not want to go back to quite this spot. He didn't want to fight the Battle of Lochwarren Castle again. A lucky shot had felled the wolf captain, and Norman knew he could never make that shot again in a million years.

"Describe it with the red Mustelid ensign and"—he paused before adding reluctantly—"the flag of the long-tailed weasels."

The rabbits gave him a peculiar look. "That's not much in the way of directions," Esme said.

"You'll have to trust me," Norman told her. "It's mysterious for me too, but it works. Just please try to write it big enough for a poor giant like me to read."

They didn't question him any further. The quiet young monk dutifully picked up his quill and began copying. Esme looked over the scribe's shoulder as he did so, frowning. He copied quickly, throwing sand on the scroll when he was done to dry the ink and handing it to Esme, who handed it to Norman.

It was perfect. The writing was just big enough for Norman to read, but the whole thing fit on the tiny piece of paper. He took it and placed it in his back pocket. "Do you think you can make me another copy?" he asked. It wouldn't hurt to have an extra around for when he was in a tight spot.

"I still don't see how that's going to help us find our way back," Esme said doubtfully. "How is a description of a mountain meadow going to help? Shouldn't we be looking for a hidden passage? A crevice in a mountain or something?"

"It's complicated," Norman told her. "You'll see tomorrow, when it's light."

He was starting to feel guilty about deceiving the rabbits. They had been so kind to him and he was going to desert them. He made a promise to himself to come back. It was one more thing on his list: find Malcolm, recover the treaty map the stoat king needed to defend his claim to the throne, save Jerome from the siege of San Savino . . . oh, and find his parents. Add to that saving the talking rabbits of England, and it was all beginning to feel insurmountable.

Esme must have sensed his discomfort, because she didn't push the question further. Instead, she watched quietly as Ambrose scribbled away.

The sound of his quill scratching on paper seemed loud now. The village of Willowbraid was closing down for the night. A few lights flickered in the taverns along the main road, but there were no voices, just the sound of birds and Ambrose's pen. Norman yawned.

"You ought to get some sleep now," Timothy recommended. "Esme's father has assembled an expedition party to accompany you in the morning—scouts and trackers mostly, but I'll see if we can sneak in one or two of the brothers to document the journey."

Out of the corner of his eye, Norman caught a glimpse of Esme's reaction. He had been around talking animals enough to read their expressions, and hers was clearly a scowl. She thought she should go. Norman didn't disagree. He wished he could tell her that no rabbits were coming with him to Undergrowth this time, but that hardly would have helped.

"I think you should come too," he told her finally. "You were the only one brave enough to come out of that meadow, after all."

Esme didn't answer him right away, just waited for Ambrose to finish his second copy. "Just so you don't get any ideas," she warned him as she handed it over, "there are archers stationed up in the high branches. So don't think you can sneak off in the night."

She said it with a smile, but Norman knew she wasn't joking. He put the second page in the pocket of his backpack and nodded in thanks.

"I'll sleep here, I guess?"

They left him there on the grass outside the scriptorium. Tired as he was, he didn't drift off right away. First he had to eat the page that the rabbit monk had copied for him. As he chewed, he surveyed the dome above him. He couldn't pick out any movement or glint of light between himself and the stars, but he didn't doubt that the sentries were up there. What were they thinking as they watched him eat the piece of paper? To them, he was just a crazy two-footer. For all they knew, every human boy ate a page of paper before he went to bed each night. They couldn't guess that he was escaping right before their eyes.

When he was done eating, he curled up on the grass to fall asleep. The night had grown cold, so he tugged George Kelmsworth's school sweater from his backpack and pulled it over his head slowly, trying not to alarm the sentries with any sudden movement. The sweater helped, but it wasn't enough. The only other cover was the canvas knapsack itself. If he slipped both arms into it backwards, it covered most of his chest and stomach, providing a little extra warmth. It wasn't much, but it was enough that he could fall asleep.

Wanted

When you have slept in as many strange places as Norman had, waking up in a field of heather on a sunny summer morning is a kind of luxury. Even before he opened his eyes, he knew that the bookweird had worked. There was something in the air that told him he was back in the Highlands of Undergrowth. It wasn't just the smell of pine and highland flowers; you could get that on a camping trip. No, it was a special bright smell—more of an idea than a smell, maybe, like opening a new book that you know is going to be a favourite. Whatever it was, Norman filled his nostrils with it and sat up.

He didn't even need to stand to see it. It was right there across the lake: the castle on the crag, overlooking the dark grey waters of the loch. From here, Norman could see the dock from which Malcolm's father, Duncan, and Uncle Cuilean had escaped on the night the wolves overran the castle. He could also see the little chapel where Malcolm had been crowned. By all rights, the stoat ensign should be flying now on the highest tower, but the banner was the red Mustelid pennant, the flag flown by the weasels and the snow ermines.

So he'd arrived at the right time. The wolves had been defeated and the stoats and weasels still contested the throne. Norman wasn't worried. The wolves were gone, and that was the important thing. So what if the long-tailed weasels occupied the castle for now? They were distant relatives of the stoats. Their argument with Malcolm and Cuilean was a legal one, and it would all be settled when they brought back the treaty map from Jerome's library.

Norman stood up and shook the grass from his clothes. The canvas knapsack was still firmly strapped to his stomach. He removed it and pulled off his sweater too. It was warm enough already for just a T-shirt. He stuffed the sweater back in his pack and reassured himself that Ambrose's second copy was still there. If he'd been smart, he would have asked for some extra paper. Once you set off bookweirding, you could never have enough.

There were two ways around the lake. The high road was shorter, but it was tougher climbing. The low road went through the village of Lower Warren, which settled it. The British coins jingled in the pockets of Norman's knapsack as he set off down the trail. How many lingonberry pies could you buy with a giant ten-pence piece? he wondered, and smiled to himself.

The path closed in quickly and became one of those narrow forest trails that were wide and high to animals but tricky for humans. Pine branches were arranged at about eye height. Roots stuck out at just the right level to catch his toes or his ankles. Norman stumbled a few times and took a few swipes from branches to the forehead, but it hardly bothered him. He was back in Undergrowth! It was better than being home, and soon he would be seeing Malcolm again. They'd be feasting in the great hall of Lochwarren tonight.

The moment he thought of it was the moment he took his eyes off the path. He only meant to see how far he'd come, to see if he could spy the lake through the trees, but he chose exactly the wrong time. His foot caught on another upraised root, pitching him forward suddenly. He reached out to grab a branch to steady himself but came up with nothing. It was all he could do to protect his face as he lurched towards the dirt. He landed with a thump that knocked the wind from his chest in a sort of growling gasp.

He wasn't hurt—just a scrape on his arm—but it was a reminder that he wasn't made for this place. It went much easier when Malcolm was there to act as his lookout and guide. Norman stayed on the ground to catch his breath before rising. A familiar voice stopped him.

"That was graceful," the voice said. "I hope you weren't planning on sneaking up on anybody."

Norman looked up to see the creature that was waiting for him on the path.

"Esme! What are you doing here? How?"

The little rabbit cocked her head sideways to look at him. "I thought you were going to explain it. That's some magic of yours. Were you ever going to tell us?"

Norman didn't bother to get up off the ground. It was easier to talk to her from there anyway. "I didn't know what to tell you. I didn't think you would believe me, and I wasn't sure that I could bring you with me. I had to try by myself first."

The rabbit didn't look pleased. "Why didn't you just say that you could only bring whatever fit in your bag?"

"Is that how you did it? You snuck into my bag?" You'd think you would notice a rabbit crawling into a knapsack on your chest. She must have been very quiet. "That was clever."

Esme's expression softened a little bit. "I watched you eat the paper. You couldn't see me in the dark, but I could see you. When you ate the paper, I knew it had to be something to do with magic."

"I'm not very good at it," Norman told her apologetically.

Esme just sniffed. She watched Norman for some time, then seemed to make a decision and took a package from her cloak. "I've brought breakfast."

The package contained a half-dozen bread rolls and an apple. Norman sat down against a tree and tucked in.

"You were smart to bring these. I have some granola bars." He unwrapped one and offered it to her, but the rabbit shook her head.

"I ate hours ago. And I didn't bring these from Willowbraid. I bartered for them in the village below."

Norman was impressed. "You were up early, then."

"Humans sleep too long in the night and bustle about too much in the day," she told him.

Norman decided not to be offended. His mother was always telling him to get up earlier too.

"How are things in the Highlands?" he asked. "What do you think of the stoats?"

"They laughed at my accent, but they paid a good price for English herbs."

Norman paused long enough between bites of apple to watch Esme. She seemed very calm and collected for someone who had been transported through time and space in a knapsack. He didn't know rabbits well—all his time in Undergrowth had been spent with the stoats—but he'd always imagined them as jumpy and nervous. The only thing that seemed to bother Esme, though, was that he'd slept in.

"Was there any news in town? Did you hear anything about Malcolm or his Uncle Cuilean?"

The rabbit frowned at the question. "Stoats aren't a talkative lot, especially not with strangers, but their tongues loosen when they start to barter. Neither Cuilean nor Malcolm has been seen in weeks. They say that the regent Cuilean is sick and being looked after in the castle. No one knows where the young king has gone. The long-tails on patrol say that he's run away, that he was too young to rule and has lost his head."

Norman nearly choked on his bread roll. "The dirty liars. Malcolm never ran away from anything!"

Esme shrugged. "That's just what I heard. One of them told me, 'Once a river thief always a river thief'—whatever that means."

"Malcolm was raised by his father among the River Raiders of the marshlands," Norman replied angrily. "It's where he learned to fight. It's where he learned to be king."

Esme did not look convinced. "So you don't think he would have fled?"

"Not in a million years," Norman said with conviction.

"Then where do you think he is?"

Norman didn't answer for a long time. That was the problem, wasn't it? Where *was* Malcolm? When he didn't make it to England, Norman just assumed that he'd been sent back home too. But it could be a lot worse. Malcolm could already be in *The Secret in the Library*. If Uncle Kit was behind it, he could be anywhere, in just about any book.

"We'd better go talk to Cuilean," Norman concluded. "If Malcolm is around here, Cuilean will know where he's hiding."

He stood up to head down the trail, but Esme did not move.

"Not so fast. You can't just walk into town."

"Don't worry," he assured her, "they know me. I'm a hero here."

"Oh, they know you, all right, but I don't know about the hero part." She reached into her cloak and removed a yellowed piece of paper. It was torn at the corners, as if it had been ripped from a post.

Norman unfolded the paper to reveal pictures of a fearsome-looking giant and a sinister fox drawn in dark, menacing ink. Above them in big red letters was the word "Wanted." Below, the poster said: "Norman, aka Strong Arm, and Abbot Reynard the Fox are wanted for the theft of priceless artefacts from the Royal Treasury of the Mustelids, by order of Guillaume Long Tail."

Esme took the paper back from him. "It's not a very good likeness," she said, "but the blood dripping from the teeth is a nice touch."

Norman frowned. This wasn't really the sort of reputation he thought he'd left behind in Undergrowth.

"I didn't steal anything, just so you know."

"Oh, I know. You've proven yourself to be very trustworthy," Esme replied sarcastically. "What is it you're supposed to have stolen?"

"It's the Mustelid treaty map. It gave the stoats undisputed reign over the Highlands."

"So where is it?"

"It's hidden in a library . . . for safekeeping." He didn't bother to explain that his own mother had hidden it there, or that she'd done so trying to keep *him* safe. "Malcolm and I need to get it and bring it back."

Esme furrowed her brow a little. She knew there was much to

the story of Malcolm and Norman that he hadn't told her. She held up the poster again. "Is this fox fellow a friend of yours?"

"He's my uncle," Norman admitted reluctantly.

Esme raised her rabbit eyebrows comically. "Don't tell my father that. Foxes aren't very popular in Willowbraid."

"He's not very popular with me either." Discouraged, Norman sat down again against the tree. He felt his eyes starting to sting and placed his head in his hands to cover his embarrassment. It was just so frustrating. Every time he seemed to be getting somewhere, he hit a new roadblock. It had felt so good that morning, waking up beside the lake. Coming to Lochwarren was like coming home. He had imagined that Malcolm would be here waiting for him, and that they'd finally be able to get back to Jerome and the library. He'd expected to be welcomed by friends. To find out that he was an outlaw was a cruel blow.

He just sat there for a long time with his head in his hands. The tears didn't come, but that was about the only thing that didn't go wrong for him.

Esme finally interrupted him. "Is this Malcolm really your friend?"

Norman nodded. "Just about my only friend."

"I should take offence to that," she said softly.

Norman managed a smile back.

"If you trust me," Esme said, coming closer, "I have a plan."

The Capture of Norman Strong Arm

The news of Norman's approach travelled fast through the market of Lower Warren. It was difficult to miss the giant human boy descending from the forest path towards the village. Such a massive creature could not easily conceal itself or move stealthily, and at any rate, it made no attempt. Its giant feet slapped the ground like felled trees. Those who had seen the giant's shoe on display at the castle and had pronounced it a fake now admitted that it was actually smaller than the real thing. If possible, the human had grown since its last appearance.

The shout went up around the village, and messengers were sent to the castle. "Norman Strong Arm is here. They're bringing in Norman Strong Arm!"

The giant was met at the village gates by a squad of weasels, but the warriors lowered their lances when they saw that he was coming peacefully, and that the hard work of subduing the fugitive had already been done. They followed the giant cautiously as he made his way through the village up towards the castle. A captain of the guard led them through the centre of Lower Warren, shouting orders to the others, trying his best to make it look like he was responsible for the capture, but the crowds that lined the road could easily see who was in charge.

High on Norman's shoulders sat a small brown rabbit. In her hands she held the canvas straps of some complicated harness that had been strung around the giant's chest and shoulders. She did not look afraid at all. She looked absolutely fearless as she guided the human through town. No one could guess how she had managed to do it, but no one questioned the power she held over the beast. The fearsome giant they had heard so much about came placidly through town. He did not roar. He did not bellow. He did not gnash his teeth. Whatever the little rabbit had done to rein in the famously savage creature, she had done it well.

Every now and then, the rabbit seemed to lean in close to the human boy's ear and whisper some command. The human never answered, save perhaps for the occasional nod. Some of those who'd gathered that day insisted they saw him wink. The children especially were sure that he'd smiled at them in kindness, and that he was really a good giant. Their parents assured them that this was preposterous: the giant was just blinking in the harsh sunlight.

Norman wasn't as calm as he appeared. Esme had told him to look powerful but not menacing. Norman didn't think he was that good an actor. He stomped and smiled, stomped and smiled, and all the while Esme was whispering in his ear. "All the tradesmen and shopkeepers are stoats, but the soldiers are long-tailed. It's easy to see who's in charge here. If you see anybody you know, just nod or wink. I'll be able to find them later."

Norman did as he was told. There weren't many of Malcolm's former companions in the village that day, but those who were saw those winks and guessed what they meant. The tinker standing by the side of the road was Mackie, not the brightest of the River Raiders but as good a man in a fight as any. The farmer chewing a blade of grass under a tree just outside of town was Harald Bead Eye, a captain of the archers who'd fought at the side of Malcolm's father, Duncan. Norman had seen him bring down two ravens with as many arrows at the ambush in the Glace Hills.

Norman could hardly contain himself when he spied them. He wanted to thrust his arm in the air and shout at the top of his lungs, "All hail King Duncan, the hero of Tista Kirk!" and "Long live King Malcolm the Brave!" But he did what he was told and kept to the plan.

The knapsack that they'd strung across his chest didn't really bind him in any way. Esme had tied it in such a complicated fashion that it looked like she was guiding a horse. It wasn't the straps that fooled people, though—it was Esme herself. She was magnificent. The stern, unconcerned look she put on her face convinced everyone that she was in charge. While the people of Lochwarren stared on in awe, stepping out of the way as the giant approached, Esme stood calmly and imperiously on his shoulders like a conquering hero.

The troops that met them at the castle wore the polished armour and the tawny black-tipped cloaks of Guillaume Long Tail's household guard. Their beady black eyes peered out from behind their glinting helmets, and they did not seem to blink or flinch at the sight of the outlaw human.

Esme greeted them with her usual poise. "I am Esme Leporid, constable of the Great Cities. I have brought the human boy known as Norman Strong Arm in response to your warrant. By order of Prince Leopold of Santander, I hold him in custody until trial."

She held up the scroll that she and Norman had composed that morning. She had excellent rabbit penmanship, and between them, she and Norman had done a good job of counterfeiting the court language of the Great Cities, but they hoped that the long-tails didn't inspect it too closely.

"By the same order, I request an audience with Prince Cuilean. I have messages to him from Leopold. It is Leopold's desire that Prince Cuilean act as legal counsel to the human captive. When is the trial scheduled?"

A small weasel in orange-and-black livery stepped forward and gave them a little bow. "Milady Ambassador"—he sounded flustered and out of breath—"King Guillaume was not expecting you."

"Never mind," she replied breezily. "Take me to Cuilean, and prepare lodgings for two squads of Santandarian Guards. They stopped in the lowlands to clean up some wolf stragglers. They should be here tomorrow."

The little weasel gulped. He seemed to struggle for a response.

"Guillaume has ordered that Prince Cuilean not be disturbed. He is not well."

"Sick?" Norman asked, unable to contain his concern. The crowd surrounding him gasped at the sound of the giant beast, and the squad of household guards seemed to flinch. "Is he all right? Does King Malcolm know?"

The weasel steward was too shocked to reply.

Esme wasn't to be put off so quickly. "I am a trained herbalist. I was sent here for this very reason." She patted the pocket of her cloak.

The steward's little black eyes shifted from side to side as if he was searching for a response. "Very well," he said finally. "Come along."

He led them through the inner court and into the Great Hall through the huge doors normally reserved for wheeling food carts into the castle for feasts. They were the only doors that Norman could fit through. The guards followed, slamming the doors closed behind them ominously.

Norman freed himself surreptitiously from the straps of his knapsack and surveyed the Great Hall. Last time he was here, he was celebrating the victory at Tista Kirk and the crowning of King Malcolm, but the room was sombre today. There were no decorations, no trays of food, no revelling soldiers. Esme stared up at the high walls and rafters of what was the largest room she had ever seen. Norman's own sneaker was still there, up on the wall for all to marvel at. He wanted to tell Esme all about that celebration, so she could imagine for herself what it was like to be part of it, but the emptiness of the room made them both quiet.

A messenger appeared and whispered something in the steward's ear. He nodded and turned to address Esme.

"Cuilean can see you for a moment now, Ambassador Esme." He cast a wary eye towards Norman. "But, uh"—the master of ceremonial greetings struggled for the right way to address the human boy—"Sir Strong Arm, I am afraid this room is the only one that can accommodate you. You will have to wait here."

The steward held out an arm to point Esme in the direction of Cuilean's rooms. She hesitated for a moment, casting a glance towards Norman.

"I'll be okay," he told her, not at all confidently. "These are my old stomping grounds."

She nodded silently and then reluctantly followed the steward out of the hall. Norman thought how lucky he was that she had stowed away in his backpack. He'd never have got into Lochwarren Keep without her.

The moment she'd left the room, the guards took up their posts by the courtyard door, and Norman suddenly wondered whether he should be so pleased with himself. He had faith in Esme, but being cooped up in there made him nervous. He needed to find Malcolm and resume their search for the map.

He scanned the faces of the guards. They watched him without looking him in the eye.

"Did any of you fight at Tista Kirk?" he asked. He knew they hadn't—the weasels had not come to help the stoats fight the wolves for their kingdom—but their silence made him nervous.

That silence was soon broken. Norman heard an order given outside in the courtyard, followed by the clang of metal on the cobblestones. The doors to the Great Hall flung open, letting sunlight pour in and sending Norman staggering back into the shade. More weasel soldiers. For a moment they were only silhouettes in the doorway, dark forms surrounded by bright blue sky, but as Norman's eyes adjusted, he could see that they had come in their heaviest armour. Covered in steel from head to foot, they looked and moved more like robots than weasels, their limbs rising slowly and clanking down in unison. There was nothing to indicate that these steel machines encased tiny woodland creatures. Even their eyes were hidden by heavy visors. In his arms, each soldier carried a long halberd. Norman eyed the pointed spikes and took another step backwards into the hall.

The weasel knights marched forward two steps and formed two ranks across the open doorway. The first soldiers kneeled and planted their halberds in the ground. The second ones stood behind them, their weapons at shoulder height.

Norman raised his empty hands to show that he was unarmed.

"What's going on?" he called out, his voice cracking. "I'm not doing anything."

There was no answer from the phalanx of armed weasels. It suddenly became very quiet. The only sound was the clank and scrape of plate armour as the knights shifted and swayed. Maybe, Norman thought, they are as scared as I am at this point. People always say that about animals—that they are more afraid of you than you are of them—but did it apply when they were covered in metal and armed to the teeth?

"Where is Lady Esme?" he asked, a little more bravely.

"Come out into the courtyard!" a voice bellowed. Norman couldn't tell who had spoken. The knights stepped back, leaving a path for him to the courtyard, but their weapons stayed drawn and pointed.

"I gave myself up willingly. I came here to clear my name. King Malcolm will be furious if you hurt me."

"Bonnie Prince Malcolm is a scoundrel, not a king!" the voice shouted. It was coming from the parapets out in the courtyard.

"That's not what the Mustelid treaty map says!" Norman fired back. Despite the blades pointed in his direction, he stepped into the doorway to see who he was arguing with.

The knights shifted and growled, but they held their ranks.

High on the walls above the courtyard stood a large weasel surrounded by archers. He was big, but not fighting big; there were rolls of fat around his neck, and his big belly rested against the walls of the parapet as he sneered down at Norman. On his head he wore a crown that was too small for him. This had to be Guillaume, the weasel usurper.

"Search him," Guillaume ordered.

Four weasels inched nervously towards Norman. Two grabbed his knapsack, and two began to climb the legs of his jeans.

"Hey!" Norman yelled, lifting a foot to shake off a harasser. Then he saw the archers on the parapets raise their bows. "Lady Esme will not stand for this!" he yelled, submitting to the search.

Two weasels checked his pockets, removing and returning the blank pieces of paper he'd stashed in his jeans. The other two rifled through the canvas knapsack, casting its contents onto the cobblestones.

"Some sort of monster, eh? Needs his little bunny maiden to protect him!" Guillaume mocked. "Where's the map?" he demanded. "Does he have the map on him?"

The weasels who had frisked him shook their heads.

"Where is it, beast?" Guillaume growled. "Where is this map you say you have?"

"Where's Malcolm?" Norman countered. "Take me to Malcolm and we'll both bring you the map. We'll show everyone who's the rightful king here!"

"There is only one rightful king, and that is me!" Guillaume said, snarling.

Norman bit his lip. Until he actually had the map, it didn't do any good to provoke Guillaume. He wasn't here to fight the weasels. He was here to find Malcolm.

"I don't want to argue with you. I just want to talk to Malcolm. If you let me see Malcolm, we can explain everything."

Guillaume bared a yellow tooth and growled a sickly, hissing growl. "I don't need an ugly giant to explain anything to me. This is *my* castle, *my* kingdom. You are *my* prisoner, and you'll keep that foul gaping mouth shut." He shook his paw like a fist, then clutched the stone walls of the parapet as if he wished he could crush them. "You don't have any treaty map. You've got nothing," he spat. "You're a desperate little traitor. We'll have our trial for treason instead of theft. Your mincing little rabbit dupe can argue all she wants, but we're having an execution too!"

Norman glanced down towards the weasel knights, who were now slowly closing in around his feet.

"Take him away!" the tyrant ordered.

Norman stared defiantly for a moment, but one halberd poke at his ankle was enough to get him moving.

The guards marched him out of the courtyard and into the forest, half the squad leading the way, the other half behind prodding him forward. He trudged along despondently. There wasn't anything he could do. In an open field he might be able to make a break for it, but in the thick forest around Lochwarren Castle he wouldn't get more than a few feet.

The narrow trail descended towards the shore of the loch. As the castle receded into the distance, fear began to grip him. They could be taking him anywhere. He stared at the closed visors of his captors and wondered what their orders were. Guillaume had said there would be a trial, but Norman wouldn't put it past the sneaky weasel to skip straight to the execution.

He did his best to make conversation, to remind them that he was a friend to the Mustelids, but nobody answered him. Not a single head turned when he pointed out the spot where he'd first seen Lochwarren Castle and reminded them of the miracle shot that had brought down the first wolf. Inside their steel helmets the weasel knights were silent. A chill ran through Norman, and it wasn't just the cold wind coming from the loch.

The trail ended at a dock at the edge of the loch. Just this morning, he'd looked down at the lake and felt hopeful about seeing his friend again. Now the sun was low in the sky above the mountains, casting a long streak of silver across the lake, and he was further from Malcolm than ever. If he was going to make a break for it, it would have to be now. But the rowboat tied up at the dock was far too small to carry him, and the water looked cold and uninviting.

Norman wasn't a great swimmer, but he could probably outswim the weasels, especially if they had to remove their armour before jumping in the water. But where would he go? How far would he get? His kept his best escape route in his back pocket. To reassure himself, he patted the back pocket of his jeans and felt the outline of the tiny pen and the few sheets of paper. If he dove in the lake now, he'd wreck the paper.

The weasel squadron brought him to a halt at the edge of the water and turned him to face the cliff. When he saw the cast-iron portcullis that barred the cave opening, he realized where he was: this was the dock from which Duncan and Cuilean had escaped so many years ago.

"Get in there," a gruff voice ordered. The gate creaked as it was raised.

Norman hesitated for a moment. Even with his paper and pencil in his back pocket, he didn't like the idea of being locked in a cave. Another poke from a halberd got him moving once again.

The cave was large enough that he didn't have to duck to enter. The walls were smooth, carved from the rock by wind and water. At the back of the cavern, a set of stairs had been chiselled into the rock. The stairs climbed halfway up the wall to a tiny stoat-sized door in the rock face.

This was one end of a tunnel that led all the way to the castle.

Lochwarren Castle fell to the wolves at the very beginning of *The Brothers of Lochwarren*. Malcolm's grandfather was king then. Bodyguards had whisked Malcolm's uncle and father down this tunnel and to this cave, where boats waited to take them to safety. The wolves overran Lochwarren, but the two princes slipped away. Years later, Cuilean and Duncan would return to reclaim their kingdom and make Malcolm king.

It was strange to be here where it all began. The portcullis might be slamming closed behind him, but Norman felt strangely calm, as if he knew he was in the right place.

He hardly bothered with the mocking jibes of the guards.

"Whatever happened to that lumbering oaf of a giant who came to save the stoats?" one guffawed.

"Run off, I think," another answered, chuckling to himself inside his helmet. "Like his friend the boy king. Just goes to show, you can't trust a stoat . . . or his pet human. They'll bolt on you as soon as you turn your eye."

Norman took the tiny rabbit-made quill from his pocket and rolled it between his fingers. You don't know how right you are, he thought to himself.

It was only when he sat down to actually write something that he realized what a jam he was in. He could write himself out of the cave, but to where? Where was he supposed to go?

There was no point going back home as long as Uncle Kit was messing with reality at the Shrubberies, and he didn't want to return to Willowbraid without Esme. He could imagine the reception he'd get there if he came back alone. His face was probably already on another wanted poster.

In his back pocket he had Ambrose's second copy of the Lochwarren description. That might work, but it would only bring him back to where he'd started that morning—in the meadow on the other side of the lake, looking down at this very cave. He'd never actually tried this, using the bookweird to move from place to place inside the same book. It wasn't predictable at the best of times, and he had no way of knowing whether this would work.

No, the place he really needed to get to was San Savino. He needed to rescue Jerome—and Malcolm's treaty map—before the library burned down. Norman was just delaying things. He'd wanted Malcolm with him, because he always felt braver with the feisty stoat at his side. But there was no delaying anymore. He had to write himself into *The Secret in the Library*.

Norman held the quill and squinted at the paper through the pink air of the highland sunset. In a moment the sun would drop behind the mountains and it would be too late. Perhaps it was already too late. He wouldn't admit to himself that he was afraid to go back to the burning fortress in the desert.

It was a dangerous book, perhaps the most dangerous one he'd ever been in. Black John of Nantes was prepared to burn down an entire desert fortress to get his revenge. It terrified Norman, but that was exactly why he had to go back. It was about more than the treaty map. If Jerome died in that fire, it would be because of him.

He cursed under his breath and vowed for the eighth or ninth time in his life to give up the bookweird for good once this was sorted out. The bookweird always did this to you: no matter how you tried to fix things, you always ended up breaking something else.

By the time he'd finished scolding himself, it truly was night. The sun had descended behind the mountains and the cave was in complete darkness. Norman was angry with himself for putting it off. He was angry with himself for feeling relieved that he didn't have to go just yet. But he promised himself he would act quickly in the morning. He'd stay up all night if he had to, and at first light, he'd write himself a good description of Jerome's library and have it for breakfast. He could sleep after breakfast and wake up ready to rescue Jerome and the map.

It should have been easy to stay awake. There was plenty to worry about, and the stone floor of the cave was anything but comfortable. He did manage to stay up long enough to see the moon rise above the mountains, but not much longer than that. Even the guards were still awake when Norman dropped off.

Reunion

The voice that woke him seemed to come from nowhere, a whisper that echoed around the cave. There might be someone hiding in one of the dark crevices of the cave. There might be someone whispering right in his ear.

"Wha?" he asked groggily. Norman was used to waking up in strange places, but the darkness of the cave was more disorienting than most.

He'd heard a voice, but he hadn't heard what it said. He wasn't even sure whether he'd really heard it or simply dreamt it.

"I said that this is one of your more unusual rescues," the voice said cheerfully.

Immediately Norman was completely awake.

"Malcolm?"

"Keep it down, Strong Arm," the voice replied. "Those lazy weasel guards will sleep through almost anything, but your din could wake the dead."

Norman's eyes adjusted to the darkness a little. High up on the wall at the back of the cave, a light flickered. He scrambled to his feet and stepped towards it.

There it was, not much higher than his head: the little portal in the rock above the stone staircase. Barred by a rusted iron door, it was the ancient escape route of princes. Behind those iron bars, a torch illuminated the familiar sharp-toothed grin of a stoat prince he knew well.

"Malcolm! What are you doing here?" Norman whispered, pressing his face to the bars to see his friend at long last.

Malcolm nodded, rubbing his sleek forehead against the tip of Norman's nose through the bars.

"I can't believe you're safe." Norman's voice cracked as he struggled to contain his excitement and relief. "Guillaume told us you were gone, abdicated."

"Why would you believe anything that traitor told you?" Malcolm asked.

Norman didn't bother to answer the question. "Can you get out of there? Do you have a key?"

"I was hoping you'd brought one," the stoat said hopefully.

Norman stepped back and gave the bars a long look. "Stand back. Let me try something."

Reaching up, he wrapped his fingers around the iron bars. Bracing his feet, he took a deep breath and summoned all his strength, then pulled. The hinges began to creak and screech. Dust fell down into his eyes, making them sting and blink, but it did not stop him pulling. He closed his eyes and strained against the bars. His arms felt like they were going to come out of their sockets, but Norman would not give up.

The screeching of the straining hinges echoed around the cave.

"Stop," Malcolm whispered. "The guards are waking up."

But Norman wouldn't stop. The hinges seemed to shift, as if they were about ready to give. If he could just give one good pull, they might snap.

"Stop," Malcolm repeated more urgently.

Norman's fingers lost their grip on the bars and he fell defeated in a heap on the ground.

From the cave mouth came the low grumble of voices and the distinctive clang of armour.

"Put out the light," Norman ordered.

The torch winked out, and Norman covered his head with his hands and feigned sleep. Inside he was anything but asleep. At a word, he would have jumped up and thrown himself at the door again. He was not going to abandon his friend once more.

A chain rattled in the gears above the cave mouth. From his position on the ground, Norman could see the portcullis outlined against the inky sky as it began to rise. The guards must have heard him. They were coming in to investigate. He lowered his eyelids until only the smallest slit of his eyes remained, and then watched as the gate drew up.

Three figures entered the cave. The glint of moonlight off their armour marked two of them as guardsmen. Between them was a third person. Shorter than the guards, this one moved slowly. He wore a hood and a long dark cloak of some kind. He made a sort of scraping sound as he came towards the spot where Norman lay. It was a sinister, menacing sound, as if he was dragging something—a noose or a net or something. As they loomed closer, Norman closed his eyes for real.

The scraping sound stopped inches from his head. Norman tried to breathe normally, like a person just lying there, asleep, but his heart was racing and he could hear the ragged edge to his breath. What were they going to do to him now?

"Are ye aright there, Master Strong Arm?"

It was not the voice or the question he was expecting, but Norman did not stir.

"What 'ave they done with yer?" the questioner continued, anxiety cracking its voice. "They have na killt yer yet, 'ave they?"

Norman knew that voice. It was, in fact, one of the first voices he'd ever heard in Undergrowth.

"Norman, are you all right? Are you injured?"

He knew this soft voice too.

"Esme?" His eyes snapped open. Sure enough, it was the little rabbit under that hood. She stood there between the two armed guards, and even in this light, Norman could see the concern on her face.

"I'm all right," he said, pulling himself to his knees. "Are you okay? Did the guards hurt you?"

"Och, Master Strong Arm, we'd no sooner harm Lady Esme than we'd harm our own wee sisters." The guard lifted the visor of his helmet to reveal the snaggle-toothed grin of Mackie the River Raider. "Pleased yer all in one piece," he said.

The second guard lifted his helmet from his head and held it deftly under his arm as he executed a quick bow. "Strong Arm," he said formally, snapping a salute, "it is a pleasure to serve with you again."

"Mackie, Captain Harald—am I glad to see you. But how . . . ?"

The archer captain stopped his question short. "There'll be time aplenty for stories anon. Let's get you out of here."

"Wait," Norman said. "It's not just me. Malcolm's here too."

As if on cue, Malcolm's torch flickered back to life at the portal overhead.

"I sure hope you lads have brought some keys," he called down. "Strong Arm wasn't living up to his name when you arrived."

Mackie grinned, exposing the full crooked armoury of his teeth, and held up a ring of keys.

"The guards were very obliging," Esme said with a smile. "They were quite happy to be relieved an hour early."

"Especially when we promised not to report them for sleeping on duty," Captain Harald added. He shook his head. "Wouldn't be tolerated in my regiment."

Norman took the keys and began trying each one in the lock.

"You'll have to make for the forest," Harald explained as Norman worked his way through the keys. "It'll be easier now with King Malcolm. He knows the pathways better than most men in his kingdom—better than these weasels, anyway, and no stoat will help them—but you'll have to be quick."

Norman finally found the key that turned in the lock. Rusty after so many years of disuse, the mechanism lurched and grinded as he turned it, but finally it clicked open. Malcolm gave the iron door a good shove and pushed it open.

"Well done," he said. "Now can you give us a lift down?"

"*Us?*" Norman asked.

"Aye," Malcolm growled. "They've got the whole royal family locked up in here." He turned and bent to pull a figure from the ground behind him. It was another stoat all right. He looked injured or ill, or maybe he was just old. He was almost silver grey, the colour of his ermine cousins, but the proud head on those tired shoulders was unmistakably Cuilean's. With Malcolm's help, he limped towards the hole in the cavern wall and cast a skeptical eye downwards.

"Last time I did this, there was a rope ladder to the steps and a boat waiting below."

"Don't worry, Your Highness," Norman told him. King Malcolm was always just Malcolm to him, but Prince Cuilean, his regent, always inspired the title Your Highness. "I can get you down." He held out a hand like a landing dock below the opening in the rock.

Prince Cuilean hesitated. "If we're to be escaping overland, I'm afraid I should stay here. I'll only slow you down."

Malcolm was having none of it. "I'm not leaving without you."

The old prince smiled gratefully at his nephew but did not budge towards Norman's offered hand.

Harald and Mackie looked nervously towards the open gate and the mouth of the cave.

"I'll carry you," Norman offered. "It won't be a problem."

The stoat prince stiffened, as if offended by the suggestion.

"If you will allow me, sir," Norman said more formally. "When Malcolm was struck by Raven fire at the Glace Mountains ambush, I had the honour of carrying him to safety. I consider it my greatest service to your family. It would be my honour to do it again for you."

Cuilean smiled ruefully and nodded. "Now is no time for an old soldier's pride. Your offer is a gallant one." He stepped onto Norman's palm. Norman lowered him to the ground and held out his hand for Malcolm. The stoat leapt nimbly from the opening to the outstretched hand, then bounded up his arm to his shoulder. He tapped Norman gently behind the ear with one of his tiny paws and whispered into his ear, "Knew I could count on you, Strong Arm."

Norman took a deep breath and smiled. The weight of the little stoat was never a burden. He was never happier than when Malcolm was there on his shoulder chattering into his ear.

"We should be moving," Harald told them. "The next shift could be here any minute."

Cuilean was already sitting down on the floor of the cave, exhausted just by his efforts to clamber out of the portal. Norman wondered if it really was a good idea for him to come. Last time he'd seen him, Cuilean was in the prime of his fighting years, but now he looked years older. He was clearly very sick. It would be a struggle for him to hang on to Norman's shoulder like Malcolm did.

Esme seemed to understand the problem too. "Will this be of any help?" She held up the strap of Norman's knapsack. "I was hoping I didn't drag this down from the castle for nothing. The weasels wanted to make a tent out of it, but I claimed it for the Great Cities. Do you think you could be comfortable in there?"

Cuilean eyed the knapsack approvingly. "I think I could be very comfortable. Thank you, Lady. It's a joy to hear a Santandarian accent again. I spent my university years in Santander."

Norman held his bag open and the silver-haired stoat slowly manoeuvred himself inside.

"Very comfortable, indeed," he said, once settled. "My command tent during the wolf campaign wasn't as commodious. Nor did it smell so pleasantly of oats and honey."

Norman smiled to himself. The bag had held a lot of granola bars. He was about to lift the knapsack to his shoulder when a noise alerted them to some movement outside the cave.

Their heads all snapped towards the cave mouth. They heard voices, it was certain, and the rhythmic *ching-chang* of marching armed men.

"Aw, Bead Eye, we're too slow. It'll be the relief guard," Mackie muttered. "I was hopin' not to have ta fight. My sword arm's awful rusty." He waved his sword tentatively, as if trying it out.

"Put your sword away and get your visor on," Harald commanded. He replaced his own helmet as he spoke. "Come with me and let me do the talking." He strode to the cave mouth, and Mackie tripped after him. "You two get out of sight," he told Esme and Malcolm.

"In here," Cuilean whispered from deep inside the knapsack. He might move slowly, but his brain was still agile enough to command. "Malcolm, extinguish that lantern and both of you get in here. There's plenty of room. Norman, lie back down and pretend to sleep. Harald will handle the guards and buy us some time."

Esme and Malcolm scrambled into the knapsack, pulling the flap over the opening, and Norman threw himself back down on the ground, concealing the sack behind him. Again he squinted towards the front of the cave. Two guards had arrived to meet Mackie and Harald.

"Why is the gate up?" one of the new guards asked. "Are you mad?"

"We heard a sound," Harald explained. "Have you ever heard a human snore? It's something you're likely to hear in hell. Like a badger cornered. We thought it was going to gnaw off its own paw or something."

"Then why in the Maker's name did you open the door?" the new guard raged. "Are you simpletons?"

"We, er . . ." Mackie stammered. "Harry here wanted to give the beast a good poke with his lance, to shut him up."

Harald must have been biting his tongue.

"Then you're both fools. That thing is dangerous," the guard spluttered. "The orders were to leave it alone. Report to the Captain of the Guard. He'll have you transferred to the Sangbord Fringelands, no doubt. You can do your share of badger-baiting there if you like."

Mackie and Harald executed a pair of sloppy salutes and marched out. The new guards shook their heads in disbelief. "Blasted fools," one muttered. "They'll get us all killed. Let's get the gate down again double quick. That thing in there gives me the creeps."

Norman could not help smiling to himself. Sometimes there were advantages to being a fearsome monster. He lay there pretending to sleep for a little while longer, before daring to whisper to the fugitives in his knapsack.

"Everyone okay in there?"

"We're fine," Malcolm whispered back. "Are you going to get us out of here?"

"How do you expect me to do that?" Norman asked, opening the flap of the knapsack just a little so he could see their faces. Three sets of animal eyes looked out at him.

"The bookweird," Esme replied. "Isn't that what you call it?"

The little rabbit was adapting very quickly to his ways.

"It doesn't always work that way, Lady Esme," Malcolm protested. "He seems to be able to bookweird himself, but bringing a passenger is a challenge."

"But he brought me here with no problem."

"To be clear: you were a stowaway," Norman said.

Esme wrinkled her nose. "Well, we have to try. Hand me the paper and pen. What do you want me to write?"

"We need to go to San Savino," Malcolm declared. "We need to get the treaty map and we need to rescue Jerome."

"We can't all go." The idea of infiltrating Jerome's historical novel with two talking stoats and a rabbit was too much for Norman. "It's not safe."

"What is this madness you are conjuring?" Cuilean wheezed as Norman handed the writing materials to Esme. "Is this the sorcery that heretic fox was teaching you? I warned you against it. That abbot cannot be trusted." He broke down into a coughing fit.

Malcolm and Norman exchanged a worried glance.

"We can look after him in Willowbraid," Esme insisted.

"Esme's right," Norman said. "Malcolm and I will go straight from there to San Savino."

The rabbit dipped the quill into the ink and begin to write, tentatively at first, but quickly once she'd found her subject.

It was too dark for Norman to read. "How can you see in there?"

84

Cuilean read over Esme's shoulder. "Rabbits are crepuscular. They can see in very low light. It's what makes them such good archers," he said absently, distracted by what he was reading. "This Willowbraid place is new to me. This woven dome you describe is ingenious. Is it based on a design from one of the Santandarian masters?"

Esme kept writing without answering him. Her little rabbit forehead furrowed as she concentrated, and she dotted her sentences with vigorous punctuation. "There," she said, blowing on the ink to dry it. "Will that do?"

Norman held the paper up in front of him. "I'll need the lantern for a minute to read it. I don't think it works unless I read it."

Malcolm lit his lantern, pulling the flap of the knapsack around him to block the light. It was just enough for Norman to make out the tiny handwriting. It was Willowbraid all right, described better than Norman could ever have done. The way Esme described the morning light coming in through the gaps in the dome, the way she saw the differences between the various greys of the morning, on the stone of the church, in the shadows of the square—it was a very rabbitish view of the world. Norman had read a lot *about* Undergrowth, but he'd never read anything *by* an Undergrowthian.

"You should write a book," he told her honestly.

Esme curtsied at his compliment and capped the inkpot.

The lantern winked out and the animals withdrew into the knapsack.

"Goodnight, everybody," Malcolm called cheerily from inside. "See you in the morning . . . I hope."

"Hold tight," Norman advised them as he lifted the knapsack. "I hope everyone's sleepy."

Before lying back down, he stuck his arms through the straps and clutched the knapsack to his belly. He really was tired. His eyes were sore and his legs heavy, but he couldn't fall asleep right away, and the shifting of the animals in the bag across his belly reminded him he wasn't alone. Cuilean was more right than he knew: you couldn't trust the fox abbot Fuchs and you couldn't trust the bookweird. They might wake up in Willowbraid, or they might wake up just about anywhere. He only hoped that they woke up together for once.

Return to Willowbraid

ncomfortable mornings were pretty normal now. If you fell asleep on a cave floor, you couldn't complain too much if you woke up in some dusty warehouse or on a pile of pine cones. It was the trumpets that woke him this time—that and the shouting. It wasn't much more noise than Dora made when she got up early for riding classes, but it was enough to rouse him, and it definitely wasn't Dora blowing those horns and barking the orders for the archers to man the ramparts.

He resisted the urge to open an eye. It was probably what they were waiting for, with orders to shoot it out, but the trumpet blasts and the shouting made him curious and eventually he could not help himself. The rabbit was so close that it made him jump. The rabbit jumped too. It was Ambrose. The timid rabbit monk's brown eyes were huge with terror.

"Ambrose!" someone shouted joyfully. It came from around his belly. Esme poked her head out of the knapsack. "I'm home. You should have come. It was fantastic. I was in the castle of Lochwarren—actually inside it!"

Ambrose blinked but said nothing, even as Esme danced out of the knapsack and threw her arms around him in greeting.

"You look worried," she said. It was only then that she saw

the ranks of archers forming up around the square. "Oh, please," she said. "Put those down. There's nothing to worry about."

But the archers did not move. The flap of the knapsack fluttered again as Malcolm stuck out his nose. "Where's this, then? Is this home, Lady Esme? I have to say I thought you'd get a friendlier homecoming."

He emerged cautiously from the knapsack. On one shoulder he supported the weight of his uncle, who limped slowly at his side.

"Ah, my friends," the old stoat croaked, "how good to see you. So long since I saw a good company of Santandarian archers. You are Santandarians, are you not? My archery master in Logarno was a rabbit, Jost Kanin. Perhaps you've heard of him?"

The jaws of the rabbit archers dropped in unison. It was as if they had never heard an animal speak before. Norman could sympathize.

There was a brief commotion while two figures broke through the ranks. Norman recognized them immediately as Brother Timothy and Alderman Morgan.

"Lower your bows, gentlemen," Esme's father commanded. They hardly needed to be told. Cuilean's greeting had flummoxed them.

"Esme, my dear, we will speak later of this. You've simply no idea of the dangers you are exposing yourself to."

"You mean being imprisoned by angry weasel usurpers and their heavily armed guards?" Esme asked cheerily.

"Pardon?" her father spluttered. "Where? What?"

Brother Timothy took it upon himself to properly greet the guests. "Welcome to Willowbraid, my friends. I am Brother Timothy. You look as if you could use some rest."

Cuilean nodded appreciatively. "That would be welcome. I am Cuilean, regent of Lochwarren. This sturdy young fellow is my nephew, King Malcolm."

Brother Timothy and the alderman exchanged a confused look. Esme's father had not yet recovered from the shock of hearing that his daughter had been captured by weasels. The news

that a legendary figure from the past was now standing before him
was too much to handle.

Esme smiled winningly again and asked, "Do we have lodgings fit for royalty? I think Prince Cuilean could do with the ser-
vices of a doctor." She turned to the regent and curtsied. "With
your leave, sir, I will fetch what's needed from the herb store.
Brother Ambrose, will you help me?"

Ambrose stood stock still, not budging from the spot where he
had been standing for the past ten minutes. Again he blinked, but
he managed a sort of nod.

"You are very kind, Lady Esme," Cuilean replied with a
stiff bow.

It took a tap on the elbow from Brother Timothy, but the
nervous young rabbit finally sprang to life and hurried to help
Malcolm support Cuilean. Under Esme's guidance, they set off
towards the centre of Willowbraid.

Norman could not follow without crushing half the houses of
the town, but he watched from the square as the parade formed. The
rabbits of Willowbraid came out from their homes to see this marvel
that had walked out of legend and onto their main street. Malcolm
took it all in stride, shaking hands and kissing babies all the way
down the street. He was as at home here as he was anywhere.

Norman sat down in the square and relaxed. It was a long time
since anything had gone right. He was happy to sit down and
enjoy it. Father Timothy remained behind with him, making sure
that he got some breakfast too. The old monk probed him for the
details of how they'd made their trip, but he didn't push too hard.
He was happy to listen to Norman's description of the town and his
memories of the church at Edgeweir. Norman liked the old monk
and was grateful to him for staying behind when everyone else had
run off to celebrate the arrival of the stoats. He sincerely hoped that
one day, he'd be able to take Timothy to Edgeweir.

The rabbits were reluctant to let one of their honoured guests
leave the celebrations, but Malcolm managed to get free by lunch-
time and hurried to meet Norman back at the cathedral square.

It brought a smile to Norman's face to see his friend swaggering down the main street like his old self.

"Well, Strong Arm, are we ready to try this again with your magic rucksack?"

There was a lot of catching up to do, but they seemed able to do it without saying much.

"Esme is writing up some pages for us," Norman told him, "but I won't be able to sleep for hours. Would you like to meet my sister, maybe?" Waiting in the square had given him time to worry about how things were going over at the Shrubberies.

"The fearsome warrior-maiden Dora?" Malcolm joked. "Her legend is muttered across the tables of many a feast hall."

"I'll take that as a yes."

Getting out of Willowbraid was no easier than getting in. Malcolm led the way through the wicker tunnels. It was easy enough for him. He sauntered ahead at every turn and came back to tease Norman about his pace.

"You'd be slow too if you had to crawl," Norman barked back.

"On the contrary, a stoat is quicker on four feet, but it is unseemly and unfit for royalty."

Norman knew he was right. "It wasn't too unseemly when the wolves were after us."

Malcolm tutted at him, as if it were rude of him to mention it. "Don't worry. You can show me how fast you are later. I'll let you carry me when we get out in the open."

He was true to his word. As soon as they reached the meadows, Malcolm took up his customary station on Norman's shoulder. It felt good to have him there. Despite the work they had to do, Norman felt happy. Everything seemed possible with his friend at his side.

The way back to the Shrubberies was longer than Norman remembered, even without the detour to the empty stately home and its cathedral relic, so he was glad to see the silhouette of the unicorn on the crest of the hill.

"Well, I can cross that off my list of mythical beasts," Malcolm said. "That's two of the big three: a human cub and a unicorn. Do you think we'll meet a dragon before we're done?"

"I hope not," Norman said, "but I wouldn't rule it out." He made the introductions when they reached the top of the hill. "This is Raritan. Raritan, this is my friend Malcolm, king of the stoats."

Raritan snorted a greeting. He didn't seem any less grumpy than when Norman had met him. "I can arrange for you to meet a dragon if you like, but I doubt you'd enjoy the encounter."

"You heard us from that far?" Norman asked, shocked. With hearing that good, the unicorn must be aware of everything that went on in the Shrubberies. "Is Dora okay?"

"She's fine. She misses her mother," Raritan replied. "You two had better climb on."

There was no more talking once they were up and away. Raritan was quickly at a gallop, making the landscape rush by in a blur and the wind whistle in their ears. Malcolm took up station on the unicorn's neck, clinging to the mane and howling with glee as they hurtled through fields and vaulted over fences.

They pulled up short of the house so that Norman could see the changes. The Shrubberies had several new additions. On the wall where Dora's bedroom window had been there was now a castle turret. Its gleaming white stone didn't match the rest of the house at all. It rose four or five storeys, looming over the country-side. At the top were three arched openings and a conical red roof topped by a bright blue-and-fuchsia floral flag.

"Hey, Norman!" Dora shouted, appearing from behind a giant brass telescope that poked out of one of the arched windows. "You're back. Come and see my castle."

"I see Dora's still getting whatever she wants from Uncle Kit."

Raritan snorted his agreement and carried them across the new drawbridge at a trot, depositing them in the ornamental garden beside a fountain. Norman looked up at the statue that graced the centre of the fountain and rolled his eyes. It was a life-sized reproduction of Dora holding an umbrella to protect her from water spurting at her from marble dolphins at the four corners of the fountain.

Dora met them at the back door. The first words out of her mouth were "Are Mom and Dad with you?" She peered around him to check.

Her brother shook his head.

Her face fell. She looked sad enough that Norman almost wanted to say something to make her feel better.

"I called them about fifty times. They aren't answering their cellphones. All I got was two more postcards from Paris." She let them in the house and grabbed the postcards from the fridge. "Does this look like Mom's handwriting?" she asked anxiously. She hadn't even noticed the small, fully clothed animal that accompanied her brother and her unicorn.

Norman took the postcards from her, sepia pictures of Paris in the olden days. Kit was slipping, leaving paper around the house like this. He read the notes. *Having a lovely time in Paris. Wish you were here.*

"It looks like Mom's." He was by no means sure, but now that Dora was actually worried about their parents, he didn't want to make things worse.

At his side, Malcolm cleared his throat.

Norman took the hint and made the late introduction. "Oh, Dora, this is Malcolm. Malcolm, meet the giantess Dora."

The stoat gave her one of his patented royal bows with a flourish of the cloak. "Delighted."

"He's cute," Dora said with a little pout, "but tell Uncle Kit I don't want him. I don't want anything else. I just want Mom and Dad to come home."

Malcolm gave her an offended look.

"He's not for you," Norman explained. "He's not *for* anybody. He's my friend . . . my best friend."

"No fair," Dora complained. "Why do you get to go somewhere? Why can you have friends visit? I asked Uncle Kit if I could go to Penny's until Mom and Dad come home, but he just brought me more presents."

"Where is Uncle Kit?"

Dora rolled her eyes towards the stairs. They found him in the study. Or at least they assumed it was him. He was almost hidden by the gigantic computer screen in front of him, but the slow *tap, tap* of his typing gave him away. The ban on paper seemed well and truly lifted, because the desk was filled with crumpled piles of it.

"Are you writing an apology letter?" Norman asked bitterly.

The typing stopped. "Ah, the wandering boy is back—a little late for curfew, perhaps. What's the usual punishment for that?"

"Why don't you ask my mother?"

As usual, Kit didn't bother to answer his question. "I was just thinking of dear old Meg. I want to do something nice for her. Tell me, does your mother still like the opera? Would she prefer that to a trip to Versailles?"

Norman decided to return the favour and ignore Kit's question. "You have to bring them back sometime. What you're doing is wrong. This is actually kidnapping, you know."

Kit stuck his head around the side of the monitor and pulled an exaggerated sad face. "Technically it's not kidnapping because I haven't taken you anywhere, forcible confinement maybe . . ." The frown on his face turned to a smirk. "But you've shown that you can leave any time you like. Apparently you've got a secret horde of paper hidden away somewhere. Would you like some of mine so you don't have to use up your stash?" He picked up a few sheets of printer paper and offered them to Norman. Only then did he notice Malcolm.

"Oh, it's you!" Kit seemed genuinely surprised, and not altogether happy, to see him. "Where did you come from? Never mind that. You're here now. We can work you in somehow." He drummed his long fingers on the table and scratched his head as if trying to look like someone puzzling over a problem. "Actually, maybe you can help with this one, Spiny. Come on around here."

Norman bristled at the nickname Spiny. Only his father called him that. He didn't like doing what Kit told him at the best of times, but at the moment, he was curious to know what the schemer was up to at the computer. He arrived around the other side of the desk in time to see him close the file that he'd had open, and to catch the title. "The Case of Madame Lecteur," it was called. Was Kit trying to write a story? He'd closed the file too quickly for Norman to see anything more than the title, and had switched to another file that was already open on the desktop.

"Now," Kit resumed, "your sister seems bored, and I confess I'm having a little trouble getting past the setting and the characters on this one. Do you think it would help to introduce a dragon? It feels like we need some sort of conflict. Do you think a dragon would work? Nothing old Raritan couldn't handle, but it would give the little princess downstairs something to do."

"How about a vengeful stoat prince?" Malcolm asked pointedly.

Kit missed the jibe. "I hadn't thought of that. Would that work, Spiny? Do you think our sharp-toothed friend has it in him to play the villain?"

Norman couldn't resist provoking his uncle. "I thought this story already had a villain."

Kit just made an exaggerated hurt face. Everything was a joke to him.

Norman read the page in front of him on the computer.

The Shrubberies was the most perfect place on earth. No castle was more beautiful or more secure. Its gardens were the most fragrant in the world, its moat the deepest and the fish that swam there the brightest. The banner of the unicorn princess waved brightly from its tallest tower, and from there one could see as far as the hummingbird fields and the forests of tangled bracelets. Out in the far meadows, a unicorn grazed. He was the finest of his kind and belonged nowhere else than in the Unicorn Kingdom at the Shrubberies Castle.

This seemed to go on for several paragraphs more, but Norman noted that the file was only two pages in total. "Is there more?" he asked. "Does anything happen, or is it just description?"

Kit seemed bothered by the question. "Well, I have to get the beginning right. There's no point going on from a bad beginning. I have to make sure it's just right."

"And what about the other file? 'The Case of Madame Something'? Is that another story?"

"Yes, well, that's normal. I always have several projects on the go. You can't govern the imagination. You have to go where it tells you." Kit was so busy pontificating on the art of the imagination, he didn't notice Malcolm prowling around his desk and leafing through the crumpled printouts.

"So you're a writer now?" Norman asked skeptically. Out of the corner of his eye, he could see that Malcolm had found several pages of interest and was slipping them into Norman's knapsack on the floor.

"You know," Kit said earnestly, "I think I was always a writer. It's just taken me a long time to complete my apprenticeship. I'd like to think I've been studying all these years. I've really immersed myself in the world of books, you know."

Norman shook his head and rolled his eyes. "Some imagination. You didn't even make up the Shrubberies. It's real. And Dora's real too. It's not right what you're doing here. The tiara you gave to Dora is from another book. She told me. You stole it. I bet you even stole that tower and the moat and the stupid dolphin fountain. They don't belong to you. They belong somewhere else."

Kit's frown seemed real for once.

"We're not going to help you, you know. You might as well know that. What you are doing here is not right," Norman repeated. "How long do you think Raritan will play along? He knows he doesn't belong here. You've already made an enemy of the stoat king. Do you think you could handle Raritan as your enemy?"

"Well, I wouldn't call young Malcolm my enemy." Kit glanced towards Malcolm, who was now standing atop a pile of manuscript pages, scowling as if what he was reading was particularly bad. Kit paused and continued to bluster. "We've been through some adventures, you and I, haven't we, Mal? We haven't always agreed, but 'enemies' is going a little far. Am I right?" He tried to laugh, but it came out forced and unconvincing.

Malcolm looked up from his reading for a moment to stare at the man behind the desk. The look he gave him left no doubt as to how he felt about their past.

Kit had to look away. "Well," he said, more softly, "I'm sure we'll work it out."

"With Raritan too?" Norman asked.

"Raritan is no problem at all."

He didn't sound confident, but there was no point in arguing any further. There never was with Kit. He helped only when it was to his advantage or when it amused him, and he had set his mind on building this fantasy world for Dora and himself. It didn't mean that Norman had to play along, though, and from the looks of it, Dora was getting tired of the game too.

"I'll be seeing you, then," he said. Then he thought he'd put in a word for Dora. "Word of advice: if Dora is grumpy, it's because she's not eating right. Maybe she needs some fruit and vegetables before her ice cream." Among other things, Uncle Kit was a terrible babysitter.

Malcolm's parting gesture was less kind. He aimed a meaning-ful kick at the tallest pile of papers, sending them sprawling on the floor. Then he strode across the keyboard purposefully, leaving a string of gobbledygook across the screen. And they left Kit at the desk with his writing and his fantasies.

Back at Willowbraid, they had an appointment with the armourer. The talking rabbits of England had not forgotten the crafts of the Great Cities. Their blacksmith went by the traditional English name of Wayland, but he boasted of his Santandarian heritage as he laid out a selection of his finest swords for Malcolm to choose from. The stoat eyed them expertly, extending his arm and tossing each one from hand to hand to feel the weight of the blades. Wayland nodded knowingly when Malcolm made his selection. "Aye, that's the one," he said.

"It's as fine a blade as I've ever seen," Malcolm told the proud smithy as he slid the sword into its scabbard and belted it to his waist. "My last was a gift from my uncle, forged in Santander itself. This one is its equal."

He had a quiver of new arrows too, and an English-style longbow that the rabbits had copied from their human country-men. That afternoon, he spent an hour at the range befriending the archers of Willowbraid, but he still made sure he won the impromptu contest that broke out.

Norman had a weapon too. By design, it was a two-handed broadsword, meant for the burliest of rabbit warriors; in Norman's hands, it was a short dagger. He'd tucked it into his belt at first, but instead of making him feel safer, it only reminded him of the danger. It was in his knapsack for the time being, with the human-sized pen and pencil Malcolm had lifted from Kit's study and a sheaf of white computer paper.

There was celebrating that night in Willowbraid. All afternoon the town smelled like baking, and as night fell rabbit swains carried long tables and laid them in rows across the cathedral square. All the townspeople came out, carrying the trays of food they'd made for the festivities. Norman sat on the steps of the cathedral, beside the head table. Shy rabbit girls offered him bowls of salad and trays of tiny bread loaves that he ate in one gulp. The bread melted in his mouth. He had never tasted anything like it. When the rabbits saw him stuffing spare loaves into his knapsack, they brought out another tray and filled any remaining space in his bag.

"You know, when I became a vegetarian," Norman told Malcolm, "kids at school teased me that I ate rabbit food."

Malcolm raised a glass of raspberry beer and toasted, "To rabbit food—second to none!"

After dinner, the tables were pulled to the side and the square became a giant dance floor. Norman watched as the rabbits danced their complicatedly choreographed routines, forming lines, linking arms and turning in circles, making intricate patterns in the square. When the formal dancing was done, the tempo picked up and young rabbit couples danced merrily together, whirling across the cobbles. Children had decided by this point that they were brave enough to approach the human boy sitting on the cathedral steps. They made a game of creeping up on him to try to touch him. Norman waited until the last minute before feinting towards them and sending them scrambling, giggling through the square.

"What does this remind you of, Mal?" He wondered if the stoat was thinking the same thing.

"The victory celebrations at Lochwarren," Malcolm said with a slow smile. Despite this, he seemed distracted. On most days, no one enjoyed a feast more than the stoat prince. "It's like that day in more ways than one."

The victory they celebrated at Lochwarren had come at the cost of many lives. Malcolm's father, Duncan, had not lived to see the stoat banner raised again over their ancestral castle.

"Cuilean will be okay," Norman told him. "A few days of vegetable stew and Esme's magic herbs, and he'll be his old self."

Malcolm nodded. "And still, this is not my celebration. You and I still have a battle to fight." He tapped the hilt of his new sword instinctively. "More than one, it seems."

As the festivities wound down and the rabbit mothers began dragging their excited children to bed, Esme finally appeared.

"Your uncle is a tough soldier," she told Malcolm as she nibbled on whatever was left at their table. "He's been treated badly. He has a touch of cellar fever and the damp from the dungeons has worked its way into his joints, but he'll get through. He's a battler."

Malcolm snarled and tapped the sword at his side again. "I should never have left. It was reckless of me."

"You needed the map. You *still* need the map. Jerome will help us. Once we have that, we'll put Guillaume in his place." Norman's reassurance did nothing to dispel the bitter look in the stoat prince's eye.

Esme broke the solemn silence. "I've brought you your papers," she said, handing over two small pages of fine rabbit calligraphy. "I rewrote what you dictated in smaller script. Easier to digest."

Norman scanned the pages and marvelled at what she'd managed to fit in. They'd debated long and hard about what to write. The return trip was easy—if they needed to escape, they would return to this very spot in the cathedral square. It was the outbound leg that challenged them. Days of captivity had stoked Malcolm's anger, and he was ready for some fighting. He was all for getting to the heart of the matter, surprising John of Nantes in his tent and ending his reign of terror with a few well-placed strokes of his new sword. Norman wasn't so sure that was a contest they would win. The only advantage they had was surprise. Nantes had all the weapons they had and more. In battle, size and numbers often matter.

Norman's worry was rescuing Jerome. They needed to get him out of the library before John of Nantes's archers burned it down. Then they needed to escape San Savino, or at least find somewhere safe from the fire—somewhere in the cellars, maybe, or deep in the clay fort. Anywhere but in the wooden rafters among the dry scrolls.

Norman scanned the page now and wondered if they had made the right choice. Esme watched and seemed to read his mind.

"Here," she said, handing over a third piece of paper. "I wrote up the other one as well. In case you change your mind."

As Norman took the page from her outstretched hand, he wondered if he was grateful or not. It only delayed the decision yet again.

The moon was out by the time they curled up on the straw that the rabbits had laid down in the square for them. Malcolm was yawning already. Norman was tired but not sleepy, if that made any sense. His stomach was a mess of nerves.

Malcolm could see what he was thinking. "Fear is normal," he assured him. "You aren't any less of a warrior for it. Even my father was afraid." Norman found this difficult to believe. Duncan had seemed fearless. "In battle, he always said, we conquer our fears first and our enemies second, and the strength comes from our allies, the friends who fight beside us. We fight to keep them from harm, because the fear of losing them is greater than the fear of dying."

Norman thought about that and was shocked to realize the stoat was right. In all the battles he'd fought, the fear had always disappeared into the background when he thought of Malcolm. Knowing that his friend felt the same calmed him instantly. His body felt warm from the inside, like he'd just eaten soup on a cold day.

"You've made your choice?" the stoat asked, indicating the pieces of paper that Norman held in his hands.

"I have," Norman told him confidently. He ripped a corner from the page and began chewing before offering Malcolm a symbolic bite. The pages were almost as easy to digest as that night's bread loaves. Norman had eaten a lot of paper in his short life, but nothing went down as easily as fine rabbit-made rice paper.

In Paris, Encore

A lot happened very quickly, or seemingly within the same moment. A blood-curdling scream brought Norman to. It was
the kind of noise that they say could wake the dead. Norman
wasn't dead, but it woke him anyway. He rose with a start, shouting, "What?"

He didn't know who was being attacked or by what, but the
shrieking continued, rising to an ear-splitting crescendo. The
screamer wasn't the woman in the old-fashioned dress and fancy
hairdo of cascading ringlets who stood several feet away, although
she had every reason to scream. A man in a blue military jacket and
a stage villain's moustache aimed a short-barrelled revolver at her
chest, and yet she seemed remarkably calm. Her head was tilted to
one side and her arms were crossed in front of her as if she was about
to lecture her assailant on the rudeness of pointing guns at people.

Norman and Malcolm had emerged in the balcony box of an
ornate theatre. The screaming was coming from the stage below,
and everyone else in the theatre seemed to be okay with it.

"Alarm!" Malcolm cried, bursting free of the knapsack. "What
foul screeching! Is it swans attacking us?"

At the sight of the stoat in his forest gear, reaching for his
sword, the woman shook her ringleted head and blinked, as if she

wasn't sure she could believe what she was seeing. "Norman?" she cried out in shock.

While Norman stood stunned and wondered how it could be that she looked so familiar, Malcolm was all action. He leapt to one of the cushioned chairs and from there to the balcony railing, his sword already drawn.

"Lower your hand cannon!" he demanded.

The man in the military tunic and the twisted moustache whirled round in surprise, pointing his revolver at the strange woodland creature that had accosted him.

Malcolm didn't waste a second. With two deft swooshes of the blade, he marked an X across the gunman's wrist, and the revolver fell from his hand with a clatter.

The woman in ringlets sprang forward and deftly kicked the gun away. Under her ornate opera dress, she was wearing the same neon orange runners that his mother wore.

"You must be Malcolm," she said. "I can see you're handy in a fight." Under that makeup and behind those ringlets, it was his mother's voice.

Down below, the screaming had stopped. A swell of violins replaced the screeching and a man began to sing, and finally Norman came to his senses. Nobody pointed a gun at his mother. He braced himself and charged at the gunman's knees. The moustachioed officer grunted and lurched as he absorbed the blow, but Malcolm gave him another sharp poke with the sword.

Their attacker recoiled from the shock but still kept his balance. It was the slap his mother gave him that did him in. She didn't even wind up, just smacked him across the cheek with her open hand. Her assailant's head spun away from this last blow, throwing him completely off balance. He made one last grab for the railing but went flailing over it, toppling into the rows of seats some twelve or fifteen feet below.

"Lecteur!" the man howled as he plummeted. He landed among the audience, sending hats and programs flying. On the stage, the singer stopped to gauge the source of the interruption and the orchestra screeched to a halt. Norman, Malcolm and Meg Jespers-Vilnius peered over the edge and watched their assailant rise slowly to his feet. He shook his head and dusted his tunic as if to pretend he'd just stumbled and it was nothing much, but he limped as he escaped down the aisle. When he reached a side door, he turned to shake a fist dramatically.

"You have made a powerful enemy, Madame Lecteur!" he bellowed. "Tell Dupin he hasn't seen the last of me."

With that, he charged out of the theatre. The room buzzed with questions as every head in the audience and on the stage turned to stare up at the fashionably attired lady, the shabby little boy and what appeared to be some sort of forest animal standing at the edge of the box.

In the neighbouring boxes, women in even more elaborate dresses and hairdos waved their fans and gasped. Men in top hats and tails peered over to see if anyone needed rescuing or to be challenged to a duel. Too late, Norman thought.

His mother was still for a moment, then with a dramatic flourish, she blew the audience a kiss and waved. It was as if she were just another actor in the play. When she had finished waving, she pulled calmly on a silk cord, cloaking the flickering gas lamps and gilt-decorated balconies of the theatre behind a thick red curtain.

The murmur of the crowd continued for a few more moments, then the singer resumed his song. He sang alone for a moment, until finally the orchestra pulled itself together and accompanied him.

Meg Jespers-Vilnius turned to her rescuers. "You two arrived just in time. Well done."

Norman stared at her red lips as they moved, fascinated. Even on days when his mother had a speaking engagement, he'd never seen her dressed so elaborately.

"Are you going to introduce me to Prince Malcolm?" She nodded towards the stoat, who was watching the scene below through a crack in the curtain.

Malcolm turned and executed his most princely bow. "At your service, Madame Lecteur."

Norman's mother returned his greeting with a curtsy. "You may call me Meg."

Norman thought she was taking this rather well. "Malcolm, this is my mother."

Malcolm bowed again. "It is a pleasure." Then he voiced the question that needed to be asked: "Where are we?"

"The opera," his mother said. Norman had heard of the opera. It sounded even worse than he'd imagined. "The Paris opera house."

"Dora said that you'd gone to Paris." Norman was relieved to see his mother, no matter where.

"Did Dora tell you that we'd gone to Paris of the 1800s?"

Norman shook his head. "Is Dad here too?"

"He's here, but he doesn't know where 'here' is. He and Dupin are backstage searching the dressing rooms." Then, as if remembering what had just happened, she urged them to the door. "We'd better be going. I expect the gendarmes will be on their way."

Norman opened the knapsack to let Malcolm jump in.

"Oh, don't worry about that," Meg told them. "We can freak out a few Parisians. It's not like it's a real book."

Malcolm crinkled his forehead as if struggling to decipher what she said, but he decided to let it go. "At your service, madame." He jumped to Norman's shoulder, flourishing his cape. "Let us freak out the Parisians, as you say!"

They marched through the lobby, past gawking spectators and staff. Norman winked at them and gave them the thumbs-up sign. Meg took a handful of coins from her purse and handed them to the doorman. He glanced at the scruffy boy and his stoat and struggled to maintain a professional smile.

"Tell Monsieurs Dupin and Lecteur not to return to Rue Dunot tonight, but to meet me at the Gare D'Orsay tomorrow," she told him.

The doorman nodded dutifully, as if this was the sort of request he always got.

At the curb, they entered a carriage that seemed to be waiting for them.

"We're going to Dupin's house? Dupin the detective? We're

in a Poe story? Does Dad know?" Norman peppered his mother with questions. If his father realized he was in a book, he probably thought he was losing his mind.

"The answers to your questions are yes, yes, sort of and no."

Both Norman and Malcolm squinted at her.

"Yes, it's Dupin the detective, but no, this is not a Poe story, or not really. It seemed so at first, but it's dragging on far too long, and all the villains have the same bad moustache as that guy back there at the opera. There just seems to be conspiracy after conspiracy and no solution. Poe wouldn't have written this. Dad thinks we're on some sort of mystery dinner party vacation. He can't ever find out what's really happening. That's why I left that message with the doorman. He can't see you here."

"Can't you just bookweird yourself out?"

She shook her head regretfully. "I'm not so nimble with the bookweird as you are, young man. I didn't bring myself here. I can't get myself out."

As the carriage rattled along the cobbled streets, Malcolm pressed his nose against the window. "Norman, you should see this. The city is enormous and completely lit up. Some of these buildings are like mountains."

Norman ignored the stoat's interruption and tried to understand what his mother was telling him. "But if this isn't a real book and Poe didn't write it, then who . . . ?"

"I think I've figured out that mystery. This has Kit written all over it. It's the sort of thing he would try—copying Poe."

Norman thought of the file he'd seen on Kit's computer: "The Case of Madame Lecteur."

"So Uncle Kit really is a writer?"

"He wishes." Meg exhaled and shook her head. "Kit tries—he really tries—but all he can do is copy. He never finishes anything either. He doesn't have the attention span. He starts with these grandiose plans and then just gives up."

Norman could sympathize. He'd tried to write a book once, just as he'd tried to invent a board game and build an Elf Lord diorama. He almost felt sorry for Kit. His uncle wasn't much of a writer, and he wasn't much of a villain either.

Norman peered out the window. They were crossing a stone bridge, following a line of carriages over the Seine. It was strange being in the same book as his mother. She'd warned him about the bookweird, and he'd tried hard to keep what he was doing a secret. But it was all out now, and he was relieved she wasn't angry. Nineteenth-century Paris seemed about the best time and place to ask her the question he'd been wanting to ask since they came to England.

"Why are you so mad at Kit? What did you fight about?"

Meg sighed and rolled her eyes. "We fought about everything. We fought about who could name the most capital cities, who could cross the wooden footbridge in the fewest steps. We argued about who was going to be the most famous writer. We argued about which books belonged to who. In the end, we mostly argued about the bookweird. I knew we had to stop. I had realized that it was danger- ous. Your uncle didn't think any of it was *real*, but I knew that the lives of people in books were just as real as ours, and that we were wrong to meddle in them."

Norman couldn't lift his head to speak. His mother was right. She'd warned him, but he hadn't listened. He'd wanted to help. He'd wanted to dive right into a book and save the day. He'd wanted to be the hero, not just the reader, but it had never worked out that way.

His meddling had put a lot of people in danger. He thought of George Kelmsworth, fighting off a desperate criminal from hard- boiled New York with not much more than a cricket bat and his own ridiculous self-belief. He thought about Amelie, trembling as she faced the wolf assassins that Norman had unwittingly unleashed from Undergrowth. Norman had scraped by so far. George and Amelie were okay, but not everyone was. He and Malcolm were supposed to be rescuing Jerome right now.

"Mom," he began, "there's something I need to tell you." It was so hard to say. It was almost as if he needed to drag the words out of his throat with a rope.

Hearing the hesitation in her son's voice, his mother narrowed her eyes.

"It's about *The Secret in the Library*," he said reluctantly.

"Oh, Norman," she said. "Please tell me you didn't."

He shook his head. "I had to go. I had to get Malcolm's map. If he doesn't get it back soon, he'll lose his kingdom for good."

At the mention of his name, Malcolm pulled his nose away from the carriage window. "Norman's no meddler. He saved my life."

Meg Jespers-Vilnius pursed her lips, began to say something and stopped.

Norman figured he'd better get it all out now that he'd started. "They captured me."

"Who?" Meg snapped like a mother bear. "Who captured you?"

"Black John of Nantes. He thought I was Jerome."

She gasped. "Oh, Norman! Have you any idea how dangerous that was? This is what I was talking about. You could have been killed!" She grabbed him with two hands and began to rub his arms as if to confirm that he was still in one piece. "Thank God you got out of there." She stroked his hair and looked him in the eyes. "Do you understand what I mean now?"

Norman nodded. It would be so easy to stop there, but he had to tell her everything. "There's something else. They attacked San Savino. I guess they were waiting until they had Jerome. Mom, it was terrible. They were smashing the walls in with catapults. They were shooting fire-arrows at it. They were burning down the library!"

Meg's eyes widened in shock. She brought her hand to her mouth as she gasped. "Was Jerome . . . ?"

"Last I saw him, he was still in there," Norman said.

His mother put her head in her hands. "This is my fault. I never should have hidden the map there. I should have told you . . ." Her eyes were moist with tears.

Norman could barely look at her. He couldn't remember the last time he'd seen his mother cry.

"You see why I have to go back?"

107

She nodded, silently. He hadn't expected her to agree, but there she was, nodding. Tears still ran down her face, streaking her thick costume makeup.

Norman's stomach felt like it was ripping itself apart. She really must have cared for Jerome. All he could think about was losing Malcolm and how that would make him feel.

"Come with us," Malcolm interrupted. It was obvious to him that she should come along. "Come and save Jerome with us."

"Oh, I wish I could. You can't know how much I wish that!" She was trying to blink the tears out of her eyes. "But I can't just flit from book to book like Norman. I need a book, a real, complete book. I need to find a passage and memorize it. There are no books here in Kit's fake Poe story. This awful unfinished story of your uncle's is a dead end, and I can't get anywhere from here."

Norman looked out and saw they were crossing the same stone bridge again, following the same black carriage. It was like the roads around the Shrubberies, taking them in circles.

"It's the same back at the Shrubberies. It's not the real Shrubberies," Norman told her. "It's full of unicorns and magic wishing stones, and he's emptied the library. I got out only because Kit didn't know about the rabbits. We borrowed paper from them and wrote our way out."

"You can write your own ingress?" she asked, incredulous. "That's . . . well, it's amazing. I wish I could. I'm stuck here until we convince your crazy uncle to let us out."

"I've tried," Norman told her. "But he's crazier than ever. He wants me and Dora to live with him in his fantasy world."

Meg bit her lip and seemed to think about this for a while. "Kit's not actually a bad kid. He just gets carried away. We'll need to trick him somehow, make him want to let us out."

The carriage lurched to a stop in front of an apartment building that Norman recognized from his visit to a real Poe story.

"We're here," his mother announced. "Let me think about this one for a while."

In Dupin's apartment, Meg removed her makeup and put her

hair up in a ponytail, looking more like his mother again. Only the elaborate evening gown looked out of place as she brought them mugs of hot cocoa.

She asked a million worried questions about Dora. Norman assured her guiltily that his little sister was eating properly and getting to bed at a sensible hour. He told her that he'd left someone back at the Shrubberies to protect her. He didn't mention that that someone was a unicorn.

Meg listened intently as he told her about his discovery of the rabbit village and the trip back to Undergrowth.

"That's probably why you could get to Undergrowth," she reasoned. "The rabbits originate there. Their story is a real book, so there's a connection to Undergrowth. I expect you could get into the unicorn book too if you knew the story. Kit's cobbled together a fantasy world out of other books, but for the bookweird, it's a dead end. You can go backwards into the books he's stolen from, but you won't be able to get anywhere else. You need to get back to a real story, and for that we're going to have to trick Kit. Tell me more about his playworld. There has to be a way out. Kit's not that smart."

Malcolm told her everything—about the growing strangeness at the Shrubberies, Malcolm's troubles back in Undergrowth and the mess he'd made in *The Secret in the Library*. She winced when he told her how he'd made it into the fortress of San Savino, and how Black John had mistaken him for Jerome and taken him captive. She looked away when he described the siege and the fire, and when she turned back to listen, her eyes were red again, but she did not let herself cry. She covered her mouth with her hand when he told her of all the times he'd been captured or had swords and arrows pointed at him, but she never seemed surprised by anything he told her. When Norman told her that he'd been able to transport Esme and the stoats in his knapsack, she only raised an eyebrow.

"I only wish your knapsack was a little bigger!" she said, shaking her head ruefully. "You could sneak me out of here too."

When they had finished their cocoa and their storytelling, she was all business.

"The problem with Kit's Shrubberies is that it isn't real enough. You need to trick him into making it more real."

"How do we do that?"

"You have to make him write something true."

"Something true?" Malcolm repeated skeptically. "Kit?"

"I know," Meg replied. "It won't be easy, which is why you'll have to trick him. Here's the plan."

She explained it to them twice, describing carefully how to exploit Kit's weaknesses: his vanity and his need for praise. It was a good plan and she tried to seem confident, but Norman knew his mother, and the way she diverted her eyes when they started to well up meant that she was more worried than she let on.

When they had gone through all the details of the plan, Meg made a bed for Norman and Malcolm on the couch. She hugged her son tightly as she wished him goodnight, told him not to worry, assured him that everything would be all right. That hug more than anything told him that he *should* be worried. He'd never really listened when his mother warned him that the bookweird was dangerous. It made him nervous that now she'd stopped telling him.

Writer's Block

It was nice to wake up in his own bed, even if it was only his own fake bed, in the fake house in the fake story that his uncle was trying to write. It was still better than the forest or the balcony of the Paris opera house. A light snoring sound from the knapsack on his belly seemed to indicate that he had not made the journey alone, but Norman checked, just in case. Malcolm woke up with a start and reached instinctively for his sword, relaxing only when he recognized Norman's nose peeking in at him.

"So we're here," the stoat said with a sigh. "Do we have to do this?"

Norman nodded slowly. "I don't like this any more than you do."

They allowed themselves breakfast before taking up their onerous task, but they knew they were only putting it off. The cereal in the cupboard was still the colourful and sugary kind, but there was at least milk and bread now too. They even scrounged some jam and some cheese to round out a semi-complete meal. Dora came down as they were making it. Her blonde hair was tangled and her eyes red from lack of sleep. She managed a grim smile before sitting down to eat—and to eat the way Norman had only seen a stoat eat, hardly stopping to breathe between oversized bites.

"I guess Uncle Kit still isn't feeding you properly?"

She shook her head, sending toast crumbs flying. Norman noticed that she had chocolate stains on her face and was wearing their mother's sweatshirt.

"You'd better go have a bath," he said as kindly as he could. "I'll tell Uncle Doofus to get some better groceries."

Dora brightened a little at that, but there was no real spring in her step when she set out back up the stairs to clean up. At the kitchen window she looked out, as if expecting something. "Oh, look," she said dully, "there are real dolphins in the fountain now."

"Did you ask for those?" Malcolm asked. His eyes bulged when he saw the enormous sea creatures in the backyard.

"I asked for Mom and Dad to come home," she replied bitterly, and stomped up the stairs.

"All right, let's get on with this," Malcolm said, hauling himself away from the window.

Though it was early, Kit was already in the study. The piles of paper surrounding him had grown higher, but Kit looked to be in the same spot where they'd left him, behind the desk, hidden by his computer. If the clatter of manic typing hadn't told them that he was still at work on one of his masterpieces, the muttering would have. They waited at the door, not wanting to disturb his inspiration.

"Hello, boys, you're back," he said finally. "Do you have time to read something? I've had a few false starts, but I think I've really got something here." He spoke quickly, as if he'd had too much cola. His hair was a mess—a real mess, not the fake mess that he usually did with gel. It looked like he'd been trying to pull it out of his skull. He hadn't shaved either, and his chin showed the faint start of a ginger beard. When Norman came round the other side of the desk, they saw it was piled high with coffee cups and empty plates. Three files were open on the computer screen. Kit was still working on the Dupin story and his Shrubberies fantasy, but he also had a third one started now, something called "The Thrall of the Badgers."

"You'll like this one," he told them eagerly. "It's set in Undergrowth, in the time of Maltesta di Marffa. It tells the little-known story of his childhood in the Halagonia, where he was raised by badgers."

"Maltesta di Marffa was born and raised in Pantaleone della Marffa, by poor relatives of the Duke of Ansi," Malcolm said. "Every schoolboy knows that."

"Not in my version."

Norman frowned. He'd started reading the story over Kit's shoulder. It was worse than it sounded.

"You can't do that," he protested.

"I can do what I want," Kit replied petulantly. "It's my story."

Norman didn't need to read more than three paragraphs of "The Thrall of the Badgers" to know that it shouldn't—and wouldn't—ever be finished. It was the opposite of what they wanted. They needed Kit to write something true.

"Aren't you writing something about the Shrubberies?" Malcolm asked. "I'd like to read that."

Kit waved his hand as if he were swatting a fly away. "Yes, yes, that's just for Dora. Kid's stuff. My Dupin story, on the other hand . . ."

Malcolm and Norman exchanged a frustrated glance. This was going to be more difficult than they had thought.

"I'm making real progress on this one," Kit enthused, standing up so that they could see the screen. He closed all the other windows and brought "The Case of Madame Lecteur" to the fore. "I've changed it a bit. The villain is a member of the Prussian delegation now."

Norman read the page on the screen. It described a confrontation at the Paris opera. The villain was depicted as having a pointed moustache and black hair plastered to his head. It sounded like the man they'd fought with on the balcony, but instead of a military tunic, this version wore a black suit with a red cravat and a top hat. Instead of a revolver, he carried a bayonet and an explosive device.

"Why would a member of the Prussian delegation have a bomb and a bayonet?" Norman asked, confused.

Kit bit his lip. "Maybe you're right. Maybe instead of a bayonet, it's a letter opener or a chloroform rag, or perhaps a jar of black widow spiders. No, wait. Maybe that would make sense if he was from the Egyptian delegation."

Kit sat down again and began revising furiously. Norman and Malcolm looked at each other and shook their heads. This might be their most difficult mission yet. Norman had no idea how they were going to manage this, but they had promised his mother they would try. They needed to help Kit write a real story, something believable that would work with the simplest bookweirding.

Norman waited until Kit had stopped writing. It took about five minutes of frantic typing, several more of deleting, and some copying and pasting before Kit had rewritten himself to a standstill. He leaned his elbows on the table, cradling his chin in his hands, and bit his cheek as he stared at the screen.

"Something still not right about this," he mumbled.

Norman turned the screen aside so that he could get Kit's attention.

"Listen," he said, "you want us to help, right?"

"I do, actually," Kit admitted. "This author stuff isn't as easy as it might seem to you non-authors. It would help to have you around to, you know, proofread, maybe bounce some ideas off." Norman had rarely heard his uncle sound so unconfident. The last time he sounded this shaky, there had been a gun pointed at him.

"Listen," Norman said, as earnestly as he could, "my dad knows a little about writing. He sometimes teaches the creative writing class at the university."

"Uh-uh," Kit said skeptically. He wasn't exactly a big fan of his brother-in-law's.

"Well, Armin Sarmin was one of his students."

Kit didn't appear to recognize the name.

"A.S. Sarmin? Author of the Space Bounty series?" It wasn't actually true—Norman's father had never met Armin Sarmin—but his mom had told him to pick a very famous and successful writer whose name Kit would recognize.

His eyes widened. "A.S. Sarmin? Your father taught A.S. Sarmin? *Kidnapped in Space* won him his third Silver Saucer, you know. It sold a thousand copies in Andorra. Andorra! One hundred is a bestseller in Andorra."

"Well," Norman continued, seeing that he had Kit's attention, "Armin Sarmin was a terrible writer before he took Dad's class. All he could write was bad fanfiction." He made a face, watching to see if it dawned on Kit that his badger story and his Dupin story were also bad fanfiction. "Anyway, according to my dad, Armin Sarmin simply needed to find his own voice. Dad told him the first secret of writing."

"What's that?" Kit asked. He stepped forward and grabbed a pen, ready to write it down.

"I'm not sure you're ready to hear it. Dad said it was the sort of secret you have to be ready to hear."

"Of course I'm ready. Who could be more ready?" The hand holding the pen began to quiver.

Norman made a show of thinking long and hard about it. "The secret," he said in his most serious of voices, enunciating every word, "is to write what you know."

Kit dropped the pen. "But that's not a secret!" he protested.

"It's an open secret," Malcolm told him conspiratorially. "That's the most secret of all, because it's hidden in the open."

Kit nodded, stroking the baby beard growing on his chin. "Like the purloined letter," he said slowly, as if grasping a great occult secret.

"Exactly. My dad got Armin Sarmin to write a story about his childhood back in Sri Lanka, something true that actually happened to him. Writing that first *true* story made him a real author. It unlocked his voice. After that, *Treasure Asteroid* and *Mutiny on the Fusion Flier* were a piece of cake."

"Twelve hundred copies in San Marino. Four hundred in Vatican City," Kit recited. "And all it took to unlock his voice was one story from his childhood?"

Malcolm and Norman nodded encouragingly.

"I'd write about the time I first ate water chestnuts, or how my friend Sniptail got his name," Malcolm said nostalgically.

"I'd write about the time I dozed off in class and talked in my sleep about elephants," Norman offered.

Kit seemed to catch their enthusiasm. "I'd write about the time my sister stole my favourite book!"

Norman and Malcolm exchanged another glance. This sounded like one more of Kit's fantasies, but Meg had told them it didn't have to be *true* true. It just had to feel true. If it was true to Kit, that was enough.

"Did that happen here at the Shrubberies?" Norman asked hopefully.

"Yes, yes, of course. It happened right here. I remember the day like it was yesterday."

It was exactly the sort of thing that Meg had told them to get him to write.

"My mom would probably hate that story," Norman said. It was a genius stroke, and it clinched it.

"But it has to be written," Kit declared, as if it was now a solemn duty.

It wasn't as simple as that, of course. Getting Kit to sit still and focus to write a short story about his childhood wasn't easy. They needed to clear everything off his desk, not just the papers and the plates, but also the computer—especially the computer. The computer seemed to distract Kit. He started out looking things up on the Internet but soon was sidetracked. Let's say he wanted a good synonym for "house," for example; in no time, he got distracted and started listing words that started with "house"—housefly, housewife, household, houseboat.

"Did you ever notice that if you stare at a word long enough, it starts to look foreign?" he said. "Does the word 'house' look right to you?"

Norman tried closing down all the extra windows on his screen and found that he had Minesweeper open on the desktop. Evidently not all his furious clicking was typing. Eventually he and Malcolm convinced Kit to get rid of the computer and work with a pad of paper and a pencil.

"But if I need a synonym for 'house' again?"

"Just call it a house. If that's what you called it when you were a kid, that's what you should call it in the story."

Kit grumbled but slowly got on with it.

"It would be much faster if I typed it," he protested after a few sentences.

"That's not how A.S. Sarmin does it," Norman assured him. "He writes it out by hand and gets his secretary to type it up." He wondered if his mother would be proud of just how good a liar he was becoming for her. "I'll type it up for you later. Mom's always asking me to do that, but I never do."

"But you'll do it for me? You'll be my secretary?" Kit asked eagerly, pleased both to have won a victory over his sister and to have someone to boss around.

Norman and Malcolm had to be vigilant, and it wasn't fun, coaxing a true story out of Kit, making sure it didn't drift into fantasy. One of them had to be in the room at all times to make sure he didn't start doodling, or ripping up his work and starting again. They took turns watching him while the other fetched a regular supply of cookies, candies and other treats. It was obvious now why there was no good food in the house. He seemed to live on junk himself.

Kit constantly questioned what he wrote. Norman and Malcolm had to reassure him that it was good, and bring him gently back on track when he started to veer off. "Isn't this boring?" he'd ask. "Maybe I should put the dolphins back in, or just the spy car?" They had to convince him that the true story was just as interesting, if not more so.

Norman wasn't lying. He actually *was* interested in Kit's story. Kit had been a mystery for so long that it was fascinating to get a glimpse into his and Meg's childhood. They even got Dora in on the act. Whenever Norman's assurances that this was how A.S. Sarmin did something or Malcolm's exaggerated enthusiasm seemed to wear thin, Kit turned to Dora for an opinion. Maybe he thought she was still under his spell. Maybe he didn't have Norman's insight into how good a fibber she really was.

In the end, it was a sad little story about Kit as a boy, or at least how he saw himself as a boy. When they read it, both Norman and Malcolm felt a little sorry for him, although nothing particularly bad happened to make them feel that way. He lived in a nice house and had a nice family. The dad worked a lot overseas. The mother did charity work, and the boy's older sister either bossed him around or wanted nothing to do with him. The kid had a wild imagination and was always seeing crazy conspiracies and outrageous crimes going on around him. He'd tell wild stories to anyone who would listen, but nobody really did listen. The parents pretended to, but they were obviously just humouring him. The sister rolled her eyes on good days, mocked him on bad. It was strange to see his mother through Kit's eyes, or through the eyes of Kit as a boy. Not that there was much difference between the man and the boy. Norman wasn't grown up himself, but he could tell that Kit really wasn't either. As a boy, Kit had admired and hated his big sister in turns. He wanted to be like her, but he wanted to be better than her, and even though the story was told from his point of view, you could tell when he was lying about beating her at cards or getting better grades or winning the race across the wooden footbridge.

In fact, most of the story seemed to take place in the boy's head alone. It started like this:

> The Secret in the Library *is probably the rarest book in the world. Many stories are told about this book. Some say it contains some truth, and some say it's all fiction. It is the story of the last Livonian knight, the secret child of Johan Vilnius, the boy monk who would bring Black John of Nantes to justice. But some say that it is also a codebook used by German spies in the Second World War. During the war, most copies of* The Secret in the Library *were confiscated and burned. There were supposed to be only three left: one in the super-secret room of the British Library; one in the hold of the sunken* Titanic, *locked in the trunk of the millionaire prizefighter "Rockjaw" Marty Phillips; and the last in the subterranean lair of the Secret Society of Reborn Knights of Livonia. But there was one more copy, and that copy belonged to my*

father. Before that it belonged to his father, a gift from the author. By rights, that copy should have come to me. For years, it stayed locked in the drawer of his rolltop desk while he waited for the right moment to bestow this family heirloom on his only son. This is the story of how my prized inheritance fell into the vile clutches of my sneaky sister, Margaret.

Norman wondered what his mother would think when she read Kit's story. It definitely wouldn't do anything to mend the argument between the two.

"It's good," he told Kit when he'd finished reading it. He was telling the truth, but he would have said it regardless.

"You think so, Norms?" his uncle asked, sticking out his chest and looking enormously proud.

"Very authentic," Norman assured him. "Don't you think so, Mal?"

Malcolm was half asleep on the windowsill by this point, but roused by the question, he summoned an enthusiastic agreement. "Oh, yes! Very much so."

Kit rubbed a hand across his scruffy chin and nodded. "Yes, I think you're right. I can feel my voice loosening up already. Voice, voice, voice," he repeated in different notes and intonations, as if warming up to go on stage or testing a microphone. "Yes, definitely. It's coming in nicely."

Behind his back on the windowsill, Malcolm yawned a toothy stoat yawn and rolled his eyes.

As promised, Norman typed up the story for his uncle. Malcolm sat on his shoulder and watched, fascinated, as the letters blinked onto the screen.

"Is this the bookweird?" he marvelled. "This personal scriptorium of yours? Did you conjure it with the bookweird or did Kit?"

Norman stopped typing long enough to answer him, or at least try to. "It's a machine, like a loom or a musical instrument. It's not magic. A human made it." The computer was just the latest in a series of modern machines that the medieval king should never really have seen. "It's like the train we took from George's house, and you have to forget about it. Some things belong in your story. Some things belong in mine."

Malcolm nodded sagely. "And you and I? Where do we belong? Back in our own books?"

"Yes," Norman concluded after a pause. "We belong in our own books." It saddened him to admit it, but it was true.

He had turned back and resumed typing when Malcolm added, "It doesn't feel that way."

"No," he agreed. "No, it doesn't."

Malcolm curled up on the desk and snoozed in the heat of the computer exhaust while Norman finished his typing. When he was done, he printed off two copies. One he kept for Kit, and the other he slipped into what he'd come to think of as his magic knapsack. Then he woke Malcolm for dinner.

The only thing that Norman knew how to make was grilled cheese, so he made grilled cheese. Malcolm and Dora ate with glee. Kit nibbled away, distracted by reading his own story.

For dessert, they ate bowls of raspberries and blackberries that Malcolm and Dora had collected.

"I don't think I'll ever eat ice cream again," Dora declared. Her lips and one cheek were stained purple from the berries.

"Where is my real sister and what have you done with her?" Norman asked.

Malcolm, who didn't get the joke, looked from side to side, wondering what he was missing. "But isn't Dora your sister?"

Brother and sister both nearly spit out a mouthful of berries laughing at that.

"I like your new friend," Dora said when she'd finished giggling.

Malcolm licked the berry juice from his paws. "The feeling is mutual, Lady Dora," he assured her.

When dinner was done and the dishes cleared, Norman excused himself for a nap. Dora's eyes boggled at the suggestion. Neither of them had willingly taken a nap in years. She opened her mouth to say something but stopped when she saw her brother shake his head.

"Maybe if you ask nicely, Uncle Kit will read you his new story."
Dora rolled her eyes. "Why would—"

Norman stared at her and tried to get her to read his mind.

Kit didn't seem to notice the silent communication between
brother and sister. "You want to hear it?" he asked. "No problem.
I'd be happy to read it to you." He flapped the papers ostenta-
tiously and cleared his throat.

Norman mouthed a silent thank-you to his trapped sister as he
and Malcolm escaped to his room.

Though Malcolm had snoozed off and on all day, he was ready
for another forty winks, as he called it. Norman wasn't very good
at napping. It felt strange trying to go to sleep in the middle of the
day, but they had agreed this was the next step. Everything seemed
to happen while they were asleep.

"The bookweird is like a watched pot," Malcolm suggested. He
peered into the knapsack. "It's getting crowded in there. I might have
to eat some of these loaves to make room."

It took Norman ages to drop off. The moment they stopped
doing things, his mind started to fill with worries. In the desert somewhere, the library of San Savino was still burning. Back in Willowbraid,
Cuilean was lying in a sickbed. In Paris, his mother was fending off
Prussian officers or Egyptian diplomats armed with bombs or guns
or jars of spiders. To add to all that, he now had Dora to worry about
too. Would she survive a few more days with Kit?

The Library Restored

Norman was woken up in the middle of the night by a tickling in his ears. It was only Malcolm whispering to him that it was time get up, but it startled him into a shout.

"Shhh, Strong Arm." Malcolm put a tiny paw over his mouth to shut him up. "You'll wake the whole house."

But the fine hairs of Malcolm's palm on his lips only tickled him more, sending him into a giggling fit.

Malcolm stood there with his hands on his hips in mock disapproval. "Whenever you're ready."

It was still nighttime, but as Norman's eyes adjusted, the moonlight was enough to illuminate the room and his friend standing on the headboard. They were still in the Shrubberies—so far so good. Norman had purposely not eaten any paper before going to sleep, but that was no guarantee of staying in one place. Sometimes the bookweird just picked you up and put you where it wanted to.

Norman pulled himself together. "Has anything happened?"

"I dunno," the stoat replied. "Nothing changed in here, but it's the library that matters, I suppose."

"Did you hear anything?" Norman asked.

Malcolm shook his head. "Nothing but the strange bird sounds you have here in England. Does it make a sound, the bookweird, when it happens?"

"I'm not sure," Norman replied. "But you'd expect something, wouldn't you? If the world was going to change in the night, shouldn't it make some sound—a whoosh or something?"

Malcolm shrugged. "You're the expert. So what now?"

"I guess now"—Norman swung his feet over the side of the bed—"we check if there's a way out of here."

Malcolm needed no further invitation to action. "I was hoping you would say that." He sprang from the headboard to the open window. "I'll see you in five. And, Strong Arm?" He paused dramatically on the sill. "Try to make less sound than a badger at a jam tasting, will you?" With that, he disappeared outside.

Norman waited a moment before rising to his feet and tiptoeing to his bedroom door. An ear on the door confirmed that everyone was asleep, but the creak of the floorboards still made him cringe as he crept out and down the hall. At the library door he paused and listened for movement. If Malcolm was inside, he was too stealthy for Norman's human ears. The scratch and click of the key turning in the lock was the first indication he had that Malcolm was inside. Norman gave the door a gentle push. Malcolm clung to the handle and rode it as it swung open.

"Your library, sir," he declared, hanging on to the handle with one hand and gesturing to the shelves with the other.

"Thank goodness," Norman said. "I almost didn't believe it would work." He dropped to his knees to check the bottom shelf behind the encyclopaedias. Sure enough, the Intrepids series was all there. He opened *Intrepids at Sea* and leafed through it, sighing with relief. It was real—real words in real sentences. They could at least get to Kelmsworth. If they needed allies, they knew they could count on George Kelmsworth and the Cook twins.

"But how?" Malcolm asked. He leapt down to see the book his friend had left open on the floor.

Like most things bookweirdish, Norman could only guess how it worked. "I think it's because Kit really isn't in control of this world, even though he made it. It's just made up of scraps of books and other stories he's stolen. When he wrote the story yesterday, he couldn't help making it true. I guess that's why my mom wanted him to write about his childhood, because that would mean writing about the real Shrubberies, and the real Shrubberies has a library."

"So it's not a dead end anymore?" Malcolm asked, glancing again at *Intrepids at Sea*. "We can get into any of these books here?"

Norman nodded. "And from there, hopefully, to San Savino."

"Your uncle said there was a copy of *The Secret in the Library* in the British Library. You think we could get there from Kelmsworth?" He held up *Intrepids at Sea* hopefully. "If anyone can get us into the British Library, it would be Georgie and the Gingers."

"It could work. They might even have a copy of their own— Kelmsworth had a pretty big library—but I was hoping . . ."

Malcolm read his thoughts. "You were hoping that Kit's story would bring *The Secret in the Library* back."

Norman's eyes roamed the room until they lit upon the rolltop desk in the corner. The desk was new, or new to Norman, but this was the library as it had appeared during Kit's childhood. Likely the desk had been there when Meg and Kit were children.

"Do you think it's still there, like in Kit's story?" the stoat asked.

Norman tried the top left-hand drawer, but it was locked.

"Malcolm?" The desk might look impregnable to a human, but Malcolm had a stoat's eye view of it.

"Lift the rolltop for me," he urged.

Norman did as he was told and rolled up the top of the desk. The stoat needed only a couple of inches of gap to duck in among the old papers and notebooks. In a blink, he had all the small interior drawers out and had emptied their contents. Old coins, pins, stamps and paper clips were strewn across the desktop. In a flash, he dove into one of the drawer openings—just stuck his head in and disappeared inside. It looked impossibly small for him, but Norman knew that most of the stoat's apparent size was fur and he could squeeze into very tiny holes. A scratching noise now ran though the innards of the desk, as Malcolm descended through whatever gaps he found in the joinery. It was impossible to know where he was from the scratching, but it was obvious that something was in there somewhere. If they ever had to haunt anyone (and it wouldn't be the first time!), the stoat-in-the-desk trick was a good one.

All at once, the shuffling stopped, and there was a click and then silence. Norman waited anxiously, not sure what the silence meant. Was Malcolm stuck? Was he going to have to saw the desk apart to rescue his friend? But three tiny knocks from inside the top left-hand drawer stopped this line of thinking. When Norman pulled on the drawer this time, it slid open easily to reveal Malcolm standing in the bottom. The stoat blinked and shook his head, sending up a cloud of dust and woodchips that made him cough and splutter.

"This—*cough, chuff*—what you're looking for?" Malcolm managed to ask, pointing to the book under his feet. He punctuated his question with a tiny comical sneeze.

It was indeed what they were looking for. The navy blue cloth cover and the silver-embossed lettering were both newer than when Norman had seen them last, but it was recognizably the same book—*The Secret in the Library*. Malcolm stepped aside so that Norman could lift it out. He opened it to the first page, and stoat and human boy read the inscription out loud: "To my little adventurer. May it be good company on your travels."

The inscription was in pale blue ink, the script elegant and old-fashioned, a little blurry around the edges, the mark of a fountain pen. There was no signature.

"Was this there when we last saw it?" Malcolm could not recall reading any inscription.

"Not that I remember, but we may have missed it. Or maybe it's new. This was the inscription in Kit's story, so maybe it used to be there. He could have conjured it as he remembered it, or maybe the paper was cut out by the time we got the book. I never looked that closely."

"So what now?" Malcolm asked eagerly. "We find a nice page for you to enter and you have a little midnight snack?"

"I suppose," Norman said hesitantly.

Together they leafed through the pages of *The Secret in the Library*. The first time they'd stumbled across it, the book had grabbed them right away. There hadn't been time to read beyond the first two chapters, but boy and stoat both agreed that they knew how the novel was supposed to end. *The Secret in the Library* didn't have two plot lines for nothing. One plot was about Jerome, who was delivered to San Savino on horseback by a dying knight. The other was about Johan Vilnius, the leader of the Livonian Knights, and his escape from the dungeons of the evil Black John of Nantes. It didn't take a genius to see that the boy had to be the Crusader's long-lost son. At some point, they would be reunited to defeat Black John together. Norman and Malcolm would have to read more of the novel to find out how, but there was no time for that now. They just knew that they had to get into the book before John of Nantes's threatening first visit, before Norman was captured, and before Nantes launched his attack on San Savino. And this time, Norman had to do a better job of hiding.

For an hour, they sat on the carpet in the library and pored over the book together, arguing about where to ingress.

"Let's let the book decide," Norman suggested, putting the book down and yawning. The excitement of sneaking into the library had worn off and he was exhausted.

"Do they talk to you now, then?" Malcolm asked, not completely sarcastically.

"No, let's just put it down and see where it opens." He hadn't really meant it when he'd first said it, but it was starting to sound like a good idea. Why not let the book decide?

Malcolm rubbed his eyes and shook his head in disbelief. "And if it opens to John of Nantes running someone through with a sword?"

"Then I guess we'll know not to trust the book to decide."

Malcolm shrugged. It was worth a try. Norman closed the book solemnly and then placed it spine first down on the carpet. It flopped open to a page about a third of the way in. The boys read it eagerly.

Jerome lay awake in his tiny cupboard and watched the stars through the narrow slit that brought in the cool night air and what little light he had. San Savino was the only home he had ever known. For as long as he could remember, this sky had been the last thing he saw before falling asleep. He could not imagine it otherwise, but that was exactly what Sir Hugh and Father Lombard were suggesting. Something had changed with the visit from John of Nantes. Jerome had heard the shouting from his hiding place in the corridor behind Sir Hugh's rooms, but had not been able to make out the conversation. Some threats were made, some accusations. Only now was he learning that the argument had been about him. But why? Why would the man they called Black John care about him? What was it that Sir Hugh and Father Lombard were keeping from him? There was a secret at the centre of Jerome's life. Everything revolved around it. He himself was a secret, hidden away here in the library, but he was not even allowed to know the cause. He was a secret even to himself.

Now he was to leave the fortress—to leave the only home he'd ever known—and travel to the other side of the world. The caravan left in the morning. He had only this night to worry and fret, and he was using all of it. Godwyn would accompany him on the journey to England. That was some comfort, but otherwise he would be separated from everything and everyone he'd ever known.

"This won't work. It's after Nantes visited the castle, after he captured you. You're already tied up in the tent outside. The attack will start any minute."

"Let's try again."

Norman closed the book and once again placed it down on the carpet spine first. Once again they watched it flop open.

"Same page!" Malcolm cried when he saw where it had opened. "Try again."

They performed the test again and again. Each time, the book opened to the same page. Boy and stoat exchanged significant looks.

"When this book decides something, it doesn't change its mind," Malcolm concluded.

Norman nodded and gulped. "I guess this is it, then." His hand hovered over the page. To be honest, he felt a little uncomfortable about eating a page from this book. If it was as rare as Kit claimed— if all the other copies were locked away somewhere—they might be destroying the last available copy. Norman was afraid of losing his ingress, but more than that, he felt guilty removing a book from the world. And it was his mother's favourite, after all.

He got a firm grip on the page and prepared to give it one good tug to get it over with, like yanking a tooth or pulling off a bandage. He even closed his eyes. But still, he couldn't do it. Closing the book again, he considered his options.

"Let's try this," he said, opening the book to the first page again. "We'll copy it out, but we'll use the book's own paper. That's as close as I dare come to eating a real page."

The closest thing to a blank page was the fly-leaf on the inside of the front cover. The inscription was on one side, but the other was entirely blank.

"Let me," Malcolm offered, whipping out his sword. Norman nodded for him to proceed, and the stoat king went to work. He made quick work of it, running the blade along the edge of the paper, closer to the stitched seam than Norman would have been able to. The cut was clean and straight. The book appeared undamaged. If you didn't know that the page was supposed to be there, you would never know it was missing.

"Well done," Norman told him, and he set about copying the page they'd selected, or rather the page that had selected them. "I wish Esme was here," he said when he was about halfway through. "Her handwriting is so much better."

"And smaller," Malcolm agreed. "Your chicken scratch is an insult to chickens."

Norman ate the page right there, still sitting on the rug in the library. There was no point waiting.

"What'll we do with the book, then?" Malcolm asked as he watched Norman laboriously chew and swallow the page. "Should we put it back?"

Now that they'd finally found it, Norman didn't like the idea of letting it go. "There's still some room in the knapsack."

"You're turning into a right paper hoarder, aren't you? I have to be careful now in here. I'm liable to die of a paper cut." But Malcolm made some room for *The Secret in the Library* among the granola bars, rabbit baking and various loose sheets of paper.

Back in Norman's room, they both waited for sleep to come to them. They'd thought that if they woke up and did the book-eating business in the night, they'd save a day waiting for the bookweird, but the whole plan depended on them being able to fall asleep again before dawn. Only minutes ago in the library, they had both been yawning and rubbing their eyes. Now, knowing where they were going and what they might find there, sleep didn't come so easily.

The sound of Malcolm fidgeting in the knapsack told Norman that he wasn't the only one struggling to get back to sleep. "Funny," he said. "Jerome is lying awake and worrying right now too."

"I never could sleep the night before a battle," Malcolm replied, his voice muffled by the canvas of the bag.

"If we're lucky, we won't have to fight."

"Aye, and we've been famously lucky so far," the stoat replied. There was a long silence before he said anything else. "Besides, I'm spoiling for a fight myself."

That was the last thing either of them said, but it was still a long while before they managed to return to sleep.

San Savino

The scent gave it away—the smell of old wood, books and dust, and beneath that, the dry smell of the desert. They had done it. The room they had woken up in was completely without light, but there was no doubt that it was San Savino. That scent of Jerome's desert hideaway was unmistakable.

A rustling of paper and canvas was all that gave Malcolm away. Even this close, Norman could not see him, unless perhaps that was the glint of moonlight reflecting off the blade of his sword. Norman felt the stoat before he heard him again, just a gentle tug on his arm that told him Malcolm was climbing up to his shoulder, then the swish of his tail on his neck.

"We're not alone," Malcolm whispered in his ear. "Wait here while I circle round."

Norman remained as still and silent as possible while the stoat reconnoitred the room. Malcolm's hearing and night vision were much better than his. Already the stoat was proving his usefulness. Norman would never have known there was someone else in the library with them. But who was it? Was it Brother Godwyn, finishing up for the night? Surely Godwyn would carry a candle, unless he had come here to sleep, guarding Jerome's hiding place. Norman fervently wanted to believe this. He did not want to believe that there was another intruder in the castle, one of John of Nantes's spies or assassins skulking around in the dark, perhaps. Where was Malcolm? He certainly was taking his time.

It seemed ages before he heard Malcolm speak. Then it was so sudden and so fierce that it made Norman jump a little.

"Who goes there?" the stoat demanded. "You, lurking in the dark corner—reveal yourself."

There was no reply. The only sound Norman could hear was his own breathing. Maybe Malcolm was wrong? Maybe they were alone in the library after all.

"Declare yourself and your purpose. Don't think of running. I have a bead on you," Malcolm threatened. It would not be an idle boast. Somewhere in the darkness, the stoat king was poised with an arrow between his knuckles.

There was the sound of movement somewhere to Norman's right, the scrape of a shoe on the rough-hewn floorboards, so close he might be able to touch it. He gulped and felt his heart beat a little faster in his chest.

"You will not lay a finger on Jerome tonight," Malcolm declared. The anger was building in his voice.

"Who's this Jerome, then, and what makes you think I'd hurt him?" It was a girl's voice, but so close that it still made Norman jump.

"Never mind that," Malcolm pressed. "What is your name and your purpose?"

"Please don't 'urt me, sir," the girl begged. "I'm only Gwendolyn. You'll 'ave seen me in the kitchens, per'aps."

There was something about her voice that was not quite right. Norman couldn't put his finger on it.

Malcolm did not let down his guard. "What are you doing up here, girl?"

"I only came up here on a dare. I was just curious about these books, is all. Please don't, sir." There it was again in her voice. The words were right, but her voice never cracked. She didn't sound scared enough.

"Get yourself down to the kitchens, then, girl," Malcolm commanded in his roughest voice.

"Yes, sir. Right away, sir," she agreed meekly. "But only . . . who is Jerome, pray tell?"

It had been a mistake to mention him by name, but who was this girl who was brave enough to ask the question rather than scurrying back down to the kitchens?

There was only a moment of hesitation before Malcolm's clever reply. "Jerome is my mouse," he said. "If you were thinking of feeding him to one of those mangy cats you keep down in the kitchen, you can think again."

But then she made her move. She might have had a chance, had her path to the stair been clear, but she could not have known that Norman was crouched just steps away from her. She ran right into him. He felt what might have been a forearm smash into his nose. The pain shot up his face into the top of his head, and he fell backwards uttering a low grunt. The girl's limbs tangled with his, and they tumbled to the floor together. She let out a short squeal of pain as she hit the floor. Only then did Norman hear the arrow. What was Malcolm doing? It wasn't like him to fire in anger.

"I've got her," Norman yelled. "Hold your fire. I've got her." He wasn't absolutely sure he did have her, though. That felt like an ankle he'd grabbed. A swift back-heeled kick to his nose made him sure of it. He wrestled with the bony bundle of limbs in the dark. When she tried to rise, he heard her squeal again and he knew he'd managed to pin her somehow.

"Jerome, Jerome," she cried out, "get up. They've come for you. Run!"

That was a surprise, to say the least. They heard the sound of wood scraping and of feet frantically hitting the floor. The kitchen girl was still writhing in his grasp, grabbing his ears and his shirt and struggling to free herself, so Norman couldn't be completely sure what he'd heard when Jerome's voice called out. It sounded like "Margaret."

The light of a torch seemed to stop them all, and Jerome repeated what he'd said. "Margaret?"

Norman blinked and covered his eyes with his both his hands to protect them from the bright light of the torch. Beside him, the girl again tried to rise to her knees, but immediately she fell back down to the ground as if yanked by the hair.

"Margaret? Is that you? And Norman? Norman, I thought they'd got you. Didn't the black knights take you?"

The scullery girl had scrambled out of Norman's reach. She was struggling with something behind her head. It took him a moment to realize that she was undoing the long braid of hair behind her, the bow of which was pinned to the floorboards by a tiny arrow of rabbit manufacture. Now that she could see what was holding her down, she made quick work of untying the black ribbon that held her braid in place and pinned her head to the floor. She was poised to make another run for it, but she was still casting around to see where her attacker was. Expecting a human archer, she would not have seen the little flash of movement as Malcolm ducked behind a chest.

"Wait—Margaret?" Norman said, slowly coming to his senses. "You said your name was Gwendolyn."

"But it's Margaret, Norman," Jerome said, lowering his torch so that it wasn't in everybody's eyes. "You know that. You told me you knew each other."

It finally dawned on Norman. "M-m-ar . . . Meg?" he stuttered, starting with one name and finishing with another. He had not expected her to be here, and yet here she was: his mother as she'd looked at his age, or maybe a few years younger. When she bookweirded into *The Secret in the Library*, Meg was always the age she was when she had first read it.

She jumped to her feet. Now that he could see her face, he could recognize her features: the same pointy nose, the same straight brown hair pulled back into a ponytail, the same thinly pursed lips, the same furiously blazing eyes. This was exactly how his mother looked when she delivered an angry lecture.

133

"I don't know what this lackey told you, but I've no idea who he is. He's probably one of Nantes's men. You should report him to Sir Hugh immediately." The scullery maid accent was gone now. She sounded exactly like herself. She stood protectively between him and Jerome and peered down on him accusatorily.

Norman couldn't even begin to respond. He was dumbfounded. The bookweird had brought him face to face with talking unicorns and evil knights, but this had to be the strangest meeting of his whole life. He was looking at a childhood version of his own mother.

"Norman, you told me that you were Meg's friend. You said that you knew her and Kit back in England." The young librarian sounded more hurt than angry.

At the mention of Kit, Meg's eyes narrowed even further. "Is that it? Did Kit send you? Are you Kit's friend? I didn't know he had any!" She had realized now that the archer, whoever he was, was gone, and she wasn't afraid of confronting the boy alone.

"You don't recognize me?" Norman asked.

"Why should I?" she demanded.

Norman realized his mistake: he'd assumed that this was the adult Meg returned as her childhood self, but in fact this was the true young Meg. "No, no. Let me explain." He shook his head, not sure that he *could* explain. "I'm sorry, Jerome, but I lied." He wondered where to begin.

The young archivist's face was full of confusion as he glanced from Meg to Norman and then back again.

"I know Meg, but she doesn't know me." What could he say? He couldn't just tell them that she was his mom. "I live in the neighbourhood. I guess I've always wanted to know her."

Meg was having none of it. "That's a lie. I know everyone for miles around the Shrubberies. I would have noticed even a little pipsqueak like you. What school do you go to?"

"Erm, I . . ." Norman caught a glimpse of Malcolm climbing the rack of parchments behind Meg and stumbled on his answer. "I go to boarding school at St. Edwards," he blurted, naming the only British school he'd ever heard of.

Meg rolled her eyes and scoffed. "Right! With George Kelmsworth? Are you best pals with the Famous Five too?"

Truly worked up now, she leaned in close now and whispered angrily in his ear, "I don't know what you think you're up to, but you'd better get out of here fast. Tell your pal Kit that if he ever tries to meddle with my book again, I'll rip up that favourite little bunny book of his." Seeing Norman's stunned face, she added, "Don't worry. He'll know what I mean. I know he still keeps his furry bunny book."

Norman stammered, unable to get out a sensible response. It was so strange to hear his mother sound so vicious and cruel. He knew she was only defending her friend, but it was still hard to take. He wanted to say, "Mom, it's me, Norman. Don't you recognize me?" but he knew it was an irrational urge. Instead he reached for his knapsack.

"Don't you dare reach for a weapon." She made a fist and waved it threateningly in his direction.

Norman did not know how to react to this version of his mother. If he closed his eyes and listened, it was his mother, but if he looked, it was just another bossy girl. She looked like an older version of Dora.

"Come on, Jerome," she urged, pointing to the tiny arrow lodged in the floorboard. "That crossbowman has probably sounded the alarm. We'd better get out of here."

Norman's brain scrambled to catch up. The "crossbowman" was now rifling through ancient scrolls a few feet behind her. "Malcolm fired that arrow," he explained breathlessly. "You remember Malcolm, don't you, Jerome?" He stared pleadingly at the boy, who stood behind Meg with a gentle hand on her shoulder. He needed to get a grip on the situation, and he needed Jerome to believe him. "Malcolm shot the arrow. He won't tell anyone."

"Don't believe another word this liar says," Meg warned, tugging at Jerome's sleeve.

"But she's right," Norman continued breathlessly. "We do need to get out of here. It can't wait for the morning. John of Nantes is going to attack the fortress tonight."

Meg gave him the evil eye and wrinkled her nose, but she took the time to check the little window at the end of the library. A gust of night air blew in as she opened the wooden shutter. Outside, the campfires of Nantes's men burned at even intervals across the edge of the desert.

Up high on the shelf amongst the parchments, Malcolm held out his empty paws and shrugged.

"Black John thinks I'm you, Jerome," Norman explained. "He thinks he's captured you."

"But you are here. You escaped?" Jerome asked. "You are unharmed?"

Jerome's concern helped him snap out of it. The girl who would grow up to be his mother may not care that he had been captured and tortured by an evil knight, but Jerome had a kind heart. It reminded him why he was here.

"I'm here to help Jerome. That's the only reason," Norman said, reaching into his knapsack. "Read this if you don't believe me." He removed the copy of Kit's story and thrust it towards Meg. "But hurry—we don't have much time."

Meg took the stapled sheaf of papers from his fingers. She glanced down long enough to read the title and the name of the author, then flashed a questioning look at Norman.

"That sweater . . ." she said, suddenly recognizing the burgundy-and-yellow piping of the grey V-neck that George Kelmsworth wore in every cover illustration.

"It's George's," Norman said quietly.

Her brow furrowed and she returned to the pages in front of her.

"Where is Malcolm, then?" Jerome asked, relieved now that his two visitors had made some sort of truce. "I've been dying to tell Meg about him. If she could meet him for herself, that would be even better."

"Don't be too sure," Norman started to say, but Malcolm had finally decided to show his face.

"Don't worry. I'm here," he announced. "Just looking for something of mine, that's all."

He bounded across the floor and began to pry his arrow free. "Can never have too many of these," he said, pulling on it and the ribbon it held. "Lady Meg, I believe this is yours." As gallant as ever, he presented the ribbon to the girl. She still had not closed her mouth, which had dropped open the moment Malcolm revealed himself. "My apologies for loosing an arrow upon your lovely hair. I pray you are not harmed. In the darkness, I could not tell that you were a maid. I dare say that in a fair fight, you would have bested young Strong Arm." He didn't hide his admiration.

Meg finally found the voice to express her outrage. "I cannot believe this!" She turned·on Norman, throwing the pages of the story at him in disgust. "You're just like Kit. You can't leave a book alone. Have you any idea what you've done? Has anybody else seen the talking weasel?"

Malcolm bared a sharp tooth and let out a low growl.

"Stoat," Norman corrected her hurriedly. "He's actually the king of the stoats. The weasels aren't our friends at the moment."

Meg snatched the ribbon from Malcolm's paws and turned on Norman. "Stop it! Stop telling us this. We can't know. That's another book altogether. You can't keep mixing things up like this. What do you think you're doing bringing him here?"

"To tell the truth, Lady Meg"—Malcolm leapt to Norman's shoulder so that he could meet her eye—"*you* brought us here. You are the one who took the Mustelid treaty map and hid it here."

"What?" She put her hands on her hips and widened her eyes in an expression of outraged disbelief that Norman recognized instantly. "What are you talking about?"

Norman, Jerome and Malcolm exchanged confused glances.

"But, Meg," Jerome said, "do you not remember? You told me to keep it safe for you. You said that by hiding it here, you were protecting someone you held dear."

Now everyone was confused. This Meg, the childhood Meg, had never seen the map. The adult Meg wouldn't bring it to the library for another twenty years, and yet it was always this library at this time to which she returned. For Jerome it had already happened.

Norman had thought that he was getting used to the bookweird, but this was hard to get his head around.

"I what?"

The sound of a thousand whips lashing the air interrupted her latest outrage.

Malcolm was instantly on his guard, grasping his bow and an arrow as he dashed to the window. "Heads down, everyone!"

But no one obeyed him. Drawn by the sound, they followed him to the window in time to see the arrows unleashed from the desert camp inscribe their fiery orange arcs across the night sky.

Malcolm made a rough estimate of their numbers as arrows rose and fell. "Two hundred archers. That's a party of some size, and well outside my range."

Back in Undergrowth, the stoat king was a sharpshooter of some renown, but he'd only witnessed human archery once, and that was Norman's one lucky shot, which had felled the wolf at Lochwarren. Seeing the work of these professionals, he could not help marvelling at their power.

They were all a little speechless standing there, watching the arrows rise and then ever so gently begin their descent towards the fortress. Two hundred tiny points of light hurtled in their direction. They would have been beautiful, had they not meant their destruction. The three human children held their breath as the arrows began to fall. Malcolm continued to count, estimating the distance and the range. At the end of their arcs, the arrows plummeted steeply towards the ground, until one by one the fires blinked out, extinguished by the sand.

Collectively, they exhaled.

"Does that mean we're safe?" Meg asked.

"They're just getting their range," Norman and Malcolm answered together—Malcolm because he knew his siegecraft, and Norman because he had seen it all before from a tent out in the desert.

"We have to get out of here," Norman urged them.

Meg shook her head. "We can't. Jerome can't reveal himself. He has to stay hidden."

"There's no use anymore. They're going to burn the whole fort down. We have to go," Norman urged her. Then in a lower voice, hoping only she would hear, he added, "I've seen it from the desert out there. The whole fort burns down."

Her eyes glinted with understanding. She knew how he knew. Still, she couldn't move. "But the book. We're wrecking the book."

"I . . . I know." Norman felt bad for her, but they had to get moving. "But if Jerome dies here, there will be nothing left of the book to salvage."

The *whoosh* of the second volley of arrows finally made her budge.

Jerome needed no more persuasion. "Let me get my things," he said.

Unlike Meg, the young archivist seemed eager to be moving. He'd spent his whole life hiding away in this library, and now finally he was being asked to do something. He ducked into his cubby and drew out the small sack of belongings he'd packed for the trip to England. From the writing table in the middle of the room, he plucked a small scroll from where it had been lying, in plain sight, ever since Meg had asked him to hide it for her.

"Your map, Your Majesty," he said, presenting it to Malcolm. The stoat nodded thankfully and held it appreciatively before stuffing it into the ever-useful knapsack.

"Let me lead the way. It's easy to get lost," Jerome said, striding to the first stair.

Norman well knew it. The last time he was here in San Savino, he'd walked right into a squad of Nantes's men. He'd been forced to duck behind a curtain. It had not worked very well and had ultimately led to his capture.

Now they tumbled down the stairs one by one, trusting Jerome to lead them through the dark, but letting Malcolm run ahead at each corner to make sure the coast was clear. The steps descended in twists down to the main clay walls of the fortress. Norman was relieved to be out of the dry wooden tower that housed the library. The scrolls and paper were just so much kindling, and the image of them igniting like a giant torch was hard to forget.

He couldn't remember the turns he'd taken through the hall-
ways last time. The baked-clay passages all looked alike to him, but
Jerome seemed to know exactly where they were going. Clearly
this wasn't the first time the young archivist had snuck out of his
hiding place to do some exploring.

"There are three main ways out of San Savino," Jerome explained.
"The Jerusalem Gate is the main one on the north side. The Sinon
Gate to the west and the Desert Gate to the east are smaller."

"We have to assume those are being watched," Malcolm
warned them. "We'd have to be prepared to fight our way out."

"Is there another way?" Norman fervently hoped there was.
He trusted Malcolm in a fight against his own kind, but he was no
match for Nantes's knights.

The archivist paused as he peered around a corner, holding up
a hand to make them wait. When the coast was clear, he beckoned
them on again. "I've seen some of the boys throw ropes through
the lower windows so they may come and go at night," he said
breathlessly. "But we'll need some rope for that."

At the next window, Norman stopped to check the distance to
the ground. At that very moment, a volley of arrows landed. Some
clattered off the clay walls and others struck the straw roofs below
them, setting them instantly ablaze. The sudden light illuminated just
how high up they were. "Let's keep going down," he urged them.

They could hear the shouts of the men in the courtyards
now—shouts of "Fire!" and "Water!" and a few high-pitched
screams of terror.

"I know a way out," Meg blurted, as if breaking a vow of
secrecy. "Through the cellars, there's a passage."

Norman didn't have to ask how she knew. He knew how. *The
Secret in the Library* was like a second home to her.

"Follow me, this way." She urged them down a narrow
passage, away from the main corridor. They met people rushing
here and there through the fortress—men rushing down to the
courtyard to help in the firefighting effort; women hurrying to
fetch their children and find safety. Norman wondered what would

happen to them. He had not seen anyone escape the conflagration of San Savino.

"They've found their range now," Malcolm told them solemnly. "The siege engines will begin soon."

He spoke prophetically. They were too deep in the fortress to hear the first projectile being launched and hurtling through the air, but they felt its impact. All of San Savino seemed to shudder. Ahead of Norman, Jerome stopped dead in his tracks, a look of terrified realization on his face.

"Come on," Norman told him, grabbing him by the shoulder to urge him on. "Don't give up now."

"But the others—" Jerome whispered. "I had not understood the destruction. So many will die here if we don't warn them."

"There's nothing we can do!" Norman argued. He could feel the heat coming from down below and was beginning to panic. He fought a sudden cowardly desire to devour a piece of paper and curl up somewhere to try desperately to fall asleep.

"But Godwyn—he's an old man. He needs my help." Jerome did not stay to argue with them, but set off in the opposite direction.

Norman, Meg and Malcolm stood in stunned silence for a moment, then realized they had to follow him. After all, he was the reason they were all here.

As Jerome hared through the corridors, he began shouting out warnings. "Hurry to the courtyards! Save yourselves!" If anyone wondered who this strange boy in a monk's habit running through the fortress was, now was not the time to ask him his name.

The interlopers could only follow. They were climbing back up towards the main apartments of San Savino, towards the maze where Norman had been captured last time. "We have to warn Sir Hugh and Father Lombard!" Jerome shouted back to them breathlessly. "How big is this passage you spoke of, Meg? Could we all escape that way?"

"I—" She shrugged her shoulders helplessly. "Not big," she told him.

"But some could escape with us, right?"

There was no arguing with him. The catapults continued their bombardments. San Savino was rocked by tremor after tremor as each flaming projectile struck the town walls. Below them, the screams became louder and higher pitched. A giant crashing sound was heard as some inner building finally gave up under the heat and the flames and fell in on itself.

"Sir Hugh's rooms are through here!" Jerome shouted, rounding the corner.

Norman thought he recognized this corridor—the iron lantern brackets, the enamelled shields that punctuated the walls.

They were running so frantically now that they didn't notice who passed them in the other direction. Jerome yelped in pain and surprise as a strong hand grabbed his arm and spun him round.

"Where on God's earth do you think you're going, young man? Father Lombard's pulling out what's left of his hair worrying about you."

Jerome looked up into the familiar grey eyes of his protector, Sir Hugh.

"Sir Hugh!" he said. "We all need to flee. They won't be happy until all of San Savino is rubble."

Sir Hugh had seen his share of fighting in his life. He'd walked with a slight limp since the day a horse was taken down beneath him at full gallop, and his tunic hid many old scars. But he had long ago given up the sword and learned that most fights could be avoided.

"Ah, it may take some doing, but I think we can get Nantes to call off his dogs," he told them, sounding perhaps more confident than he was. "What we need is a parley, a truce so we can discuss how to resolve this without losing any more lives. I'm heading down to open the gates now. You need to get yourselves to the shelter of the cellars."

"That's just where we were going," Norman interrupted. He couldn't help himself. He had to tell Hugh what he knew. "But, Sir Hugh, they won't stop. They think they have Jerome. All Black John wants now is vengeance."

Sir Hugh was not accustomed to interruptions. "Who are you?" he asked, turning angrily. "And what do you know of Black John?" As he spoke, another boulder struck the outer walls; the shudder it sent through the fortress seemed to underline his anger.

"I'm the boy they found in your chambers," Norman continued, undaunted. "They think I'm Jerome. They think they've captured him."

Sir Hugh looked him over. "The thief from my chambers, eh? So it is," he concluded. "Captured you, did they? And yet here you are now. How to explain that?"

"I escaped."

"Escaped the clutches of evil John of Nantes and ran back here to save us all?" he said mockingly.

"Yes," Norman assured him. "And I'm no thief."

"And Nantes thinks you are Jerome here?" Sir Hugh continued. "And what would the most powerful knight in the Holy Lands want with our little archivist, eh?" The scorn almost hid the worry in his voice.

Close by in the shadows, a growling Malcolm was spoiling for a fight, but Norman did not need his help just yet. He looked Sir Hugh in the eye and said solemnly, "He knows who Jerome really is."

Sir Hugh's right eye twitched. With Jerome standing there, he could not ask what Norman meant or how he knew. He cast a quick sideways glance at his ward before responding. "Well, if Nantes wants you"—he stared pointedly at Norman—"let's let him see that he doesn't have you. Come with me to the Jerusalem Gate. Jerome, go with Father Lombard here. He will get you to safety."

Norman didn't protest, letting himself be turned around and pointed down the stairs again. He looked over his shoulder, meaning to catch Meg's or Jerome's eye, hoping to silently communicate his plan, but Meg had melted into the crowd of escaping San Savinans or ducked into a dark corner. All Norman could do was shout, "Remember the plan!" and trust that she cared enough about Jerome to get him safely to her cellar escape route.

Just then, he felt the familiar tug of stoat claws on his legs. In the confusion and the darkness, no one noticed Malcolm climbing into his knapsack.

"No," Norman muttered. "Stay with Jerome."

The stoat hissed his refusal. There was no telling that animal what to do sometimes.

Sir Hugh pushed Norman ahead of him as they continued down through the fortress to the courtyard. He was not a cruel man, but Norman had put San Savino in danger and Sir Hugh was only just curbing his anger.

"A talk with Nantes will sort this out. We'll see what Black John really wants from you, and what you said to him to bring all this on. Perhaps I misjudged you. Perhaps you are more than a thief after all. Perhaps you are a spy."

Norman knew it was pointless to argue. Sir Hugh would find out soon enough what John of Nantes thought, but if Norman could keep Black John believing he was the boy monk a little longer, perhaps he could buy the real Jerome enough time to escape.

The walls of San Savino were still standing, but inside the fortifications, the little desert outpost was a tangle of fallen timbers and blazing straw. It would take all night to reduce it to rubble. Norman had lived through it once. He could take a little rough handling from Sir Hugh if he could put a stop to the bombardment.

As they stumbled through the debris of the courtyard, Malcolm whistled gently inside the knapsack. It was that same old tune of the Great Cities that the rabbits of Willowbraid sang. It was a strange time to be whistling—while San Savino fell around them—but Norman was grateful. His friend was letting him know that he wasn't alone.

He was so distracted by the whistling that he didn't hear how the sounds around him had changed, but as they approached the gate, he realized that it was quieter somehow. Men and women still ran around, shouting to be heard above the flames and the creaking of falling timbers. But where was the thud and shudder of the catapults? Where was the ominous *whoosh* of the arrows? Was it possible that the assault had stopped?

Sir Hugh seemed to notice it too. He did not let go of Norman's collar and continued to push him towards the big gate at the end of San Savino's only street, but his face betrayed a self-confident smile. "Just as I told you. Even Black John wouldn't raze a town just to sate his anger."

Norman couldn't help arguing. "Maybe he's just realized that I escaped and he's come looking for me. He thinks I'm Jerome, and you know that's who he's looking for. He's looking for the son of Johan Vilnius. This is about Vilnius and the Livonian Knights."

Sir Hugh stopped in his tracks and turned fiercely to Norman. "That's enough of that! If you say a word of this to Nantes, I'll have you put in stocks."

Norman gulped and nodded. "Jerome is my friend. I'm trying to save him."

"Then keep your mouth shut, boy," the governor of San Savino commanded. "Open the gates!" he called out to the small party of guards ahead of him. They were a scraggly bunch, too fat or too skinny or too short to be mistaken for real soldiers and with barely a full suit of armour between them. They froze at the order. "Do it now!" Hugh directed, even more firmly. "And raise a white flag for parley."

They may have needed to be told twice, but now they reacted. It took six of them to lift the two giant logs that barred the gate. The smallest of them scurried up the stairs of the guard tower to find the flag. It was already dangling from the tower window by the time the other guards had put their shoulders to the gates, pushing them outwards until the fortress was wide open to anyone who wished to march in.

And then they waited, Sir Hugh and Norman side by side in the middle of the road, the old governor with a restraining hand upon the boy's collar, in case he decided to make a run for it. The guards stood a respectful, or perhaps cautious, distance behind them. No one was sure how many would be coming to meet them, and in what mood.

They stood there for a long time, gazing out through the open gate at the campfires of their besiegers—long enough to wonder whether this pause in the hostilities was just a tactic, whether even now the catapults and troops of archers were being moved to forward positions. Certainly there was movement out there. The fires blinked as men strode back and forth in front of them. The screeching of large machinery being trundled across the dunes did nothing to improve the confidence of the tiny band of defenders.

Finally the camp seemed to settle into a sort of silence. The fires burned lower and the sound of creaking wheels ceased. Norman shifted from foot to foot, his legs tired from standing there. In the knapsack over his shoulder, he could feel Malcolm also shifting impatiently. To keep him updated, Norman periodically repeated, as if to himself, "No one coming yet." Or, "Nothing happening." Sir Hugh began looking at him as if he might be crazy.

They heard the approaching rider before they saw him. It was just one rider—they could tell from the thudding of the hooves on the packed dirt road—but it made them wonder. Why send a single horseman after such an overwhelming show of force? Was he just a messenger, delivering the conditions for their surrender? They prayed that they would be spared. Finally something appeared on the road, a darker shadow against the night sky, and then suddenly it was upon them: a huge horse and rider. A blacker horse would be difficult to imagine. He was a big animal, even for a noble horse. And noble he was. You could tell from his gait, which was proud and springy despite the knight in full armour who rode upon his back. The knight was all in black too. Was it Black John himself? Surely no two men in the Holy Land could afford such a fine suit of plate armour, polished to such a bright shine, yet pure black like the horse he rode.

It was worries like these that kept Norman from noticing the obvious—and it *was* as obvious as the nose on his face. It was only when the knight stopped, planted his ebony lance in the sand and raised the visor of his helmet to grin down on them that it all came together. This was not Black John. It wasn't anybody who should be riding up the road to San Savino—it was Uncle Kit. And the horse he rode was no horse at all. How could Norman have failed to see the twisted ivory horn that sprouted from the steed's forehead?

"Raritan," he whispered under his breath, as much to himself as to Malcolm, hidden away in the knapsack.

The guards had seen it too, as had Sir Hugh, who said nothing right away, but was astonished enough to relinquish his hold on Norman's collar.

"Never fear," said Kit in a haughty voice that was not quite his own. "I have prevailed upon the Duke of Nantes to curtail his attack."

He smiled the same self-satisfied smile that Norman had seen too many times on too many of Kit's different faces.

"You may be wondering who you have to thank for this," he said, the grin never disappearing from his face. "I am Reynard, Prince of Kelmsworth. Perhaps you recognize my heraldry." He indicated his shield, which was painted with a red fox rampant over a black unicorn guardant.

Inside the knapsack, Malcolm heard the voice and growled again.

"Of course," said Sir Hugh, obviously not recognizing it at all, but not wanting to offend their apparent saviour. He still had not taken his eyes from the magnificent horn on Raritan's head. "And your retinue? They are farther down the road? Shall we keep the gates open for them?"

"I have no retinue," Kit answered. "Kelmsworth rides alone. Surely you have heard that. I'm disappointed that my legend has not spread this far."

"Of course, of course," Sir Hugh assured him. After the rough handling Hugh had given him, Norman was almost glad to see him put on the back foot, even if Kit was the one doing it. "But it is not often that the man lives up to the legend so magnificently."

Kit beamed. Even his unsteady dismount did nothing to dint his bravado. He struggled out of the stirrups and required the assistance of two guards to set himself upright on the ground. When he had finally made it safely to ground, he removed his helmet completely and revealed a long mane of red hair.

"As long as I am in the Holy Land, I am England and England's will. The Duke of Nantes may be a blackguard, but even he would not defy England's will. He will join us tomorrow to parley in your chambers. I will enforce a truce between your two parties."

"You have our gratitude and our best bed, Your Highness," Sir Hugh replied. "Shall we take your . . . your steed to the stables?"

Kit removed his armoured glove and patted Raritan's neck. The unicorn, which until now had stood there impassively, neighed a sharp warning, and Kit backed away.

"Of course. Prepare a new bed of straw and bring him loaves of bread. No unbaked grains for Raritan here. He is a prince in his own right, and must eat like one."

The guards, mesmerized by the twisted ivory horn, did not protest. Not one of them dared to hold Raritan's bridle as they marched alongside him to what was left of San Savino's stables.

Norman wished that Raritan had stayed hidden away in the stables for the night, but while Kit was happy to retire to Sir Hugh's chambers for a drink and a rest, the unicorn was too proud an animal to watch the people of San Savino struggling to clean up the destruction of their town by themselves. He was discreet about it. He didn't shout orders or wave magic cleanup dust from his horn. He just whispered the occasional instruction to Norman, helped pull ropes when ropes needed to be pulled and trampled a few of the remaining fires with his massive hoofs. His greatest contribution to the clean-up effort, however, was his presence.

After a night of bombardment, the people of San Savino were in shock. Their houses were in ruin, the street and squares of the town filled with rubble and burnt debris. Some were badly injured, and a few had lost loved ones to the flames and destruction. The appearance of such a magical creature in their midst lifted their spirits the way only a miracle could. Besotted children could not help creeping towards Raritan to get a look at the magnificent horn. To the smallest and the luckiest, Raritan bowed, letting them touch the horn with the tips of their fingers. Some squealed in delight and ran away, holding their hands aloft; some just stood in silent awe, staring now at the hand that had touched the unicorn's horn. And it was not only the children who marvelled. Grown men and women fell into hushed silence when they saw him, and under his gaze, they seemed to redouble their efforts, lifting more, carrying farther, singing more cheerfully through their labours. If this inspirational effect was the only magic Raritan possessed, it was still a magnificent thing.

Norman worked alongside him, as tirelessly as anybody, but without the same sense of experiencing a miracle. He'd been battling a sinking feeling since Kit lifted his visor to show his annoying grinning face. He was making a huge mess of this book, worse than he'd done anywhere else. He could only imagine what was going to happen when his mother . . . uh, when Meg found out. She was going to kill him! He'd already introduced a talking stoat into her favourite book. When she saw the unicorn, she was going to freak out.

It was lucky, then, that he did not see her again through the night. Busy as he was helping to clear out the rubble and extinguish the last of the fires, he didn't have time to go looking for her. Instead, Malcolm went off in search of her and Jerome. When the men and women of San Savino decided they'd done all they could for the night, Norman followed Raritan to the stables. The boy probably could have fallen asleep on his feet, but the unicorn recommended the hayloft. Norman was climbing the ladder unsteadily when Malcolm returned from his scouting mission.

"Is that your stealth look?" Norman asked. The stoat was nearly black with ashes.

"All my looks are stealth looks," the stoat replied cheerfully. "You look like a chimney sweep."

There wasn't a single mirror in San Savino, so Norman could only imagine how filthy he was.

"They've hidden Jerome away in the monk's quarters with Lombard and Godwyn," Malcolm reported. "They're fussing over

149

him and asking questions, but the boy knows how to keep a secret and he's sticking to his story. He ran from the library when the bombardment started. He's never met you or Meg before in his life. The first time he ever saw you was in the rush down to the cellars."

"And where did Meg disappear to?" Norman asked as he laid his weary body down on the fresh hay.

"Your mother?" Malcolm replied with a grin, apparently enjoying Norman's discomfort at having to deal with a version of his mother only a few years older than himself. "Resourceful as ever. She's helping with the injured. They've set up a hospital in the tavern. It's the second miracle of the night. First the unicorn appears, then the tavern is left standing."

"You're enjoying this," said Norman. He couldn't understand how. He was exhausted. His bones felt like they were made of lead and his muscles of Jell-O. He supposed hay was scratchy, but right now this felt like the most luxurious bed in the world.

"San Savino is saved," Malcolm replied, unable to see why he shouldn't be happy. "I have my map. Jerome still breathes. A good day's work, I'd say."

"But the book's wrecked." Norman groaned as he said it. He couldn't imagine how to fix it now.

"It's not wrecked!" Malcolm protested cheerily as he made a little burrow for himself in the hay. "Not as far as I can see. A bit messy, I'll admit, but it's just gained a unicorn. Surely that'll make up for the mess."

"My mother won't think so."

"Mothers see messes everywhere," Malcolm assured him. "She probably thinks your room's a mess even after you've tidied up."

He was right.

Norman didn't remember much of the conversation after that, if there was any. Malcolm slipped away to clean himself off, but Norman was too tired to bother. He fell asleep right there in the hay. For the first time in a long time, he was too tired to worry whether he'd wake up in the same place tomorrow.

Parley and Melee

For once, Norman did wake up in the same place. He hadn't eaten any books the day before, but that was no guarantee of remaining in the same book. The bookweird had a mind of its own sometimes, and sometimes, like yesterday, Uncle Kit did some meddling. So it was a relative relief to wake up in a hayloft in a burned-out medieval fortress with soot all over his face—at least until he heard his mother's voice. And this time, it was exactly his mother's voice. If he kept his eyes shut like he did now, he could make himself believe that it was the grown Meg who stood at the top of the ladder and shouted into the hayloft.

"You didn't think you'd done enough? You didn't think a scruffy American boy and a talking weasel were enough to mess up this book?"

"Stoat," Malcolm corrected her again, though Meg was just winding up and ignored him.

"So you had to bring a unicorn? It's all the town can talk about. What's next? Do you have a few space aliens or some cowboys you'd like to introduce? Who are you, anyway? Are you one of Kit's friends from school? Did he teach you how to do this?"

It was difficult for Norman to interrupt her, and he had met a few bossy girls in his life. Dora was the worst, but she was small enough to ignore. In *Fortune's Foal*, Amelie was just like this, but he'd managed to stand up to her and hold his own. Staring at Meg there on the ladder, he just couldn't get past the fact that she was his mother, and though he usually grumbled and procrastinated, most of the time he did what she told him to.

It was Malcolm who finally leapt to his defence. "Norman didn't bring Raritan here. It was your kid brother."

"Kit did this?" she asked, a hint of worry entering her voice.

"Pranced right in here and declared himself our knight in shining armour. Calls himself the Prince of Kelmsworth," Malcolm scoffed.

Meg closed her eyes momentarily as if she was trying to wish it all away.

"It's actually a good thing he turned up," Norman said. "He managed to call off the attack, after all."

"It's never a good thing when Kit turns up," Meg replied bitterly.

"Listen," he said, "let's just find Kit and talk to him. He obviously came here to help."

Her ponytail whipped from side to side vigorously as she shook her head. Somehow she'd found time to clean herself up and fix her hair. It was just like his mother. She'd probably gone for a quick morning jog too. Norman still looked like a chimney sweep.

"He's obviously here to cause trouble, like always."

"Kit's a little crazy, we all know that. But I think we made a bit of a breakthrough back at the Shrubberies."

Meg rolled her eyes.

"It's worth a try," Norman insisted.

Before they cleaned themselves up and went in search of some breakfast, Norman had an urgent question for Raritan. It had come to him in the night and haunted his dreams.

"Raritan, if you and Kit are here, who's looking after Dora?" He whispered it into the unicorn's ear as he passed him in the stables.

"I've asked Lady Esme to stay with her," Raritan assured him.

Norman nearly screamed out, "What?!" A talking rabbit really shouldn't be babysitting his little sister. But as he thought about it, his outrage quickly evaporated. After Uncle Kit, Esme was a distinct improvement. At least Dora could count on a nutritious meal. He patted the unicorn on the neck and thanked him for his thoughtfulness. There would be plenty of time later to worry about what his mother would think. He had his hands full with the child version of her.

Since Meg knew San Savino best, they followed her lead. The town had not been built as a single structure but had grown from a small church and garrison inside the original fortified wall. There were individual homes and shops, but they tended to merge into each other, sharing walls and roofs and courtyards. The stables were across the courtyard from the monks' dormitory and workroom, which shared a kitchen with the governor's residence. From the kitchen, you could get to the guards' quarters, and from there through a passage between the walls to the armoury. Then it was only a question of climbing one of the towers to the dining hall and sneaking down a back corridor to the chambers of the governor and his staff. This all seemed simple when Meg explained it, but in practice, it was easiest just to follow her.

"Now can we count on your stoat friend to stay hidden in that knapsack of yours?" she asked. Norman had told her that Malcolm was royalty, but she refused to treat him with deference.

The muffled voice of the stoat king replied from inside the canvas. "You can count on me to do as I please and as I think, right?"

Meg ignored him and continued her instructions. "If we meet anyone, let me do the talking," she warned as she and Norman ducked into the mayhem of the kitchen. "The cook and the kitchen staff think I'm the personal maid of Lady Vorgogne, who occasionally visits Sir Hugh. Sir Hugh's people think I help in the kitchen."

"Aren't you afraid that someone will ask this Lady Vorgo-whatever about you?" Norman was both impressed and a little bit outraged by how easily she made up her cover story.

"Oh, they wouldn't dare," she told him. She nodded self-importantly at the kitchen maids and proceeded to grab two large earthenware jugs of water from one of the many broad wooden tables. "Here," she said, handing them to Norman to carry. "And besides, there is no Lady Vorgogne. I made her up."

Norman's arms sank under the weight of the jugs and he staggered after her. Behind him he heard the snickers of the maids watching him struggle. By the time they reached the dining room, his arms felt like they were going to burst into flames under this burden.

"Do you think you could carry one of these?" It hurt his pride to have to ask, but lugging the huge earthenware jugs hurt his arms more.

"Oh, that wouldn't do," Meg told him, barely looking over her shoulder. "Lady Vorgogne's personal maid doesn't carry water jugs to the governor's tables. That's a job for lowly kitchen boys."

Norman had no choice but to carry on behind her. When they finally reached Sir Hugh's chambers, they were surprised to find the door watched by two of Hugh's better guards.

"We've brought water for Sir Hugh and his guests, as requested," Meg told them.

"Plenty of water in there," the guard told her. "Wine too, though it be early for that."

Meg tried to argue, but the guards were unmoved. She'd been so bossy and self-assured all morning, it almost made Norman smile to see her falter. But they really needed to get in there to see Kit, and the pain in his arms had started to spread to his shoulders and neck.

"Important parley with the Duke of Nantes today," the guard insisted. "Nobody is to disturb Sir Hugh and Prince Reynard."

"Black John is coming here?" Norman asked nervously.

"Aye," the guard replied, grinning cruelly. "And I hear he likes to flay a few little pipsqueaks the likes of you each morning. Now get ye gone."

Meg glared at him, but there was no arguing left to do. They retreated down the corridor, and after the first corner, Norman finally put down the jugs that were pulling his arms out of their sockets.

Meg was furious. "I told you not to say anything."

"And you said you could get us in there!"

"I would have, if you hadn't stuck your foot in it with your whimpering about Black John." She crossed her arms in front of her and rolled her eyes exactly like Dora did. It was even more infuriating when Meg did it.

"Easy for you to say," Norman shot back. "Have you ever been captured and tortured by the Duke of Nantes?" He hadn't actually been tortured, but he exaggerated to make the point that he was no coward.

"No, but I'm not stupid enough to get myself caught."

"I wasn't stupid. I was—"

The argument could have gone on for much longer had Malcolm not stuck his head out of the knapsack to interrupt.

"Would you like me to slip in there and have a word with your lovely brother?" he asked cheerfully. "Or would you like me to stay hidden away inside this sack?"

Meg frowned. For some reason—perhaps because he was a talking animal in a book he shouldn't be in, or simply because he was Norman's friend—her nose always wrinkled when she caught sight of him. She inhaled deeply as if she was gathering breath to start lecturing him as well, but she seemed to realize that it would do no good.

"Can you get in there without being seen?" she asked reluctantly.

Malcolm didn't answer her, just winked and bounded to the nearest window ledge. "Be back in two shakes," he told them before Meg could reconsider, and with a flash of his tail, he was gone through the window.

Norman and Meg ducked into an adjacent room while Malcolm did his scouting. The two human children barely looked at each other. When they did, it was just to glare. The argument continued inside each child's head, where each one was able to win it.

The sound of movement in the hallway froze them for a moment. Meg was first to the keyhole, leaving Norman stuck standing behind her and wondering what she was seeing. He could guess. The sounds of medieval knights stomping down a hallway were familiar enough by now. The thump of their boots on the thick timber planking indicated a large troop of them, marching in unison—more feet than Norman had seen among San Savino's guards, and better unison than they'd seemed capable of. There was too much chain mail and plate armour jangling and rattling out there too. These were professional soldiers.

"Black John," he concluded in a whisper, "and his thugs."

"I know," Meg replied. "I can see, can't I?"

It amazed Norman just how annoying his mother was as a girl. He could see where Dora got it from. He was glad when he spotted Malcolm slipping back in through the open window behind them. It was difficult being alone with her. Meg, still crouched at the key-hole, didn't notice the stoat's return. Norman let her kneel there, all her attention focused on the corridor outside, as Malcolm leapt silently to the top of the jug beside her.

"Bla—" he began in a whisper.

Startled by the sound of the unexpected voice in her ear, Meg let out a little shriek of fright.

Norman caught the wink from Malcolm and couldn't help snickering.

"Black John and his lads are in there with Hugh and Kit," he told them. "There's a balcony we can all look in from—if you can manage not to squeal again."

Meg scowled as she regained her composure, but followed the stoat king's lead as he ducked back out the window. The ledge outside the window barely looked wide enough. If it had been a path marked on solid ground, Norman could have walked it easily without fear of stepping off, but they were three storeys above the ground—high enough that falling was not an option. High enough to make the path seem narrow and precarious. Looking down, he recognized the little courtyard that Jerome looked into from the library. Above, he noted with relief that the wooden tower had survived the night. It was blackened but still standing.

Malcolm danced across the narrow gap from the window ledge to the railing of Sir Hugh's balcony. After a quick check that the coast was clear, he beckoned them on. Norman knew from experience that it was best not to think too long about these things. He took a deep breath and made the jump. It was hardly brave, but he was proud of himself for not hesitating. Behind him, Meg peered down at the courtyard and paused. After all her bravado and bossiness, Norman thought he would be happy to see her waver, but the moment she showed vulnerability, she was his mother again, and he hated to see the fear that now flickered in her eyes.

He held out his hand to her. It wasn't very far from the balcony to the ledge. In fact, he could reach all the way across to her. But at the sight of his hand, she shook her head vehemently, and he withdrew it. Spurred on by the offence of a helping hand, Meg screwed up her courage and made the jump. The grown-up Meg, Norman thought to himself, was a whole lot nicer.

From the balcony, the children and the stoat had a perfect view of Sir Hugh's chamber. Norman recognized it as the room in which he'd been captured. Across the corner on the other wall hung the curtain he'd hid behind. From this vantage point he could see what a terrible hiding place it was. The curtain stopped inches from the floor. His ankles and half his shins must have poked out, giving Black John an easy target.

It was difficult to stand there and watch while Black John sat just feet from him again. There were four of them around the table: the duke, Sir Hugh, Father Lombard and Kit. Father Lombard looked sombre and thoughtful in his monk's robes. He'd spent most of the night administering last rites. Sir Hugh wore the same clothes he'd worn the day before. He looked tired. No doubt he'd worked through the night putting out fires and helping the wounded. To impress the royal emissary, the duke had put on his finery. His doublet was of black velvet with silver brocade, the colours of his dukedom. The big ring on his finger would be his signet ring, another symbol of his status. He tapped it loudly on the table as he spoke.

Kit looked distinctly unimpressed. He sat silently on the other side of the table with that knowing expression he always had, half looking away, as if the meeting bored him. He looked older than when Norman had left him back at the Shrubberies. His hair was longer, ginger red again, but falling to his shoulders like a lion's mane. On his chin he had a pointed beard of the same colour. He stroked it pensively while Hugh and Black John argued.

"I want that boy, Hugh," the duke growled. "You saw what I'm capable of when defied."

"I did see what you are capable of," Hugh replied gruffly. "But if I'm not mistaken, you already had the boy when you launched your attack."

"The boy's escaped," the duke barked. "You well know that. He couldn't have done it without help. He must be here. I want him back."

Sir Hugh sighed as if he was weary of the whole discussion and had better things to do. "If the boy is here, then I assure you I know nothing of it. I don't even know who the little scoundrel is, or why he was hiding in my chambers."

Black John glowered at Hugh. "You know just as well as I do who the boy is. You've known all along who he is and whose blood he carries."

Sir Hugh's quick reply betrayed his irritation. "I tell you, I have no idea who he is. Are you sure you do? He is English, I know that much. He called out for his mother in English when you nearly broke his head open. What would you want with a wretched little English boy?"

He looked pointedly at Kit, who so far had only watched in amusement. The fake prince cocked his head to the side and appeared to remember something. "You know, I do recall my chef de camp saying something about a runaway. One of our boys, a squire—No, not even a squire," he corrected himself. "A scruffy peasant boy who helped the squires. Simple little thing, baffled by the desert. I think he actually thought he could run home to England."

Norman seethed as he listened. Did Kit know he was watching or did he always say things like this about him?

A glance at Meg beside him told him that she wasn't any happier with him. "Kit always seems to bookweird in disguise," she whispered. "His age and costume changes, and that helps him fit in. No matter where I go, I'm always myself."

It was one of the strange things about the bookweird—how it affected people differently. Meg didn't know the full story: that even as an adult, she would always appear in *The Secret in the Library* as her childhood self. When she'd come to hide Malcolm's map in the library, Jerome had not noticed any difference in her.

"Shall we try to signal to Kit? Tell him we're here?" Norman asked.

"Don't!" Meg replied, louder than she intended. Inside the room, the murmur of voices halted. The two children cowered in silence, expecting someone to come to the balcony any minute, but the conversation quickly resumed.

"If you do find the boy, bring him to me," Kit continued. "If it is our lost stablehand, I can arrange to have him flogged before we put him back to work."

"Of course, Your Majesty," Black John replied, his voice oily whenever he thought he was talking to a superior. "If it please Your Majesty, we could flog him for you."

Kit smiled and shook his mane of red hair. "Do not trouble yourself, Nantes. We'll have the squire do the lashing. It is he who has been inconvenienced."

Black John smiled obsequiously and returned to the subject of Jerome. "It is this other boy who concerns us most. We have had news of a revival of the Livonian conspiracy. The boy seems important to them. It is our belief—"

"Livonian Knights?" Kit repeated, suddenly animated. "They were disbanded years ago. That was your triumph, wasn't it? Is that not how you earned the Order of the Cross that I see around your throat? Are you saying the task remains unfinished?"

Black John appeared to bite his tongue before speaking. "Even a felled tree sheds its seeds, Your Highness. We did not know that Johan of Vilnius had a son."

There was that name again—Vilnius, the name Norman shared with Jerome. It made him uncomfortable to read it, and even more so to hear it spoken.

Sir Hugh, as amused as he seemed by the duke's attempts to win the prince's favour, did not appear pleased with this turn of the conversation. "Your Highness," he said, trying to change the topic, "I fear my old eyes deceived me last night when you arrived. Please tell me what extraordinary beast it is I now house in my stables."

Kit puffed out his chest. "Your eyes deceived you not. It is a unicorn, a most spectacular creature, no? I discovered him in the far south, at the source of the Nile, where the sand dunes turn to verdant forest and the natives speak the original language of Adam—a veritable paradise. He was wild, of course, but I tamed him myself." Norman wasn't the only one Kit lied about behind his back.

Kit probably would have gone on for hours, telling ridiculous stories about his adventures, making himself out to be some brave explorer and unicorn tamer, as well as the prince of England, but he was interrupted by a knock on the door. Sir Hugh rose to answer it, but before he could, the door was pushed open to reveal six of Nantes's black-clad knights and a small, sweaty, sunburned man in white stockings and tunic.

One of Sir Hugh's guards burst belatedly into the room behind them. "Ambassador Fitzgibbon," he announced breathlessly.

"Arrest this scoundrel!" the sunburned man cried, pointing a finger at Kit.

Kit rose from his seat. "What is the meaning of this? Who is this offensive little man?"

The six knights who had been reaching towards Kit hesitated.

Sir Hugh turned to the angry little man. "Surely there is some mistake, Fitzgibbon. Don't you recognize Prince Reynard?"

"P-p-p—" Fitzgibbon stuttered. "Prince Reynard! There is no

Prince Reynard. There is no such man, no such title. How could you let yourself be fooled like this?"

Sir Hugh's face went blank with disbelief, but he wasn't fooling Norman. He must have known all along. "Ambassador Fitzgibbon, I had no idea. When a man rides in here astride a unicorn and calls himself Prince Reynard, who am I to contradict him?"

As he watched this all unfold, the Duke of Nantes rose slowly from his seat, his eyes growing ever wider. "What is going on here? Hugh, is this some stratagem of yours? I'll see you both hang, but not before I finish the job of razing this pile of dung!" He made a lunge across the table at the man he had been trying so hard to win over just a few moments earlier.

Kit scrambled to his feet and edged towards the door. "Who is that at the window?" he cried, pointing to the balcony where Norman and Meg stood. There was no time to duck out of sight. All eyes turned towards them. It bought Kit just enough time to get to the door. He allowed nothing to stand in his way, not even Ambassador Fitzgibbon, whom he sent flying. Sprawled on the floor, the little man made a grab for Kit's ankle, but the fugitive kicked himself loose and fled.

"Get them!" the enraged duke cried, slamming an angry fist on the table.

Nantes's men dashed in different directions—half of them towards the door after Kit, and the others towards the balcony—but Meg and Norman were already in motion, and Malcolm, perched on the railing, had his bow drawn. At this sort of distance, his aim was deadly, but he chose his targets to cause mayhem rather than fatalities. His first arrow struck the duke in the hand, pinning it to the table as securely as he'd pinned Meg's hair ribbon to the floor.

Black John's howls of anguish froze everyone for a moment as they tried to figure out what had just happened. When the knights finally realized that their leader had been struck by some sort of dart or crossbow bolt, they reacted according to their characters. The brave planted their feet, drew their swords and scanned the room for the source of the arrow. The cowardly took cover behind tables, chests and, if no other obstacles presented themselves, the backs of their braver comrades. The ambitious ran to the duke's side, attempting to win his favour by appearing to stand by him. One poor fool tried to remove the arrow, but the shaft was too small for him to get a good grip on it. The duke screamed in agony and cursed as the hapless knight yanked on the projectile.

"It's the Saracens, for sure," Sir Hugh cried loudly and convincingly. "They're inside the gate. God help us all!" He knew a diversionary attack when he saw one, and he made sure that this one succeeded. He lunged at poor Father Lombard, tackling the surprised cleric to the floor, perhaps bruising his old friend more than he wanted, but blocking the passage to the door. "Save yourself, Father!" he shouted as the priest began to recite a prayer for their salvation.

In the chaos, Malcolm unleashed two more arrows. He caught one knight in the back of the knee, causing his leg to buckle under him and sending the hulking warrior crashing to the floor like a pile of empty armour. His sword went sliding away from him across the wooden floor.

Another knight wheeled, flourishing his blade towards the sound of the bowstring. Norman gasped at the evil glint in the man's eye. The knight had only to take two steps and the point of the blade would be at Norman's throat, but the warrior froze when he saw the furry creature dressed in hunting greens and wielding a tiny bow. His hesitation cost him dearly. The next arrow was aimed squarely between his eyes. Malcolm let the arrow go and dove for cover.

Norman was rooted where he stood. He had witnessed battles before, but he had never seen medieval combat up close. It was bloody and hectic and fantastically noisy—all shouts and clanks of armour and futile swishes of swords through the air.

The knight who'd spied Malcolm fell to his knees clutching his face. At the sight of his bloodstained hands and the sound of his high-pitched shrieks, the remaining knights suddenly found their inner cowards. They stumbled over themselves, diving under furniture and cowering behind each other.

Black John strained to free his pinned hand and shrieked orders that went unheard above the din of battle. His wild eyes darted from corner to corner, unable to locate the attackers. Finally, they lit upon the children standing at the window. They narrowed as they locked on Norman, and he mouthed the word "You!" With a grimace, he yanked the arrow from his hand and lurched towards the children. But his revenge was thwarted. One of his own guards slipped as he backed away from the fight, falling across the duke's path and sending them both tumbling to the floor.

Sir Hugh added to the chaos, slapping one knight across the back with the flat blade of his sword, sending him lurching into a comrade like an armoured bowling pin. He continued to call out the alarm, insisting that the Saracens were in the fortress, but he was the calmest of the lot, the only man in the room who seemed to realize that this attack was a diversionary tactic.

"Run! Save yourselves!" he cried, seemingly to no one, but he looked directly at the two children on the balcony as he said it.

Sir Hugh's command snapped them out of their reverie, and they sprang into action. Meg led the way, leaping from the balcony back to the ledge.

"There's a window there." She pointed out the unshuttered opening on the far side of the courtyard.

There was no time to think of how high up they were or how narrow the ledge was. Norman just followed her lead. Meg leapt from ledge to ledge, so agile now that he had a hard time keeping up. Behind them, Malcolm discarded his dignity and fled on four feet, rapidly catching up with his human friends. He was a forest creature by nature and a River Raider by birth. His childhood had been spent in the riggings of the Raider ships. He'd walked ropes higher than this. To him, the ledge was like a highway in the sky.

Meg hauled herself through the open window and tumbled onto the floor, followed quickly and clumsily by Norman. They were both gasping there and revelling in their narrow escape when Malcolm appeared.

"Does someone want to close these shutters?" he asked nonchalantly. "They're a little large for me, and if someone with half a brain were to look out, he'd have a good idea where we got to."

Norman leapt up to do it, but he found there was someone else there already. The darkness of the room after the brightness of the desert sun made it difficult to pick out anything. As the shutters swung shut, it became darker still and Norman's stomach sank. Had they just walked into a trap?

"Is anyone injured?" the voice asked. Norman didn't immediately recognize it, but Meg of course knew it right away.

"Jerome!" she cried out in relief. "You're safe!" She jumped to her feet and embraced the young archivist. He staggered back at first, abashed and surprised by the greeting, but soon returned her hug.

"Yes, I'm quite safe. I watched you from here. You were fearless on the ledge. I thought you were afraid of great heights."

Suddenly self-conscious, Meg released Jerome and, apparently not sure what to do with her hands, began to brush the dust from her clothes. "Well, I think Norman and Malcolm have cured me of that, though I may have a little problem with blood after what I've just witnessed."

Norman frowned and looked away. This childhood relationship between his mother and Jerome made him uncomfortable.

"Are Father Lombard and Sir Hugh all right?" Jerome asked. "I tried to watch from here, but I could not see anything."

"They're fine, Jerome," Meg assured him. "Black John's men took all the casualties. Our furry Robin Hood put on quite a show back there."

"Robin Hood?" he asked, unaware of the reference.

The hero of the moment interrupted. "We ought to be moving."

The obedient young archivist shook his head. "Sir Hugh told me to stay here."

"But Black John is still out to get you," Norman argued.

"That's surely a mistake. What would the Duke of Nantes want with me?"

Norman opened his mouth to say something, but Meg silenced him with a sharp look. "They're right. We need to hide, or even better, to leave the fortress. You were meant to have left for England today, were you not? Where is Godwyn? Is he ready to go?"

As a veteran of the bookweird, Norman could see that she was doing her best to get the book's plot back on its original track.

Jerome shook his head solemnly. "Godwyn was injured in the fire. He breathed in a good deal of smoke. He will not be able to travel for some time, and I fear—"

He was interrupted by the sound of horse hooves. The children rushed to the window, but even through the narrow slats of the blinds, they could tell that there was no horse in the courtyard. As the clatter of hooves came closer, they realized that the sound was coming from inside the fortress.

"Black John?" Norman asked nervously.

Tunnels

The childish whoop from the corridor answered Norman's question. Whoever was riding his horse through the fortress was now singing the theme to the Lone Ranger TV show. It could only be Kit.

Malcolm poked a head out the door to check, but Kit must have already known where to find them. "Hi-ho!" he cried, ducking down from his perch on Raritan's back to peer in on them all. "Let's get out of here. Who wants a ride?"

Meg flung the door open. "Kit, this has to stop! You are destroying this book. You need to get out of this fortress."

"Lighten up, Sis," he protested. "I'm not destroying anything. This is what it's all about!" Now that his cover was blown, he had dropped his royal airs and any pretence of belonging in the book.

His sister shook her head sternly. "It's not what it's all about."

"Come on, Mega-Sis," he teased. "Let's go—me and you and the kid. We'll be the new Intrepids."

"Don't you dare—" Meg retorted in a rage.

Raritan interrupted her. "Maybe you two children could have this discussion later."

He was right. This was not an argument you should be having in the corridor of a desert stonghold when you are riding a unicorn and being chased by angry knights. His deep voice put a stop to the argument at once.

"Miraculous day!" Jerome cried. He had been gazing at the unicorn in silent awe, until the creature had actually spoken. "Do all the princes of England ride fabulous beasts?"

"You bet!" Kit replied, all traces of his princely accent gone. "The Queen rides a seahorse down the Thames! Come to England with us, kid, and I'll buy you a flying pony."

"Kit!" Meg shouted, but she did not have time to finish her lecture. Black John's reinforcements had arrived. Their angry shouts could be heard echoing around the corridors.

With that, they were on the run again.

"See you later!" Kit cried as he tapped Raritan's flanks with his heels. "If I remember this book right, there's something about a well and a palm tree."

Norman had not got that far into *The Secret in the Library*. As he hurried down the hall after the childhood version of his mother, he hoped that she knew what Kit was talking about.

Noises bounced and carried strangely through the baked-clay passages of San Savino. At times they were sure that they were about to be found out. The sound of chain mail jingled and resonated behind them, and they would quicken their pace until the same sounds were heard ahead of them, at which point they tiptoed forward, uncertain whether they were falling into a trap. So they ran and then crept, stepped warily and then ran full tilt, never sure whether they were running into or from danger, as they made their way out of the monks' chambers and through the dining halls towards the kitchens and the cellars.

On their dash through the kitchens, they sent pots and pans flying in their wake. They did not stop to apologize to the cook staff. If Black John's knights were after them, the cooks would understand their haste. A stair behind the food crates led down to the cellar. It was as big as the kitchen itself, though its ceiling was barely higher than Jerome's close-cropped head. They huddled silently in the darkness behind the barrels for a long time before anyone spoke. Crammed with barrels, the cellar was a perfect place to hide, but Meg knew an even better one.

"There's a tunnel beneath here. It leads out of the fortress to a small oasis."

"I can't leave San Savino," Jerome responded instinctively.

"You might not have to," Meg assured him. "We can just hide down there in the tunnel."

"It might not be a bad idea to leave." Norman looked at Meg meaningfully. "Wasn't Jerome supposed to leave for England anyway?"

She bit her lip and nodded silently. Sending Jerome off on his journey might be the easiest way to start repairing this book.

Malcolm seemed to guess what was going on. He never fully understood Norman's worries about the bookweird. Because he was a fictional character himself, he thought that everyone was, and that every world was just another book. "Well, I'd better go about gathering some supplies for this trip we're making," he said, breaking the uncomfortable silence. "Anything need fetching?"

Jerome held up the sack with his meagre belongings. "Everything I own is here."

"You'd like to eat on the journey, perhaps?" Malcolm asked. "Any special requests?"

Jerome thought for a moment, then replied, "Coffee beans. Godwyn and I always shared a mug of coffee in the morning. He gave me this for the voyage to England." From the folds of his tunic, he extracted a miniature coffee pot. It was small enough that it wouldn't have been out of place in a stoat kitchen. Malcolm eyed it appreciatively.

"Magic beans it is," he replied with a wink, disappearing into the cellar to do his foraging.

When Malcolm was gone, Meg turned to Norman to discuss their next step. "You and Kit may be right for once: leaving may be the best thing. We could at least get as far as the oasis. That was as far as Godwyn got Jerome anyway."

"What do you mean? Why do you do this?" For the first time, Norman heard frustration in Jerome's voice. "Why do you talk of

the future as if it has already happened? Is this another of your gifts?
Can you see the future too?"

"Oh no, I can't see the future," Meg declared hurriedly. "I mis-
spoke. I heard Father Godwyn mention that the oasis of Agadir would
be your first stop, and that you were to meet there some knights who
would escort you to England. We could get you that far."

At the mention of Godwyn, Jerome seemed to become more
solemn. "It will be difficult to travel without Godwyn. Before
you, he was all I knew of England." He seemed to think of something then. "Are you sure your betrothed won't mind you travelling with me?"

"Who?" Meg asked, confused.

"I'm sorry—I have betrayed a confidence," he apologized awk-
wardly. "Norman told me that you have been promised in marriage.
I should have expected it, a high-born lady such as yourself."

"He told you *what?*" It was still dark, but Norman could feel
her eyes glaring at him. He'd forgotten all about it. Last time
Norman had come to San Savino, he'd told Jerome that the adult
Meg was married, then lied to cover his slip of the tongue. He
wasn't as good at this as either Kit or Meg.

"I'm not betrothed to anyone," Meg said defiantly. "It goes to
show that you can't believe Norman or Kit." She seemed more
than normally aggravated by the thought. "I swore long ago never
to marry. Once I realized I couldn't marry you, I swore I wouldn't
marry anyone else!"

Nobody in the cellar knew what to do with this declaration,
least of all Jerome. It was clear he was in love with this strange girl
who visited him in the library. Hearing that she wanted to marry
him left him speechless.

Norman was just as dumbfounded. His brain refused to handle
the idea. His mother loved his father, and that was the end of it.

Malcolm returned with an armful of figs, cutting short any more
uncomfortable conversation. He made three more trips, foraging
through the cellar for bundles of figs and olives, Jerome's coffee
beans and skins full of water. When they had as much as they could

carry wrapped up in burlap sacks, they followed Meg's lead deeper into the far reaches of the cellar.

"Help me with this," she demanded as she put her shoulder against one of the barrels in a far corner.

Jerome and Norman rushed to help her manhandle the heavy barrel out of its spot. The trapdoor it concealed was not obvious at first.

"Are you sure it's here?" Jerome asked.

"I think so," Meg replied, sounding none too certain. "That's an apple barrel, right? It's supposed to be under an apple barrel."

"But barrels can be stored anywhere. Maybe the barrel was moved since you last used it," Jerome suggested. "What part of the cellar were you in?"

"No, she's right. It has to be an apple barrel." Norman didn't want to explain it either, but obviously Meg hadn't actually ever used the trapdoor. She knew about it only because she'd read it in the book, and in the book it was an apple barrel they moved to get at the tunnel.

"It's here," Malcolm reported. His sharp woodland eyes had picked out the seams around the old door. Years of dirt had filled the crevices. He scratched at them now with the tip of his sword, finding the corners, but if there was a handle, it had long ago been snapped off or deliberately removed.

"Do you still have that giant rabbit broadsword?" the stoat asked.

Norman reached carefully into his knapsack's outer pocket to retrieve the weapon. It made a deadly *snick* sound as he removed it from its wooden scabbard.

"See if you can pry it open with that," Malcolm suggested.

It seemed a shame to use such a well-made weapon as a crowbar, but Norman did as Malcolm said and began to pry at the edges of the square. The stoat kept at the other edges, gouging out as much dirt as he could with his own sword, but the seams were tight and unyielding. Above them, they heard the stomps of feet marching in numbers.

"Hurry," Meg urged them. "The duke's troops are getting closer."

Sweat now began to drip down Norman's brow. He wasn't getting anywhere with this door, and they were going to be found out. Half a dozen kitchen maids had seen them duck down the stairs into the cellar. If Nantes's men charged in, there would be half a dozen fingers pointing to the cellar stair. In frustration, he jammed the sword into the crevice and stomped on its hilt like a garden spade, but the door still did not move.

"When was the last time this door was opened?" he asked between gasping breaths as he tried to wrench out the sword he'd just stuck into the seam. Nobody answered him. He was regretting standing on the hilt. The sword seemed well and truly stuck.

"Need some help with that?" Meg asked solicitously.

Frustrated, Norman snapped, "No!" He fought with the sword for a few more minutes, straining to pull the blade straight back out, his arms trembling now until he lost his grip and slipped backwards onto the wooden floor with an inglorious thud.

"Give me a hand," he told Jerome, as if no one had suggested it before.

Jerome was quick to leap to his side. Each boy grabbed a side of the hilt and pulled. The archivist was taller than Norman and stronger. Try as he might, Norman could not put the same pressure on his side, and the sword started to twist. There was no difference at first, and then they began to feel the wood shifting under their pressure.

"Press down a bit," Norman said through gritted teeth.

The planks beneath them began to creak. The blade shuddered but did not snap.

"Keep going. You're moving it," Meg encouraged them.

They both leaned into it, but the boards only groaned and resisted—until without any warning the hatch flung open, sending Norman and Jerome tumbling in a pile like the winning team in a tug-of-war. The sword sprang into the air with a twang. It seemed to spin above them forever as they all watched helplessly. Nobody moved. Nobody breathed. Finally it fell straight down through the hole it helped to create in the floor. They heard it land with a clatter on the stone below.

"We're going to need a torch," Malcolm said. In a crisis like this, the little king could not help taking command.

Norman dug into his knapsack and removed the flashlight he'd stowed there back in the Shrubberies. "This is probably not the kind of torch you mean," he said sheepishly.

Meg rolled her eyes. "Do you have no respect for history?" she hissed.

Jerome did not understand, nor did he have time to ask. They were all interrupted by the sound of footsteps on the cellar stairs. The children froze. Only Malcolm had the good sense and fighting instincts to conceal himself. The others just looked at each other with wild, questioning eyes. Should they run? Should they close up the trapdoor to conceal it? In their hesitation, they did nothing.

"Jerome?" a familiar voice called.

"Sir Hugh?" Jerome asked hopefully.

"Ah, you are all here," he said, surveying the cellar. "Even our two interlopers." He nodded with satisfaction. "I don't know who told you about this passage, but it is just as well that you made your way here. The duke's men are moving through San Savino like rats through a ship's hold. It's not safe for you here, Jerome. It is time to begin your journey to England."

"But Brother Godwyn . . . ?" Jerome protested. In the heat of their pursuit he hadn't thought about the next step, but the idea of leaving now without his mentor suddenly frightened him.

"Brother Godwyn will live a little while longer at least. He'll have a few more seasons of herbs to cultivate, but he will not be travelling anywhere."

"Then how?"

"Take the passage as you had intended. I do not know where these two strangers came from. Perhaps they were sent by your—" He stopped himself before finishing his thought. "I don't know where they came from, but they seem to know enough about this fortress's old passages to get you out. The tunnel leads to the old well and the single palm."

"Do you know the route through the tunnels?" he asked, looking to Norman. Norman could only look hopefully towards Meg.

"We keep to the left," she replied confidently.

"Correct," the old Crusader said. "The one who calls himself Prince Reynard will meet you when you emerge. I will do my best to catch up with you farther along in the journey." He placed a reassuring hand upon the boy's shoulder. "This will not be the last time we speak."

"Don't be too sure of that." The new voice was low and threatening. They hadn't noticed anybody creeping down the stairs. Their heads all snapped round now to see, but they didn't have to look to know who it was. Black John took a step towards them. A bandage was wrapped tightly around his left hand. In his right, he brandished his sword.

Behind him somewhere, Norman heard a whispered stoat curse: "Badger breath, wrong hand!"

Sir Hugh turned and drew his own sword in a single motion that looked well practised but may have been executed more rapidly in the past.

The man in black tutted as if he were disappointed, but as he edged closer, his mouth revealed a cruel smile. "Don't be a fool, old man. Give me the boy and have done with it. I've no desire to see you dead today."

Sir Hugh shifted his feet, tracking the duke's movements as he circled, always keeping himself between Black John and the children.

"You seemed to want to see me dead last night, when you sent a hundred fiery missiles over the walls." He still held his sword before him warily, but with his other hand he was waving the children towards the trap door. Escape, he was telling them. I'll buy you some time. Even in the dim light of the cellar, however, Black John followed his movements. His grin became even wider, and he moved to block their escape route.

"Oh, Hugh, a trapdoor? The Vilnius brat is going to escape this, is he?" he asked mockingly. "I think not."

Black John stepped forward slowly, thrusting the tip of his sword towards them, his bandaged hand held casually behind his back. He moved gracefully, more like a dancer than the murderer he was. Sir Hugh parried these experimental thrusts and edged backwards again.

Norman scanned the dark cellar for the only real help Sir Hugh would get in this fight. Even he could tell that Sir Hugh was too old and too slow to win this fight. Norman's own weapon lay on the ground in the tunnel beneath the trapdoor, and he doubted that he could do much with it against the duke's obvious fencing skill anyway. Where was that stoat? He had been somewhere behind them when the duke barged in. Sir Hugh would be blocking his shot. He'd have to circle around the cellar to get a clear view of his target.

They had to distract the duke. They had to delay this duel until Malcolm was in position.

"Hey, Little John!" Norman shouted. In the schoolyard, fights never got much beyond name-calling. "How do you know which kid you want?"

"I'll take both," he replied, unconcerned. "One, two." He punctuated his reply with two swishes of his sword in an X across Sir Hugh's body. The old knight parried the first blow, but the second caught him glancingly on the shoulder. He grunted and winced in pain.

"Not now," Norman heard Meg whispering to herself. "This can't happen now." She had seen a duel like this before, in another part of the book. She knew better than Norman just how it was going to turn out.

"How do you know Vilnius had a son?" Norman asked, more desperately. "Maybe a daughter was brought to San Savino."

"What do you think you are doing, boy?" Sir Hugh growled. He didn't turn to say it, but it was enough distraction that he was slow to react to Black John's next attack, which came in a whirl of slashes and thrusts. Sir Hugh staggered as he parried each blow, backing them all deeper and deeper into a corner of the cellar. Black John started to laugh, getting louder and more sinister with each blow. He was toying with Sir Hugh and enjoying it.

The next attack would be the final one. Norman knew it.

"Johan of Vilnius still lives!" he shouted, desperate to buy Malcolm more time.

"Norman, no!" Meg protested.

"What?" the two swordsmen asked, one outraged, but both disbelieving.

"You had him. You had him all this time in your own prison in Jerusalem and you never knew, and now he's escaped. He's on his way here now. He's coming to get you."

"Norman, stop!" Meg pleaded. "They can't know these things. It's not time."

"These are the fantasies of a lost boy, mourning his rebel father," Black John snarled. "I think we can see which brat I need. Now say your prayers, old man. Your time has come."

Sir Hugh didn't wait for the next attack. He seized the initiative, charging forward furiously, lunging and slashing. Black John edged back, parrying to take the sting out of each blow. Hugh grunted each time metal met metal, and each blow came more slowly than the last. Black John would just let him tire himself out.

If Norman could see it, Sir Hugh had to know it too, but he fought on desperately, slashing wildly now, his sword making deep *swooshing* noises as it sliced the air. He was fighting to buy them time, hoping to prolong this contest long enough for them to escape, but to do so, he had to free a path to the trapdoor.

Hugh seemed to take a deep breath, then he aimed one last sweeping slash of his sword at his assailant's arm. The duke parried it professionally, turning and twisting his own sword in such a way that it took all the momentum. Sir Hugh's weapon went flying from his hand, landing with a thud somewhere among the food barrels, but their protector did not stop his charge; he continued hurtling towards Black John, his bare fist now aimed squarely at the duke's chin.

The blow caught the duke by surprise. Norman heard the jarring sound of teeth clashing together, and the duke turned away to protect himself. Hugh made to grasp him in a bear hug, but the younger man twisted away from his grip and sent Hugh tumbling to the floor.

Black John stepped back and looked down at his fallen opponent. The old soldier struggled to rise, but his assailant kicked Hugh's arm from beneath him, sending him sprawling again. The duke smiled and spat blood on the floor beside his fallen opponent. "You fool," he declared bitterly.

Norman could see that there was more than just the duke's blood on the floorboards. Hugh had been caught again, in his last attack, and he was bleeding heavily now. Black John saw it too, and he raised his sword high over his head.

Just then, something cut through the stale air of the cellar—a short, sharp breath of something. None of them saw it, but Norman guessed what it was.

One moment Black John was standing there, his sword held aloft in triumph, ready to deliver the final blow. The next he was staring at his empty hand, wondering what that piece of wood was sticking out of it.

"Should have got that hand the first time," they heard Malcolm mutter to himself.

But it wasn't over yet. Even without the use of his hands, the Duke of Nantes was still dangerous. He could still issue commands. "Guards! Guards!" he bellowed in pain and rage. "Down here in the cellars."

Norman and Jerome didn't wait for him to get another word out. They moved at the same time, seemingly with the same impulse. Jerome aimed high, lowering his shoulders as he charged towards their pursuer's chest. Norman went low, aiming to tackle his ankles.

Their tormentor anticipated the blow, but he could not escape it. They caught him as he twisted away, sending him off balance. He staggered once, then again, but this second time his foot found the edge of the trapdoor. His momentum carried him backwards and he fell, plunging into the hole in the floor. There was no scream as he fell. The only sound he made was when he landed—just a grunt and a sort of sigh.

Jerome rushed to the side of his fallen protector, flinging his arms around the stricken governor.

Norman and Meg rushed to the trapdoor opening and peered down into the dark passage. They were all so stunned by what had just happened that even when Norman picked up and flicked on his flashlight, no one objected and no one declared it a miracle. The beam of light illuminated the prone body of the Duke of Nantes, twisted and motionless below them. Had he been knocked unconscious by the fall?

Norman lit the way for Malcolm to climb down into the passage. The stoat drew his sword as he carefully examined the body. Still Black John didn't move. Malcolm crouched low over his face and pressed his tiny ear to the duke's mouth to check his breathing. He listened for a while, then looked up and shook his head.

"But how?" Norman asked.

Malcolm stepped gently around the body and finally found the cause of his death. He pointed to the dead man's chest. Norman aimed the flashlight. The tip of his rabbit sword could be seen protruding from Black John's black velvet doublet.

Meg put her hand over her mouth and turned away.

Norman had seen death before, had even played a part in battles. It made no difference that the "people" were wolves or humans or that they had been trying to kill him. It still made his stomach churn and his limbs cold.

They stood and stared in silence until a sound behind them snapped them out of it. Jerome. It was a low moaning sound, like the keening of a sad animal. He was crying. The boy archivist knelt beside the body of the man who had been his protector all these years. The old governor lay where Black John had left him, one hand raised to clasp the hand of the boy who knelt over him.

Meg pulled away from Norman's side and crouched down beside her friend, putting a consoling arm around him. Norman stood and watched, feeling more than ever that he did not belong here, that he was intruding.

"I'm sorry." Malcolm had appeared back at the edge of the trapdoor. "I was too late. They kept moving . . ."

Norman shook his head. He didn't blame the stoat for a moment.

Beside the fallen warrior, Jerome continued to sob and Meg consoled him silently. The old knight struggled to make himself heard.

"I've had a good life," Hugh croaked. "And a good death, if it saves yours."

At the word "death," Meg too started to sob.

"I have seen such marvellous sights—the golden cities of Europe, Jerusalem. I have fought what seemed to be the good fight. I have tried to do God's bidding." He coughed, struggling to continue. "My only regret was that I never had a son. Since you came to this little outpost in the desert, that regret has vanished."

His voice fading, he pulled the boy closer to him.

"Go now, save yourself. Live your life," he whispered hoarsely.

"But I can't," Jerome protested, tears now streaming down his face. "Not now. Not with you like this. And Brother Godwyn . . ."

The old man wheezed and took a deep breath, summoning the energy for his final words. "Let old men finish their lives as they choose. You have your own to live."

With that, he let out one final sigh and closed his eyes. He was dead, Norman was sure of it, but it was not like the other deaths he'd witnessed. Sir Hugh had called it a good death. They'd said that about the demise of Malcolm's father on the field of Tista Kirk—that for a warrior it was a good death to die in battle and in victory. Norman didn't believe it. Death was death. It was better to live. It would be better for all of them if Sir Hugh still lived.

He stood and watched helplessly a little while longer. Meg and Jerome eventually ran out of tears. Norman did not dare disturb them. He didn't know how long they waited for Jerome to say his silent goodbyes, but finally the archivist stood, bowed his head and said a prayer in Latin. When he was done, he made the sign of the cross and they said amen in unison.

They let themselves down slowly into the tunnel, with Norman leading the way and Malcolm following to close the trapdoor behind them. Meg had regained enough of her composure to frown when Norman lit up his flashlight, but she said nothing, not wanting to disturb the solemn silence of Jerome's mourning.

They stepped around the fallen duke's body, no one giving it more than a glance except Jerome, who stopped and said a little prayer for the man who had hunted him down and murdered his protector—the man who would have killed him too had Sir Hugh and Malcolm not intervened. The others did not protest. They waited for him to finish, then stepped into the gloom of the tunnels.

Norman had expected a short walk to a hidden exit not far beyond the fortress walls, but the tunnels were much deeper and much longer than he'd imagined. They turned and twisted, winding their way around boulders and outcrops, following the cracks and seams in the bedrock. Every now and then, the passage widened into a cave. Scratched pictures on the walls and piles of broken clay indicated that these caverns had been inhabited long before the coming of the Crusaders. They followed Meg's directions, always taking the left passage when faced with a choice, like the instructions for a maze.

The silence was difficult for Norman. He wanted to talk about what had happened back in the cellar. He wanted to make sense of it for himself. The distant look on Jerome's face worried him. His eyes were open, but they were focused somewhere within, in what thoughts Norman could only guess. He was merely stumbling along.

Norman nudged the boy with his elbow and handed him the flashlight. The archivist stared down at it without reaction, holding it loosely in his hand as he took it, but he did step into the lead. Malcolm took the hint and leapt from Norman's shoulder to the other boy's, keeping him company as Norman fell back to talk to Meg.

She didn't look much better. Her tidy braid was coming undone. Loose hairs fell in her face. That face was pale and smeared with grime around the eyes where she'd wiped away tears.

"It'll be all right," he told her. She looked so pitiful that even if this hadn't been his mother as a child, he would have tried to comfort her. "We'll get Jerome to Agadir, like you said. He'll go to England, just as he does in the book. It will all be okay."

"It's not okay. With Sir Hugh dead and Godwyn remaining in San Savino, it's all changed."

"No, no," Norman protested, trying to convince himself. "We can fix this."

"Don't you understand?" She stopped and grabbed his shirt. "Hugh and Nantes are supposed to fight that duel in Jerusalem a hundred pages from now. It's supposed to be Johan of Vilnius who kills the duke, not some talking woodland creature."

"We'll adapt. We'll change it," Norman argued. "The important thing is that Jerome finds his father, right? That he learns his ancestry?"

"That's the point. Without Godwyn, it'll never happen. It's Godwyn who tells him—who is *supposed* to tell him."

"Tell him what?" Malcolm had fallen back to see what was keeping them.

"Jerome's real name," Norman explained, whispering so that the boy up ahead didn't hear. "So why can't we just tell him? We'll tell him we're messengers sent by the Livonian Knights."

"Because it's an important plot point," Meg insisted, frustrated that they didn't understand. "It can't be me. I can't just say, 'Hey, Jerome, guess what? Your real name is Edward Vilnius. Know what that means?'"

It hit Norman like a bucket of cold water. "What did you say?"

"I said I can't tell him his real name. It's the turning point of the book. It has to come from one of the characters, one of the men he trusts. It can't be me." She repeated it as if explaining something to a small child.

"Not that," Norman whispered urgently, not sure if he had

really heard what he thought he'd heard. "The other thing—his real name."

"Edward Vilnius, the son of Johan of Vilnius," she repeated, exasperated. "You know that. Why do you sound so surprised?"

"His first name is Edward?" Norman was finally realizing that there was a reason the boy looked so familiar, a reason his gestures reminded him of someone. He was speechless. He just looked at Malcolm wildly, as if to ask, "Are you hearing this?"

The stoat king stared back at him and raised his paws in disbelief. "You didn't know? All this time you didn't know? I thought that's why it was so important to you."

"What?" Meg asked, bewildered by the conversation.

"You knew?" Norman asked Malcolm. "You *knew*?"

"From the moment we met him," the stoat replied. "Couldn't you see why this book was so important to your mother?"

It was a strange sensation. This is what it felt like, Norman realized, to miss something obvious in your own story that everyone reading it could see from the start. This is what it was like to be a character and not the reader.

"Knew what?" Meg asked, completely lost. "What does your mother have to do with this?"

Neither Norman nor Malcolm answered her question.

"Whose mother?" asked Jerome, returning to find the stragglers. He shone the light on each of their silent faces.

Norman turned and recognized the face of his father for the first time.

"It doesn't matter," he said, unable to answer Jerome's question. "We need to keep going. We have to pick up the pace."

At Norman's urging, they moved faster after that. His brain couldn't really come to grips with what was supposed to happen. Somehow this boy was his father, just as this girl was his mother. But how was it possible? Jerome wasn't real. Was it just that the character Jerome was based on a real person? Was it something as simple as that? Norman doubted it. With the bookweird, it was never the simple answer.

181

Lost in thought, he didn't notice when they came to a stop in a large cave. He stumbled into Jerome and steadied himself by grabbing the other boy's shoulder.

"What?" he asked.

Jerome's only answer was to point the flashlight at the wall of rock in front of them. Between two slabs of solid rock was a pile of rubble, jamming what had once been an opening.

"A cave-in," Malcolm said, pointing out the obvious. "It must have been caused by last night's bombardment."

"Are we sure we followed the right path?" Norman asked, trying to quell the panic in his voice.

"Quite sure," Jerome replied. "But we can backtrack."

"It's wrecked," Meg muttered to herself. "It's all ruined. The whole story is ruined." She slumped down on the dirt floor of the cave and buried her head in her hands. "This is all your fault." She didn't raise her head, but Norman knew she meant him. What could he say? That it was actually her fault for bringing Malcolm's map here? She didn't even remember doing it.

It was Jerome's turn to console his friend. "Don't worry, Meg. We'll find another way out. There may very well be another passage, or we can always return to the fortress. And in the end, you have your incantation."

She just shook her head. "You don't understand."

"Come on, Jerome," Malcolm said, resuming his natural role as leader. "Bring that flameless torch. Let's see if we can find a way around this cave-in."

The archivist swept the beam across the cave's walls. The pale yellow light revealed stone that was honeycombed with circular shafts. "This must be the original cave," he said. "Saint Savino's hermitage. These holes once held the scrolls we now store in the library." He continued to turn in a circle. "Some of these scrolls are in the Adamic language, the language of paradise. The Bible says Adam gave things their true names. His language made things what they are."

The archivist seemed lost in his own musings. He wandered

off to the mouth of each of three other passages, lighting them up so that Malcolm could investigate.

Meg and Norman sat on the floor and listened distractedly to the stoat's reports.

"This one is a dead end," he called, his voice echoing down the passage. "This one too. This last is the way we came. We'll have to backtrack."

Norman did his best to convince Meg that the situation could be saved, but she was beyond consoling. She still sat with her head in her hands.

"The book is ruined. They're going to have to destroy them all. They might just think it's a massive print error, but they won't stand for it. They'll pulp every copy they find. Do you know what will happen to Jerome then?"

Norman did not know, but he could guess. Characters lived only because of their books. If their books disappeared, how could they survive? Knowing what he knew now—about who Jerome really was—he realized that this was a more important question than he'd ever imagined it could be. If *The Secret in the Library* was destroyed, would Jerome—would Edward Vilnius, that is—die along with it? Would he ever have existed? And what would that mean for Norman, his son?

"We'll just have to face it: the book's going to change. The important thing is that we save Jerome." He shook her gently. "Right? Isn't that what's important?" He tried to pull her to her feet. He needed her working with them and helping them again.

"Shouldn't I have some choice in this?"

"Pardon?" Norman asked, surprised. They hadn't heard Jerome return. He had left the torch on a rock at the far side of the cave and crept up on them.

"Shouldn't I have some choice in this?" he asked again. His voice was low but assertive. "This thing that you call a story but I call my life?"

"I'm sorry, Jerome. We're being rude. You're right—you should be involved in the decisions."

Jerome wasn't listening to his protests. "You talk about my life as if it were predestined. You call it a book as if it were already written."

"Jerome . . ." Malcolm had appeared at his side. Of all the people in the cave, the stoat king was the only one who could truly understand what the boy was going through. But the archivist was through listening.

"You think I don't know?" he demanded. "You think I'm ignorant of the plots and conspiracies that swirl around me?" His voice began to grind with indignation. "Nantes was looking for Johan of Vilnius's son. You think Godwyn hasn't dropped enough hints over the years for me to guess? I'm not stupid."

Meg and Norman were speechless. This was the secret they'd been trying to keep from him, waiting for the right time to reveal it, but Jerome had suspected it all along.

"That's why we need to get you out of here," Norman told him. "Your father is waiting for you in Jerusalem. Together you will resurrect the Livonian Knights."

"Oh, he is, is he?" he replied bitterly. "That's what will happen? You're so sure. What if I don't want that? What if I want something else? Does that matter?"

Neither Norman nor Meg had an answer for him.

Jerome turned away from them and gazed back down the tunnel. "What do I care about the great Johan of Vilnius?" he asked. "He's just a name to me. I have had better fathers. One lies dead back there in the dirt of a cellar. Another lies in his bed, gasping for breath. They, like you, seemed to think that my destiny was already written for me." He turned his eyes towards the roof of the cave and shook his head wearily. "I'm supposed to give up the books I love and become a leader of men. No one has thought to ask me."

He started to wander away to reclaim the torch, but even then no one could think of anything worth telling him. He was right about everything. To them it was a book—a book they loved, but still just a book. To him it was his life.

Jerome stopped halfway across the cave and turned to get one final thing off his chest.

"I had many fathers here in San Savino—a surplus of fathers—but I had only one friend. She came only briefly and unpredictably in the night, but oh, how I loved those nights! How I loved sitting there in the dark, talking to her. Do you know how I waited for those nights? Each night I would lie awake in expectation, hoping that the magic maiden would whisper her incantation and visit me. Even that was not in my control. Can I not have that? Can I not have a friend?"

This was too much for Meg to take. She leapt to her feet.

"I'm not leaving again. I'm staying here with you," she declared tearfully. "I meant what I said about marrying you." She threw her arms around him and put her head on his shoulder.

It occurred to Norman that a scene this emotional should be difficult to watch, but there was something comforting about this. They stood together in each other's arms, holding each other the way they always did—the way they would when they were his parents. The bookweird had shown him some strange things in the past, but this was up there.

"So are we going back to the fortress?" Malcolm asked, as if he hadn't interrupted anything. He was many things, but a romantic was not one of them.

They worked their way back towards the fortress. Malcolm darted off dutifully to reconnoitre every passage they came across, but he returned each time shaking his head. For his part, Norman was preoccupied with the paradoxes that the bookweird had presented him with this time. Meg and Jerome—or Edward, as he should probably call him—seemed fine with the situation. They were going to stay here in medieval times and live happily ever after. Never mind that their real problems lay ahead of them at the end of the tunnel. The duke was still dead—as was Sir Hugh—but his vengeful knights would be roaming the fortress in search of him. As far as Meg and Jerome were concerned, these problems were nothing anymore. They had each other. But was it even possible? Could Meg just stay in the book forever? Norman had never faced the problem of trying to stay in a book. Usually he was trying to find a way out.

And what did it mean for him? If his mom stayed in *The Secret in the Library*, would he still be born? Or would this Meg Jespers and this Edward Vilnius have a whole different set of medieval children? Would he even be able to bookweird back to reality? Or would he be stuck here in the desert, or in some other imaginary world constructed of scraps of stories like the one Kit had made for himself? He was beginning to feel very lonely.

It was Malcolm who provided the obvious answer. "Just tell her," he said, catching up to Norman and leaping to his customary place on his shoulder. "Just tell her you're her son." The stoat had developed an uncanny knack for knowing what was on his human friend's mind.

Norman supposed he'd have to in the end, but he wasn't looking forward to it. He dragged his feet as they retraced their steps to the trapdoor, examining the walls for any sign of another exit. The cave walls were covered with primitive pictures of animals and stick-figured men and strange angular writing scratched in some ancient alphabet.

"Do you think you could bookweird out of here by licking the walls?" Malcolm asked, trying to lighten the mood.

Norman hoped it didn't come to that.

Soon enough, they had a new and different problem: they arrived at the end of the tunnel to find the trapdoor closed, as they'd left it, but the duke's body had vanished.

"Are you sure he was dead?" Meg asked, voicing Norman's immediate concern.

"Sure as stoats," Malcolm replied firmly.

Norman was relieved that the body was gone—it was too obvious a reminder of the bookweird's real dangers. But its disappearance was puzzling. Someone had moved the duke's body, so somebody knew about the tunnel, and yet no one had followed them. Whoever had removed the body must have wanted them to escape. Someone was protecting them. Someone—Father Lombard, perhaps, or someone else loyal to Sir Hugh—was covering their tracks.

Fearing that someone was lying in wait for them in the cellar, Jerome pushed on the trapdoor gently at first. When it didn't budge, he gradually increased the pressure. He was pushing hard with two hands when he began to worry. Norman and Meg both lent a hand, but the door didn't move. They all seemed to realize what had happened. Whoever had covered their tracks had covered them too well, and too literally. Something very heavy was now placed over the trapdoor. They would not be able to move it from there.

For a long time, they just sat there and felt sorry for themselves. They had been either fleeing or fighting since the morning.

"Do you think anyone will hear us if they come down to the cellars?" Norman ventured hopefully.

"They might," Jerome said, "but not until the morning."

"We can wait," Malcolm assured them. "At least we have supplies."

Norman didn't like counting on the chance of someone coming down and hearing them. "What about an escape tunnel? Do you think we can dig our way out, or gouge a hole through the wood?"

"It might be the end of this fine Santandarian rapier here," Malcolm replied, "but we could probably carve a hole through those boards that I could fit through. It'll take you two lads the best part of a day."

"And if you got through, do you think you could move those barrels?"

The stoat scoffed. "Yes, me and a squad of mole-sappers. We could probably dislodge the things."

"You'll have to find Father Lombard and tell him." Norman glanced at Meg, expecting her to disapprove of yet another "miracle" in San Savino, but she did not protest. Since she'd decided to stay behind in this world, she didn't seem as bothered by Norman's interferences.

"You could always bookweird your way out," she suggested.

"I'm not leaving Jerome here," Norman replied firmly.

"Then bookweird your way out on the other side," she said. "You can move the barrels and let us out."

"That would be two days from now—one sleep for each leg of the journey."

"We can wait." She touched Jerome on the arm.

"It's a good idea," said Norman as he thought more about it. "But you'd better do it too. My ingress isn't always"—he searched for the word—"reliable."

She looked at Jerome and shook her head. "I can't leave Jerome alone for that long."

He actually laughed at that. "I've spent all my life hiding in the dark. Two more days won't hurt. Besides, I've got Norman's magic flameless torch." He held up the flashlight as if it were some wonder of the world.

"I'll stay and keep the lad company," Malcolm volunteered. "Should you magicians get stuck somewhere, you'll be counting on me squeezing through a hole and sweet-talking some big-armed scullery maid into shifting those barrels."

"I'd welcome the company, Your Majesty," said Jerome. There was nothing like a plan and a backup plan to lift everyone's mood.

The archivist started on Malcolm's escape tunnel right away. He found a crack between two floorboards and began to whittle away the wood in little slivers. It was slow work and tough on his shoulders.

"Let me try," Norman said, after watching him for a while. It would have been much faster work if they'd had the larger rabbit-made sword, but whoever had dragged away the duke's body had taken Norman's sword too.

Jerome handed him the rapier reluctantly.

"What I really need," the archivist concluded, "if I'm going to be at this all night, is a cup of coffee." Norman would have thought it ridiculous to stop to make coffee at a time like this, but he had seen what the grown Edward Vilnius was like without his morning cup.

"Won't you need a fire for that? Do you think there's enough air down here?" Norman asked.

Malcolm's nose twitched as he sniffed the air. It was one of those gestures that reminded Norman he was an animal, something that was so easy to forget. "There's some fresh air coming in. In the morning, I might even be able to find the openings. But it's too dark now. Let the boy have his coffee."

Jerome ground his own coffee beans right there on the rocks. If ever his father complained about the lack of an espresso machine, he would have to remind him of this. The archivist gathered straw and wood fragments that had fallen through the cracks from the cellar, and with Malcolm's help, he built the tiniest fire Norman had ever seen. He placed the beans and a small amount of water in the travel-sized coffee pot Godwyn had given him.

"Watch the pot for me," Jerome told him. "This fire needs more fuel." It was the first time Norman had heard the other boy speak so gruffly. Maybe he really did need his coffee.

Norman did as he was told and stood guard over the little coffee pot. His father had offered him espresso once. It was just about the worst thing that he'd ever tasted, and this was from a kid who ate books as a hobby. He wondered now if his father had ever tried eating a book.

Jerome and Meg were farther down the passage, scavenging straw and wood fragments. Malcolm sat on the other side of the fire, watching it with him. The stoat caught his eye as Norman reached for his knapsack.

"Might as well get a start on this," Norman said.

He selected a page he'd written describing the Shrubberies. He could have chosen his room, but for some reason, he'd found it easier to describe the kitchen at breakfast time, with his sister being her usual annoying self and his father grumpy before his first coffee.

He ripped the page into strips as he usually did. It felt good to eat paper like a ribbon of pasta or a long roll of liquorice, feeding it slowly into his mouth and letting it dissolve before he chewed off the end.

Malcolm watched as Norman fed two strips into the top of Jerome's coffee pot. The stoat's eyes widened into an unspoken question. Norman just shrugged. It could work, couldn't it?

They watched the pot until it bubbled over and Jerome plucked it gingerly from the flames. From inside his cloak, he removed a tiny porcelain cup, smiling as he poured the thick brown sludge into it. "Does anybody else want some?" he asked. Norman and Malcolm were quick to shake their heads. Norman had to stop himself from grimacing.

Meg took a single polite sip and handed it back. "That's plenty for me. You have it."

Jerome knocked it back in two quick gulps and smacked his lips. "Let's get back to that escape route," he urged, as if just the taste of the coffee had revived him.

The three human children took turns boring the hole for Malcolm to slip through. Norman tried to do his part, but Jerome was taller, stronger and more determined. When everyone else decided to give up for the night, Jerome insisted on pressing on just a little bit longer. Norman sat on the floor of the tunnel and watched the boy who would become his father work at their escape route. He had pitied Jerome once, felt sorry for the orphaned boy locked up in the library. Now he didn't know how he felt.

The dirt floor of the tunnel was surprisingly comfortable to lie down on. Weariness can make any bed comfortable, but it was getting cold in the tunnel. Meg was already dozing under Jerome's cape when Norman pulled on his sweater and covered himself with his knapsack. It helped when Malcolm curled up on his chest. Norman felt the warmth of his body even through the sweater.

"I'll be back for you," Norman whispered. It killed him to have to bookweird away without his friend.

"I know," the stoat replied confidently. He seemed to settle down to sleep for the night, but after a few moments, he spoke up again. "That trick with the paper in the coffee? Do you think that'll work?"

"I doubt it," Norman replied with a yawn. He really didn't think it had much of a chance.

A Final Waking

Norman could tell without opening his eyes that he was back at the Shrubberies. He knew the sound of the sparrows by now, and the smell of pancakes downstairs told him something else: his mother was home. He knew this not just because he thought Kit was incapable of making pancakes. After all, Esme could probably have managed, and they would be tiny, perfectly delicious rabbit-sized pancakes. No, a boy knows the smell of his mother's pancakes. There was just one doubt that kept him in bed, unwilling yet to discover the truth. Would his father be here too, or was he stuck in the tunnels beneath San Savino, still unaware that he really belonged in a whole other time and place?

He rolled over and dangled an arm over the side of the bed. As he dragged his fingers across the floor, they brushed against a pile of bedclothes. He opened his eyes to find a small figure asleep beneath a flowered comforter. His first thought was of Malcolm, but the lump was too big to be a stoat. He finally spotted the tattered stuffed yellow dinosaur and the little pink fingers that clutched it. Dora. What was she doing curled up with her comforter and her old stuffed animal on the rug beside the bed?

He woke her gently, and she surprised him by wrapping her arms around him and clinging to him tightly. Norman wasn't used to hugging his little sister, but he decided he was enough of a hero to manage it. When Dora smelled the pancakes she quickly released him, as if she'd just realized what she was doing, and rushed downstairs. Norman followed her more slowly, prepared for anything.

He was tired of the bookweird, but if his father wasn't there, he would have to go back. He would save him from the fire all over again if he had to. He'd stop the duel in the cellars. He'd tell Malcolm to aim for Black John's right hand first, and if it came to it, he'd dig out the floorboards of the cellar himself. He wasn't going to let the bookweird hurt anyone he loved again.

And so it was a relief to see Edward Vilnius standing there in the kitchen, leaning against the counter with a cup of coffee and a grin.

"Good morning, Spiny," he said, raising his coffee cup as if in a toast. "Slept well, as always, I see."

"Better help yourself to some pancakes before they're all gone," his mother told him.

He didn't move right away. He was watching both his parents, observing their expressions and their gestures, seeing if he could pick out any echoes of the childhood versions. Maybe something in the way his father stooped, almost apologetically, echoed something he'd seen in Savino—the tall youth ducking under the huge beams of the library, the boy hiding away among monks. His mother's eyebrows, raised in bemused expectation as he stood there thinking, was something he'd seen in the childhood Meg, but there was a softness in her eyes that hadn't been there in the young girl he'd met in the desert fortress.

"Thank you for watching Dora last night. That was very mature of you. I didn't see any emergency messages on my mobile phone and there are no reports of police or fire being called to the scene, so all in all a good night. Did Mrs. Lamley from next door at the Hedges look in on you like I asked?"

Norman wasn't sure what to say. Did his mother really believe that this was what had happened, or was she asking him to go along with her cover story? He took a largish bite of pancake and made a sound that could have been either "uh-uh" or "uh-huh."

"Where did you guys go last night, anyway?" Dora asked.

"We went to an opera," his father replied, singing the word "opera" in a deep baritone.

"Yes," his mother added breezily. "An opera based on the works of Edgar Allan Poe."

"I think I might have fallen asleep," Edward said, "but I'm pretty sure the butler did it."

"I'm sure you fell asleep," Meg scolded playfully. "The people in the box next to us thought your snoring was part of the score. And it was the Prussian field marshal who did it, not the butler."

"I should have known," his father replied, snapping his fingers as if mad at himself for missing it.

Norman could feel himself grinning. They were back, both of them exactly as they were supposed to be. He didn't care how it had happened—whether it was the trick of the paper in the coffee, or if Meg had managed it herself. He didn't even care if Kit was somehow behind it. For all he cared, it could even have been another accident of the bookweird. He was just glad to have them here as adults, back in the real world.

Malcolm! The thought struck him and wiped the smile off his face. What had happened to Malcolm? Was he stranded alone in the tunnel beneath San Savino?

His mother had been watching him out of the corner of her eye the whole time.

"We got you something at the bookstore while we were out— one of those Tattersnail or Bramblebush books. I'm not sure if you've read this one."

She removed a thick paperback from her purse and slid it across the counter. His mother knew very well that the series was called Undergrowth, but it amused her to pretend not to. It used to bother Norman, back when he didn't have bigger things to worry about. He grabbed the thick paperback from the counter and sat down to read the back cover, holding it in his left hand while he shovelled pancakes into his mouth with his right. It was hard to smile with pancakes stuffed in his mouth, but as he read, Norman did.

> *Legacy of the Mustelids:*
> *In the much-anticipated sequel to* The Brothers of Lochwarren, *readers are returned to the mountain kingdom of the stoats, so recently wrested from the hands of the vicious Wolf warlords. While the prodigal Prince Malcolm wanders distant forests, indulging his taste for adventure, the kingdom he inherited languishes. Prince Regent Cuilean lies ill, felled by a mysterious illness. The legions of the Great Cities have marched home, and the stoat armies have been disbanded. The weasel king, Guillaume, continues to press his dubious claim to the Mustelid Empire by means both legal and nefarious. Will no one stand in the way of his grab for power? Is Prince Malcolm's return too late and too little? Is the ancient document he carries enough to prove the legitimacy of his rule? And if it comes to a fight, is his small band of Santandarian archers enough to seize the throne back from the treacherous weasels?*

Malcolm's disappearance from Lochwarren and the loss of the map had turned into a whole other book! Part of Norman wanted to jump right into *Legacy of the Mustelids*, not just to start reading it but to fight at his friend's side again. He was ready to run right upstairs and start eating the prologue, but then he remembered with a pang of regret that he'd sworn off the bookweird. He'd come so close to losing everything. He'd be an idiot to start messing with that now. Maybe he'd just read a few chapters and see if he was needed.

Was that small band of Santandarian archers enough, or did he need the help of the legendary giant Norman Strong Arm? And surely that band of archers wasn't just a coincidence. They had to be the rabbits of Willowbraid. Norman had done nothing to get them back to Undergrowth. Was it Kit who had helped them—fickle, unpredictable Uncle Kit—or was it just another accident of the bookweird?

Where was Uncle Kit, anyway? Norman pushed his plate away and made for the stairs.

"Dishes?" his dad asked, tilting his head towards the sink.

"I'll look after it," his mother said indulgently. That was weird too. She was usually a stickler for chores.

He bolted up the stairs before she changed her mind. There was no sign of Kit. The main bedroom looked like his parents had slept there. The library was the usual mess of his father's papers, and the study was tidy, with his mother's laptop open on the desk. It was as if Kit had never been there—and of course he hadn't, hadn't been at *this* Shrubberies. Kit had had Norman and Dora at his own version of his childhood home, stranded and in some strange half-fictional place between the real world and a real book.

Just the thought of it made Norman check the window overlooking the back garden. No unicorn appeared to be grazing there. There was no fountain filled with dolphins, marble or otherwise, and no turret-shaped addition. In the distance, he could see the edge of the woods where the rabbits lived. Something told him that not all the talking rabbits of England had returned to Undergrowth. Maybe it was wishful thinking, but he really believed that the little town of Willowbraid still rang with the sound of church bells from the Cathedral of St. Peter the Martyr and the hammer strikes of Wayland the smithy.

But the bookweird had thrown too many surprises at Norman for him to feel safe just yet. Something still nagged at him. The image of Sir Hugh using his last breaths to bid Jerome—his father, Edward Vilnius—goodbye stuck with him. What was left of *The Secret in the Library* now that Hugh and John of Nantes were dead and Jerome had vanished? Norman remembered the knapsack. He rushed back to his room. Sure enough it was there, lying in a tangle with his bedclothes.

He unbuckled the leather strap quickly, shoving his hand down through the piles of figs and apples and assorted bits of paper until he felt the weave of the cloth-bound book. It still existed. The book itself had not vanished, but what of the world it contained? Figs and apples spilled out over his bed as he withdrew the book anxiously.

At first he could see no change. It looked like the same book. On flipping it open, he could still see the slim edge where Malcolm had sliced the endpapers with his rapier, but the next page was blank, and the page after that. Dumbfounded, he flipped through the rest of the book. The pages were all like that, completely empty. Norman had seen something like this before: when he'd first messed up *The Brothers of Lochwarren*, the letters had become unreadable. But he'd never seen the pages completely erased like this. He closed the book hurriedly and examined the blue cloth cover. It too was blank. The silver embossed lettering of the title and the name of the author had vanished. There was no lettering at all, not on the front or the back or the spine. It was a blank bound book, like a diary or a writer's notebook. Its emptiness was almost scary. He shoved it back in the knapsack and buckled the straps tight. He didn't want to look at it.

Did the world of the book still exist now that the book itself existed only as a memory in the heads of its readers? And how few were those readers? Was his mother the only person alive who had read *The Secret in the Library* all the way through? Did she even remember it now that it had been erased? He wondered if he'd ever summon the courage to ask her.

The sound of a car pulling up on the driveway interrupted his thoughts. He crossed the hall to the study and looked out. A silver station wagon was pulling up. The yellow sign on the door read Taxi. The man who opened it and stepped out wore black jeans and a leather jacket. His black hair was pulled back into a ponytail. While the taxi driver removed his luggage from the trunk, the man in black frisked himself for some money to pay the fare. From Norman's angle, it was impossible to see the man's face, but he soon obliged by looking up, scanning the upper windows of the Shrubberies as if he was expecting someone to be waiting for him. The man in black smiled when he saw Norman standing there, the familiar crooked smile of his uncle. Kit waved up to him from the driveway, and Norman couldn't help waving back. It was a reflex.

Tell Us Again How You Met

That summer in England seemed so much longer than a few months. Norman had been in and out of half a dozen books and had experienced a lifetime's worth of adventure, so it didn't seem like a vacation. The strange old country house they called the Shrubberies had begun to feel like home, and now they were leaving it, returning to their real home so that Norman and Dora could start the school year and Edward Vilnius could return to teaching at the university.

The road back to the airport was like all the other roads in England, narrow and twisty, causing his head to sway in the back seat and occasionally hit the window. Up front, his mom and dad bantered as usual, laughing at their own stupid jokes and pointing out "interesting" bits of scenery.

Beside him, Dora rattled along about whatever came into her head. "Tell us how you met again," she demanded. She'd heard the story hundreds of times, but like all little girls, she loved the romance of her parents' meeting.

"Oh, that was a very long time ago now," her mother replied, pretending not to want to tell the story. But in truth, she liked to tell the story, even if she said only half of it out loud. Norman knew the unspoken parts now and could fill them in himself. It was interesting to him to realize that you could tell half the truth and still not reveal most of the story.

"My father knew her father," Edward began. "They worked together after the war."

"Grandpa Jespers was a university professor too," Meg continued. "He was sent to Eastern Europe to help re-establish their universities. He stayed with your father's family, and they became good friends."

"Do you remember that time, Dad?" Norman asked. He wasn't trying to be mischievous. He was curious to know what his father remembered.

"Oh, I was very young. I remember only little bits of it. I remember a little courtyard garden. I remember my father teaching me English. It seemed like such a strange language. Most of all, I remember the old archive where he worked—a dark, dusty room filled with rare books and scrolls."

Norman remembered that room a little better, and could tell him a few things about it, but if Edward remembered Godwyn as his father, Norman wasn't going to contradict him.

"But that's not how you two met. Tell me how you met," Dora insisted, eager to dive to the heart of the story.

"My parents tried to help Edward's family defect. The borders were closing—the Iron Curtain and all that—and intellectuals like your father's father were being persecuted. They needed to get out. The family split up. Edward came across the border with my parents. They used Kit's passport and pretended he was their own son. His parents were supposed to come later, but something happened. There was a car crash. They might have been chased."

"So you're an orphan," Dora said solemnly. It pleased her to feel sorry for her tragic dad.

"I hardly remember my birth parents. Mostly I remember growing up at the Shrubberies with the Jespers. They were very kind to me, and the Shrubberies was a magical place to grow up." He didn't sound at all bitter about the tragedy in his past. "And that's where I met your mother. She was my best friend. The best memories of my childhood are of the days we spent in the imaginary worlds we created together: great adventures in the desert, shipwrecks, forest kingdoms." He lifted his hand from the gearshift to touch hers gently.

Norman caught his mother's eye in the rear-view mirror. She was smiling contentedly.

"Your father eventually went to school in America on a scholarship. I came a few years later."

"She followed me," Edward said with mock arrogance.

"My mother got a job in America and I followed *her*," Meg contradicted him. "But it hardly matters. I knew eventually we would end up together. It was fate, you see."

"A storybook romance," his father said. He meant it ironically, but Norman knew better.

They drove along a little farther without saying anything more. Norman wondered if this was really what his father remembered, or if he was going along with the cover story too. Did he really not remember his childhood in San Savino? Did he really not realize that he had been born and had lived among the crusading knights?

"Do you think you'd know if you were a fictional character?" He blurted out the question at the end of the long conversation he'd been having with himself in his head. It was the sort of out-of-context remark that made him a figure of fun in class back home.

His mother for once seemed to know what he was thinking, but that didn't stop her from answering the question, as she often did, with another question.

"Do you think you'd know if you were half-fictional?"

He hadn't thought of it that way.

"Do you know what?" Dora asked, moving from topic to topic as only a child obsessed with her own thoughts could. "I'm going to be a writer when I grow up."

"Oh, really?" her dad said. "Not a show jumper or a ballerina anymore?"

"That's kid's stuff. When I'm a famous writer like Uncle Kit, I'll buy myself a stable of horses."

"A famous writer like Uncle Kit, eh?" Their uncle had only joined them for the last few days of their summer in England, but he had obviously made a huge impression on Dora. "And what are you going to write about?"

"I'm going to write about Esme, the magic rabbit, and how she looks after all the orphan children in her house in the country-side and rescues them when they go on adventures."

"That's a book I'd definitely like to read," their father said with a chuckle.

"Oh, everyone will," Dora assured him confidently. "Then I'll be able to buy my own horses. I'll have a jumper and a hacking horse and an Arabian for show . . ." Norman stopped listening to the list of horses she would one day possess. The list ended at some point, and thoughts of her future fame and fortune were enough to keep her quiet for a while.

Norman watched the countryside fly by the window—the hills, the viaduct, the winding roads that were so familiar to him. At one point, he thought he spotted a big estate that looked exactly like Kelmsworth. He had hated it in England when they arrived, but the site of the familiar estate on the hill actually made him sad to leave.

"Mom," he said, opening his mouth to ask the question before it was even completely formed in his mind, "I was wondering if maybe I could come back and spend next summer with Uncle Kit."

His mother gave him a sidelong glance of warning, then seemed to soften. "Maybe. We'll see how you do in school this year. It might be nice for you to get to know your long-lost uncle."